Heartquake

by

Terry Newman

Heartquake

Contact Information: info@thewildrosepress.com

Cover Art by *Kristian Norris*

The Wild Rose Press, Inc.
PO Box 708
Adams Basin, NY 14410-0708
Visit us at www.thewildrosepress.com

Publishing History
First Edition, 2022
Trade Paperback ISBN 978-1-5092-3910-8
Digital ISBN 978-1-5092-3911-5

Published in the United States of America

His hands seemed more like paws. Not destructive mauling paws of a feral beast, but the large loving ones of an animal dedicated to protecting those he loved. She feared if he kept his hand on hers too long, she would start to think about love at first sight again. Yet she didn't move it.

When he did remove his hand from hers, she felt an immediate and crushing disconnect. She fell back to earth and experienced the gripping weight and limitation of the force of gravity. *Did an astronaut experience this remorse and loss of freedom when he re-entered the earth's atmosphere and found himself bound by gravity?*

"I apologize," he said, as he shook his head slightly. "I think I've overstepped my bounds. That's not at all what I intended to happen. That was uncharacteristic of me."

"Don't be," she said. She couldn't take her gaze from his eyes.

"Pardon me?"

"Don't be sorry."

Dedication

This one's for you, Clay!
You always believed in me.

Prologue

"No, ma'am, I don't believe we'll need you to describe it. All lions look relatively alike. I believe our officers can identify a lion when they see one…Yes, ma'am, I really am taking your call seriously."

Officer Jonathan Harris, of the Prague, Ohio, police department, slammed the telephone receiver down just as fellow officer Mike Simons walked past.

"What is it, Jon? Don't think I've ever seen you this agitated before? What gives?"

"You're not going to believe this. People keep calling claiming they've spotted an African lion. Imagine that, a lion! When I received the first report, I thought the caller was a crackpot. After all, it is a full moon. Then, another person called. And another." He paused a beat, taking a deep breath.

"Sad part is we have to send an officer out to investigate each individual reported sighting. What a waste of manpower."

Mike shot Jon half a smile. "It's good to know you're concerned about how the department spends its money. But, just for your information, on nights like this the department has a dedicated team going out to investigate these sightings. That way we don't leave the city completely abandoned, and it does save some money."

"Nights like this?"

"Oh, yeah. Every couple of months this lion-sighting thing happens."

"Do you want to know the strangest thing about these calls?" Jon began, "All the calls are—"

"—made by women." Mike finished his sentence.

"Yeah, how did you know?"

"Been in that chair on nights like this." He paused a beat, as if he were trying to recall other details of the sightings. "And I bet some of them complain the lion came up to their windows and nuzzled the panes. Like he was trying to look in." Jon nodded in disbelief at the similarity of the calls.

"And no lion has ever been found?" Jon asked.

"Nope. I'm betting after the first call, you called zoos and wildlife refuges asking if anyone was missing a lion."

"You're absolutely right," he answered. "I felt a little silly doing it, but I knew it had to be done."

"And let me guess: no one is missing a lion?"

"No one. You'd think that it would be hard to misplace an animal as big as a lion."

Chapter 1

"Something amazingly awesome is going to happen to me today, Mel!"

Charlee Lightheart sung out the refrain as she padded about the shop. She owned *That Coffee Shop* and Melanie Milan was not only her trusted employee but her best friend.

Melanie looked at her suspiciously, her head tilted with one eye squinted as if she needed a better look at her friend, then began rifling through several cabinets and drawers behind the counter.

"What are you looking for?"

Having been crouched down, out of sight, Melanie popped up like a Jack-in-the Box. "The drugs you're using and obviously not sharing with me."

"Can't a woman be optimistic about the day without being accused of using illicit drugs?"

"Sure, some women can, but not you. You're the epitome of Murphy's Law: whatever can go wrong, will go wrong."

"All of that is behind me now," she said brightly. "I've changed my ways."

"That's got to mean only one thing: you've read another one of those 'woo-woo' happy books."

"What if I have?"

Charlee took her employee's remarks in stride. She had known Mel long enough to know she was kidding.

The tinkle of a small bell on the door interrupted the conversation.

"You take this customer, Charlee." Mel picked up the coffee pot. "I'll make sure all the other customers are having"—she paused a beat before continuing—"an amazingly awesome experience."

Charlee took a moment to size up the customer as he walked toward the counter. She didn't recognize him as an early morning regular. And that suit he wore screamed money—gobs of money. She guessed it was custom-tailored to his build. How else could it so unassumingly highlight that broad muscular upper body?

She scanned all of the customers she didn't know like this. It kept her mind active while she made their coffee and filled their pastry orders. She enjoyed creating a quick character sketch of them. And it helped to pass the time, especially when it was slow.

He walked up to the counter. "Good morning. I've never been here before. I know I want three caramel lattes, but what muffins would you suggest?"

"Our most popular is the coffee cake muffin. And it looks as if you've come just in time," she said as she looked at the display case. "We happen to have three left."

"They're mine then."

As she started the order, she thought the man was quite handsome. *Such a shame those good looks are probably wasted on an oversized ego.*

It took no time at all to whip up the three flavored coffees and pack up three muffins. She reached under the counter to retrieve a cup carrier. She took his money and handed his change back to him.

Their hands accidently touched. The electric surge flew through her fingers, up her arms and, she swore, jumpstarted her heart.

Her heartbeat raced and with it a cascade of sensual feelings flooded her body. Feelings she hadn't experienced since...well, she didn't think she'd ever felt before. Not even with her last boyfriend.

Did he feel it too?

Of course not, she told herself, immediately dismissing the idea. After all, he looked like Mr. Impervious. *I bet he expected women to be weak-kneed and short of breath in his presence.*

She let out a short gasp, which of course, Mr. Impervious called her on. Thinking quickly, she said, "That's some static electricity you have built up."

"So I've been told."

She wanted so much to mock him, but when she looked at his face, she saw a lopsided smile packed with a boyish charm instead of the smug grin she expected. That's when she took a second look at his hair. Tawny brown and curly. Certainly not the type of hair befitting a man who would be trying to win high-powered negotiations.

She could easily imagine him in a pair of jeans and a tee shirt. And he would be every bit as comfortable and every bit as...dare she say...handsome.

He stuffed his change in his wallet, closed it, and put it in his pocket. "Sorry, if I gave you a jolt, miss."

As he left, she leaned over the counter so far that she practically climbed over so as not take her eyes off him.

Mel returned with the coffee pot and found her in that position. "What is this all about?" she asked as she poured what little coffee was left in the sink, rinsed out the pot, and prepared another pot.

"I think I experienced my 'amazingly awesome' moment."

Chapter 2

Riley Brockton, CEO of Brockton Enterprises, ambled into the corporate offices on the twenty-second floor of Brockton Tower.

He strode across the spacious lobby where visitors were made as comfortable as possible while waiting for their appointments. When clients walked into the room, they usually commented how calming it felt. They also said it felt as if they were transported to the plains of Africa. The walls, painted a sandy, eye-pleasing ochre, were the backdrop to original oil paintings of large African cats hung throughout the lobby. In addition to the many lions, there were one or two leopards and cheetahs thrown in for good measure.

There was even an occasional painting of giraffes and hippos—all original works of art, as well.

As he walked past the desk of the secretary, Renee Mathers, he greeted her with a warm and friendly good morning and offered her one of the coffees.

"Oh, Mr. Brockton, you startled me," she said. "You would think after all these years I'd be able to hear you walk in."

"How thoughtful." She took a quick sip. He also set a coffee cake muffin on her desk. "Now, isn't this a surprise. Thank you so much, Riley."

He chuckled. "Sorry to give you such a start."

He flashed a short but sincere smile. "I'm sure my

brother is already in his office."

Riley found his brother reading the *Prague Bugle*. He set their coffees and muffins on the desk.

"Good morning," Quinn said, as he looked up momentarily.

"What's so interesting in today's paper?"

"I'm reading all about the soiree you threw the other night."

"I would have thought you'd be reading the stock market numbers."

"I have to admit, your soiree made quite an impression on the society reporter. They devoted a good deal of space to it."

"My dear brother, my soiree, as you call it, *is* the society section today. What else ever happens in this town? Besides, you know as well as I do, if I lived and died by what the society pages had to say about me, I would have been dead years ago. I know for a fact you never paid much attention to them when you were single."

Quinn began to unwrap his muffin and answered quickly. "Yeah, but it's fun to read when the story is about your event."

"Listen to this." Quinn began reading.

Riley Brockton, billionaire playboy, held another soiree at his multi-million-dollar mansion Saturday night. The guest list read like a veritable list of who's who of the rich and famous within a two-hundred-fifty-mile radius. Riley is the younger of the Brockton brothers and oversees the East Coast operations of the firm.

Recently, Riley has been seen in Prague more and more, raising speculation that he has either moved here for an extended stay or is considering a permanent move back to his hometown roots.

Riley gave a quick, low guttural sound when he heard the last few words. "I never thought I would have to issue a press release about where I'm living now, as if it's anyone else's concern but mine and, of course, yours, Quinn. You know, family."

Quinn agreed. "It might be a cliché, but it's the best description I can think of. We're living in a fishbowl. Our every action is scrutinized." He paused a beat. "I'm glad you moved back home, Riley. While the press and the populace are focusing on you, they're leaving me alone."

"Very funny."

"Maybe not funny, but it's true." He took a sip of his coffee. "Oh, and here's an article you might be interested in." Quinn handed him the front page.

As soon as he saw it, he winced. Before reading it out loud, he rose and paced.

The headline read: *Phantom Lion Spotted Again*

Prague residents deluged the police department Saturday night with repeated sightings of an African lion.

More than a dozen individuals called. The first sighting occurred at 9:04 according to police records.

The last reported sighting occurred about 1:08 a.m.

According to Officer Jonathan Harris, the department sent a dedicated team to investigate each sighting. "We take the safety of our citizens seriously and ensured that each sighting was investigated on its own merits. The department called all zoos and wildlife sanctuaries in the area but none was missing a lion."

He put the paper down. Quinn stood up as if he were challenging him on the issue. "Do you know anything about those sightings?"

"Why do you ask?"

"Oh, no reason, I guess."

By now, the brothers were standing practically toe-to-toe as they bantered. It never occurred to Riley that they could be holding the same conversation seated. Riley gave Quinn a quick brotherly shove on the shoulder, something he had done since childhood.

And before you could say "wildlife refuge" they were tousling each other, punching each other in friendly ways. As they enjoyed this reenactment from their childhood, they got carried away and the punches came a bit harder. Before either of them knew what had happened, they were on the davenport across from Quinn's coffee table playing like two overgrown cats making a variety of guttural sounds that sounded like growls.

So absorbed in the moment, Riley didn't hear Renee come in and close the door behind her. "Excuse me, boys, but your growling is disturbing the visitors in the lobby."

They never heard her.

"Okay guys, you leave me no choice." Nor did they hear her tread quickly across the office to the bar and pick up the pitcher of ice water. As she walked back toward the brothers, she said, "I'm giving you fair notice. If you don't lower your growling, I'm going to treat you both like a couple of tomcats fighting over territory."

Again, the men ignored her. "All right. Here goes nothing." She poured the entire contents of the pitcher over their heads.

"Huh?" They finally parted and looked up. "What the…?" Riley appeared irritated at first, but when he turned to his brother, he laughed. Quinn joined in.

"I was having a difficult time explaining the growling coming from this office," Renee told them. "I tried to break you up without resorting to those methods, but obviously it didn't have an effect. I thought that water might do the trick."

Both men quickly shook their heads to get as much of the water out of their hair as possible, getting Renee wet in the process.

"Good day, gentlemen," she said dramatically as she walked out the door and closed it behind her.

Riley stared at the door for a moment. "Does she know?" he asked his brother.

"Does she know what?" Quinn replied.

"That we're…well, you know."

"How could she?"

"Well, for one thing, her unorthodox method of separating us."

Quinn shook a little more water from his hair and scratched behind his ear. "Let's find out," he said.

He walked to the door and asked Renee to come back in. She brought in all the overnight and early morning messages and memos.

The pair stared at her as she walked in and closed the door behind her and sat down. "What? What did I do? Well, aside from drowning the two of you?"

"Do you know that we're…?" Quinn let the question hang in the air.

"That you're what?" she asked. She paused a beat. "Don't answer that," she said. "If you tell me what you are—presuming you are that—then when someone asks me, I may slip and tell them."

She stopped again before saying, "But if you don't tell me, then I don't know, and if I don't know then I can't tell anyone because I can't tell someone something that I don't know. You know?"

The brothers looked at each other bewildered.

"Can I go now, Mr. Brockton?" she asked formally. Quinn nodded. Before Renee opened the door to leave, she said in a low voice, "But if you ever plan to tell anyone, please let me know because I would love to see everyone's reaction to who you may be that I don't know about."

Chapter 3

Silence filled the room when Renee left. Riley stared at his latte as if he were scrutinizing its contents. "What's so fascinating in your cup?"

"Just wondering why you can't tell your fortune from coffee like you can from tea."

Riley expected a snarky answer, but instead got what sounded like sympathy. "You haven't been the usual fun-loving brother I know and love. What's wrong?"

"Nothing's wrong. Just deep in thought, that's all."

Riley continued to stare into the cup.

"I don't mean to pry, but we've been confiding in each since we were kids. Like the time you switched desserts in your lunch bag with Suzi because she had a delicious-looking cupcake and you only had a couple of Oreo cookies."

"Really? Are you going to bring that up again? At our age?" Riley glared at his brother. That prompted the beginning of one of their good old-fashioned stare-downs, another vestige of their childhood. He stared hard into Quinn's eyes, studying the amber coloring, very much aware of how similar the two of them looked. They were often mistaken for twins. When that occurred, his brother was quick to point out he was the older brother.

And befitting an older brother Quinn won the stare-down just as he had done when they were younger.

Riley stood up and paced. Then stopped and adjusted a sleeve on his suit coat. "How did you know," he formed his question slowly, "when you met your lioness, your soulmate?"

"You were with me at the community playhouse. I just knew."

"No, I think there's more that you're not telling me."

Riley walked to the receiving chair and gripped the back of it. He knew he could never hide anything from him, not even this. Their bond was deeper than most brothers. As members of a dwindling lion-shifting community, they were part of a closed, sadly secret group.

Riley couldn't remember a time when lion shifters were welcome in Prague and treated like everyone else. His grandparents had told him and his brother about the original colony of shifters, started in the late nineteenth century just outside of Prague, that grew into the small town called Lionsville. The residents of the two towns lived together peacefully and eventually, as both populations grew, Lionsville was incorporated as part of Prague.

That changed abruptly in the mid-twentieth century. And it was only getting worse with the current xenophobic atmosphere. Their parents and grandparents had told them the problems they had dealt with during those hard times. As boys they were told of the gossip their parents endured and the surreptitious looks people gave them. While the stares had lessened, it was only because the majority of Prague residents didn't believe in lion shifters.

Many people now thought those stories to be merely urban legends, but Riley felt like he needed to keep his guard up, because there were occasions when someone would bring the topic up in his presence.

"Why don't you start by telling me the real reason you came back to town. I think once I know that, I'll be able to provide a bit more advice. At least, I'll try."

Quinn's comment brought him back to the present.

Riley took a seat on the davenport. "I thought I had met my lioness—my forever soulmate. We were together for nearly a year. And we seemed so happy. Looking back on it, I was happy. On second thought, happy doesn't seem to be the right word.

"It was a contentment that nearly defied description. I guess that's what love is like. Then we woke up one morning and were leisurely lying in bed. I wrapped my arm around her, and she told me she was bored.

"I thought she wanted to go out and do something. When I asked if there was anywhere, in particular, she wanted to go, she gave me the strangest stare. She said, 'I'm bored with our relationship. I don't think I love you.' "

He paused a beat.

"It's just that it seemed so easy for you, bro. I was there. I saw it for myself. You didn't even need to enter the theater. You knew while we were still out in the parking lot, and you knew she was inside. And you were right."

Everything Riley said was true. They had attended a charity bachelorette auction. Quinn was in a nearly unstoppable one-man stampede toward the lobby.

"I remember that like it was yesterday." Quinn

smiled. "I guess I never shared all those times I experienced…well let's just call it a false sense. Times when I was so confident I found the love of my life and she just walked out without any explanation.

"And that, by the way, is how I got the reputation of being a playboy. The press naturally thought I was carving notches in my belt. That wasn't the case at all."

"And you really thought that you had found your lioness with each encounter?"

"Yes, that's exactly what I'm telling you."

Riley nodded. "Now I understand your reluctance to wear that playboy label."

Silence filled the room for a bit before Riley said, "I guess I came home to lick my wounds. I've told myself I'm never going to be fooled again. But this morning…"

His words trailed off as he thought about his experience with…he realized he didn't even know her name.

"I can't believe I'm saying this, but when I ducked into *That Coffee Shop* down the street, I think I met my lioness. Can you believe my stupidity?"

Riley was relieved when Quinn responded with "Tell me more."

"All the hallmarks were there—or so I thought. A sudden surge of electricity flew through me when we accidently touched. My heart pounded faster and louder than a drum in a heavy metal group. But even as I opened the door, I experienced a heightened awareness of all my senses. Especially my smell. I swear, the moment I walked in, I could detect the wafting of the lavender fragrance she wore."

Riley felt his brother's eyes on him before he heard his words. "You know what you have to do."

Chapter 4

Charlee leaned with her back against the front counter, her elbows resting on the flat surface. As she faced the coffee pots and watched as Mel idly wipe the counter and arrange the accessories, she confessed, "I'm a bit disappointed Mr. Impervious hasn't been back. I guess there really wasn't anything there but—"

She stopped talking suddenly, when she saw Mel making slashing motions along her throat with her index finger. Every muscle in her body froze. As quietly as she could speak, she said, "You're trying to tell me he's right behind me, aren't you?"

Even though Mel hadn't seen him, she must have recognized him from Charlee's description.

Mel gave her a slight nod and then looked at Mr. Impervious.

She did the only thing any respectable woman would do who got caught talking about a gorgeous man within his earshot. She dipped down immediately below the counter and hyperventilated. Her breaths came faster and faster. She sat for several seconds, trying to will her body to control itself.

"It's no use hiding," Mr. Impervious said. He leaned over the counter and gazed down at her. "I can still see you." She smiled weakly and gave him a timid tiny wave with her forefinger.

"There's no way I can get out of this one with my

dignity intact."

Mel extended a hand to help her get to her feet and beelined to the kitchen. Heat radiated off of Charlee's cheeks. She knew her face turned a bright red. She stammered an apology to Mr. Impervious.

The man stood with both palms down on the counter but said nothing. She involuntarily squirmed as her words were met with silence. Without thinking, she touched his hand. The electric surge occurred again, just like it did the first time. Before she could pull her hand away, Mr. Impervious took his other hand and placed it on top of hers.

This surge of electricity—no, now she knew it was more, much more than electricity, static or otherwise. It was, without a doubt, a sexual surge. A bonding of sorts. As hokey as she knew it was, it was nature's way of alerting her that she just experienced what others would call love at first sight.

As soon as that thought popped into her brain, her mind rejected it. *Holy Heavens! Where did that come from?* She didn't even know his real name and her mind is jumping to "love at first sight." *Ridiculous.*

She looked him in the eye—his amber eyes—as she sized him up. The longer she gazed into those eyes, the more ensorcelled she grew.

She marveled at how the track lighting above the counter elicited every nuance of color in his eyes. His hands seemed more like paws. Not destructive mauling paws of a feral beast, but the large loving ones of an animal dedicated to protecting those he loved. She feared if he kept his hand on hers too long, she would start to think about love at first sight again. Yet she didn't move it.

When he did remove his hand from hers, she felt an immediate and crushing disconnect. She fell back to earth and experienced the gripping weight and limitation of the force of gravity. *Did an astronaut experience this remorse and loss of freedom when he re-entered the earth's atmosphere and found himself bound by gravity?*

"I apologize," he said, as he shook his head slightly. "I think I've overstepped my bounds. That's not at all what I intended to happen. That was uncharacteristic of me."

"Don't be," she said. She couldn't take her gaze from his eyes.

"Pardon me?"

"Don't be sorry."

****

Her simple answer, spoken quietly, startled him and at the same time emboldened him. He recalled his conversation with his brother, and he decided that there was only one way to know for sure if this were his lioness standing in front of him or simply his hormones and pheromones run amuck.

The downside of all this, of course, was that he put his heart on the line…again. In an instant he wondered how many times he would do this to himself. Twist himself up inside like a pretzel, only to feel the painful unraveling of the relationship within several months. Could he put himself through all this yet again?

Then he looked in her green eyes. And caught another incredible whiff of that unmistakable lavender swirling about her. *What if she really is my lioness? Could I bear being a nomad lion for the rest of my life? That's it. It's now or never.*

She had just given him the perfect opportunity to discover what was happening between them. All he had to do was take it. All he had in mind was one date—a test date, he labeled it in his mind. A horrible description, he knew, but then he was never accused of being a wordsmith. If things went south on the date, he could assume that this was not his soulmate.

What then?

Simple, he told himself boldly, *I'll buy my coffee at another coffee shop.*

They stood there for what seemed an excruciating long time in silence. She—oh, my goodness, he didn't even know her name—not saying a word, really not making a move. He gathered up the courage and asked, "So, how 'not sorry' should I be?"

When she laughed, it sounded like an angel.

"That depends," she said.

"Could I tell you that from the first time I saw you, the first time we touched, I wanted to ask you out? And if I asked you out now, what do you think the chances of your saying yes would be?"

Again, she laughed. And, again, he heard angels. He noticed she was blushing. He couldn't remember the last time he saw a grown woman blush. The women he met in New York were too sophisticated to blush.

This was not, he thought, how playboys seduce women. If he were true to his reputation, he would have already given her some shallow line and they would have been finalizing the details.

Before she had a chance to answer, he said, "I would be honored if you would consent to go out to dinner with me."

"You really don't need to be so formal," she said.

"A simple 'Would you like to go to dinner?' would work."

"Well, would you? Please don't tell me you put me through all of this just so you can say no?"

"I would like to go out with you, Mr. Imp..." she stopped when she realized his name wasn't Impervious, "I don't even know your name. I'm Charlee, by the way, Charlee Lightheart."

"Riley Brockton, very nice to meet you. Can I pick you up tomorrow evening at seven?"

"Consider it a date."

****

Charlee played it cool and calm until Riley walked out the café door. Then she ran into the kitchen to hunt down Mel. She wasn't there. Marco, one of the cooks, said she had just taken a meal to the floor.

"You should have seen her if you were at the counter."

"Yeah, I was bit distracted." She didn't pause long enough to worry about the puzzled look he gave her.

She raced toward the door and nearly collided with Mel who entered through the swinging metal door she rushed to exit.

"You'd never guess what just happened," she said, breathlessly.

"What?"

She pulled her near the counter area for some semblance of privacy. Of course, at *That Coffee Shop* privacy was nearly nonexistent.

"Riley Brockton? That's who he is?" Mel said.

"Does that matter?"

"I know you pride yourself for not following the news much, but you have heard of Brockton

Enterprises, haven't you?"

"He's that Brockton?"

"I'm sure he is. One and the same."

Her lips fell, her previously inerasable smile now flatlining. She tried to open her mouth to form words, but none came out. It didn't matter, there were no words to describe her horror, her newly found trepidation. Mr. Impervious was one thing, but she knew a Brockton was seriously out of her league.

What did I get myself into?

Chapter 5

Riley looked like a teenage boy when Charlee opened the door, a small bouquet of Stargazer lilies in his hands.

"I hope you're not allergic to flowers," he said. He extended the lilies toward her awkwardly, as if he wanted to get the moment over.

"How thoughtful."

"Stargazers are my favorite," he said.

"Mine too."

They stood there for several seconds, on either side of the threshold in an uncomfortable silence.

"Where are my manners?" she said at last. "Please do come in."

"Let me put these in water, and I'll be ready to go. How cool. They come with their own vase." She knew it wasn't much of a comment, but in her nervous state that was all she could think of.

She walked through the living room and was in the dining room on her way to the kitchen when she turned to look behind her. He still stood at the door.

"You can come with me. It's a small house, I'm sure you won't get lost."

He smiled that lopsided, boyish grin she noticed at the coffee shop.

"I'm sure it's far smaller than the place you live."

She watched as he entered the house and took in

her living room. He glanced at the fireplace to the left. And she noticed he gave a quick glance to the couch on the right. She wondered what was going through his mind. *Why did I ever invite him in? I'm sure none of this even compares to where he lives.*

As he crossed the dining room, which she had decorated in an art deco motif, he commented.

"Love the prints. You have a great eye for decorating."

"Posters."

"What?"

"Fooled me," he said as he glanced back into the dining room.

She clipped the ends of the stems. She picked up the white packet that came with the flowers. "The official name for this is 'powdery stuff.' I don't care what the florists call it."

"Good to know," he said. "That's much shorter than what I call it."

Charlee had just finished pouring it into the water. "What do you call it?"

"That stuff-that-makes-the-flower-last longer." He winked at her.

She carried the bouquet the short distance into the dining room and placed them in the middle of the table. She stepped back to admire them and gasped.

"What?" Riley asked, "What's wrong?"

"Nothing. They just look so beautiful here against the black of the plates and cups of the place settings. What a delightful contrast. Thank you again."

"Any time. Are we ready?"

"Absolutely."

The initial strained silence had been replaced with

small talk. She felt relieved and hopeful as she locked the door as they left.

****

"What a comfortable, welcoming restaurant," Charlee said as Riley pushed her seat under the table. He lingered a moment longer than needed as he basked in the fragrances of her hair and her cologne. And the third fragrance? He called upon his leonine abilities to separate even the smallest amounts of fragrances. Freshness, he decided. She didn't overuse any cologne. It was refreshing in every sense of the word.

The scent only added to his conviction that he did make the perfect choice of restaurant. It was an out-of-the-way place called *Red's*. The lighting was low, the customers sparse and well separated from each other, and the lit candle on the table whispered romance.

A remarkable woman. Utterly devoid of pretense, unaware of her own natural beauty. He finally pulled himself away from her and took his own seat at the table.

"This isn't at all what I expected," she said as she looked around.

"What did you expect?" He tilted his head as he posed the question.

"A setting that was a bit flashier, I guess. I didn't have you pegged for the type of man who appreciated nuance."

He let out a hoarse, husky sound mixed with a chuckle. "You're not disappointed, I hope. Because if you are, I know many places we can go instead of this." He began to rise to leave.

"No. No." her voice rose a pitch. "Sit down. This is perfect. Absolutely perfect."

"I've visited enough of those places to last a lifetime," he said. "Most people go there to be seen by other people who are there to be seen...well, you get the picture. Trust me, most people don't frequent places like that because they're interested in good food. And they aren't there so they can get to know somebody better.

"To be truthful, I've only been here once before. Both the food and the service were excellent. It's the perfect place to come when you want an evening of fine and intelligent conversation—without the need to wonder who's looking at you and why. I was hoping you would like it."

"I think it's perfect."

At the reassurance of her approval, his muscles relaxed. He didn't even know he had tensed them up. He wondered how long they had been like that.

Because he knew he had so much riding on this date—like learning if Charlee were his lioness—he had taken a certain amount of time in planning the perfect evening. He wanted the most romantic spot in town. He hoped to get as far away as possible from the prying eyes of those in Prague's highest social circles.

He desired to steer clear of the women who eyed each other up like lions stalking their prey. They were quite polite in front of each other, but, oh, the backbiting. And it wasn't just the women, he thought. He had found himself to be the object of gossip among the men more than once.

But mostly he stayed away from the trendy places because he tired of random individuals walking up to him and asking about his business ventures. People he barely knew. People who had no right posing those types of questions and even less rights in getting an answer.

Now that he was back home, his privacy seemed more important than ever before. He didn't want to wake up in the morning to discover their picture in the *Prague Bugle*. Charlee deserved better treatment than that.

Oh, who was he kidding? Part of the reason he brought her to such a quiet place was to placate his bruised and insecure inner lion. It was a precaution, though, he would never regret.

The server came to the table to ask their wine preference. Riley nodded to Charlee to get her opinion. When she said she had none, he ordered one of his favorites.

"I hope you like this," he said.

"I'm sure I will. I don't drink enough of it to have much preference," she replied.

The server returned with the wine and poured a small amount for Riley to taste. He nodded his approval, and the server filled Charlee's glass.

"This is exceptionally good." She paused a beat.

"I may not know wine but ask me the differences in the types of coffees and teas. Knowing that is nearly an occupational hazard. It ranks up there in providing most individuals with too much information. But after all is said and done, I can lead you to your perfect cup of coffee."

She asked for his recommendation on an entrée. They both ordered chicken cacciatore. While they sipped their wine waiting for their meals, he tilted his head and gazed into the face of the beauty across the table. He was struck by her long blonde hair.

"What is it?" she asked, as she placed her hand over her mouth. "Do I have something stuck between my teeth?"

"No. No. Not at all. This is the first time I've seen you with your hair down. I've only seen it a ponytail."

"It's easier to handle that way," she answered.

"This style suits you well." He dropped the conversation there, but his thoughts continued. The candlelight's glow teased the most luscious shades of gold from her flowing tresses creating a halo effect around her head.

Throughout the meal, he purposely moved the conversation along, fearful if he didn't, he would touch her hand or worse, her thigh, and the intense sensual surge of desire would overwhelm his senses.

He respected her more than that. And he needed, more than anything, to show her that respect. Every minute more he spent in her presence, he became more confident he had found his soulmate, his lioness. He didn't want her to flee because he couldn't control himself.

****

Riley escorted Charlee to her front door. As she unlocked it, she kept her hand on the doorknob. "Would you like to come in?" He didn't answer right away. She marveled how he had transformed from the self-confident wine connoisseur to that awkward teenager unsure of the proper response.

If he wouldn't answer, then she would. "I really would love for you to come in."

She prayed she wasn't being too forward. Darn it, though, she wasn't sure she could simply let him walk away without at least a kiss. God, right now what she wouldn't give for his touch.

But there was a part of her that feared it, feared she wouldn't be able to control the near animalistic urge he conjured within the recesses of her body. As trite as it sounded, she would ask him in for a cup of tea and let it go at that. If anything else occurred, so be it. If not, she would have to accept it.

"Of course," she quickly added, "you're not obligated." Perhaps she was wrong, perhaps he had no further desire or yearning to touch her again. Maybe he didn't feel that surge anymore. Or worse yet, maybe she made some social faux pas during the meal that turned him off…maybe…

"I'd love to come in," he said, stopping the wild roller coaster of her thoughts. Once inside, he confessed, "I really don't need a cup of tea."

"Neither do I," she replied.

By this time, they were halfway through the dining room. "I want to kiss you," he said.

"I want you to kiss me."

"But I'm not sure," he warned her, "if I do, that I could contain my emotions to only a good-night kiss. I'm afraid I'll take you, all of you. And you don't seem to be the type—"

"Just kiss me," she interrupted him. "I'm a big girl. You might discover I've been waiting to be taken the entire evening."

As they moved closer, she was fully aware of what had occurred every other time they casually touched.

What would happen when they kissed?

Chapter 6

Charlee held her breath as Riley moved toward her.

Her lips met his, and electricity rushed through her body. Her body trembled as he wrapped an arm around her waist.

"Are you okay?" he asked in a hoarse, husky, barely audible voice.

All she could do was nod.

"Should we continue?"

She nodded once more, this time quickly. She couldn't stop now, not even if she wanted to. An unseen magnetic force pulled her toward him.

"The bedroom," she quietly said, trying hard not to interrupt the intense feeling, "down the hallway to the right."

Once in the room, she wrapped her arms around his waist, wanting every part of her body to be up against his. His muscles, starting with his shoulders all the way to his legs, were firm and inviting. She moved carefully as they inched their way to the bedroom, she didn't want to—she couldn't bring herself to—allow their lips to separate.

She had one brief moment of trepidation, but she immediately dismissed it. She started to undress him, all the while keeping her lips on his, not wanting to be deprived of one second of their sweet taste.

Her movements were interrupted when his tongue

parted her lips and he hungrily explored her mouth.

She faced another doubt. This one of apprehension. But wasn't this the moment she had been pleading for all week long? Wasn't this what consumed her dreams, enveloped her nights, and haunted her days?

He raked his hands through her long golden tresses. "I can't believe what a beautiful woman you are," he said quietly.

They undressed each other. Her mind shut the entire world out. Only the two of them existed in a place of unspeakable splendor.

He suckled her breasts, her hips rising in response. She heard a soft husky moan. It took her a few seconds to recognize that she was moaning in passionate, almost uncontrollable delight.

Their lovemaking had only begun, and she was nearly insanely charged with sexual emotions. Where were they going? How much better could it possibly get?

Ripples of sexual pleasure flooded over her body numbing her with the magic of the moment. She reached for him, felt his hard organ grow harder. He made a noise that sounded like a growl and nuzzled his face between her breasts. His hair, silky against her breasts, was unbelievably soft.

He let out another barely audible hoarse moan. She felt it more than heard it as his body was taut against hers. As he continued to nuzzle her, she marveled at his actions, his concern for her pleasure. She swore that every move he made was tailored to her needs at that exact point in time. How did he know? She had never experienced such satisfaction with anyone before.

She admired every part of his body, taking in the

fragrances that made him so irresistible. She ran her hand through his deliciously brown, curly hair. She purposely filed the silky touch and the intoxicating scent of the shampoo into her memory, knowing that always and forever that just a hint of this mixture of scents would be linked with this intimate moment in time.

He took her hand from below his waist and intertwined his fingers into hers and held them above her head.

Charlee felt him gently ease into her and push against her body. She closed her eyes as the fullness satisfied her. She wriggled her hands from his paws and grasped his hair as she rode with his slow, tender, measured moves for several moments of sheer delight.

Then she let go of his hair and moved her attention down his back, exploring his body. Charlee's eyes never left Riley's as she delighted in the sensations as her fingers traced his back. When she reached his butt, she squeezed it with both hands, her eyes now on his smile. His movements grew faster.

Her desire grew in intensity until she could stand it no longer. She raised her hips higher; she closed her eyes. Let it be now, she thought. Let it be—

"Are you ready?"

"Yes! Yes!" There was no need to think. The desire inside her had been building from the moment he undressed her.

She felt a sheer release of pleasure. She sensed he, too, had released his emotions, his energy. He collapsed on top of her. His nose again nuzzling her breasts, tickling, teasing her and sending prickles to every inch of her skin, his curly hair tickling her lips.

Her breathing was deep and heavy in response to the pent-up sensations she had from the moment of the first kiss to now.

His deep breaths vibrated on her skin. She knew it was an impossible wish, but she didn't want either one of them to move from this spot. Ever.

Chapter 7

The following morning Charlee woke up alone in her bed—disappointed. *Something magical happens when the guy you shared such an intimate bond wakes up next to you the morning after.*

She knew he was a busy executive, but still she mourned the fact that he didn't stay. She sat up in bed, raked her hand through her hair. That was when she smelled it.

Coffee?

Definitely coffee. What the...?

Then he appeared in the doorway with her "Kiss the Cook" apron on and the chef hat she received as a gag gift. And nothing else.

He appeared to be entirely comfortable dressed in the apron-only costume as if he wore the attire every morning. And for all she knew he might.

His legs were bare, and the area of the apron with the word "cook" printed on it protruded. When he twirled around to show her the entire "outfit" she got a glimpse of his tight bare butt. Perfection.

"Coffee, my dear?" he asked as he sat on the edge of the bed and offered her a cup. "As I recall from last night, you drink it black."

She took the cup nodding. "Thank you," she said and took a sip of it. "This is just the way I love my French roast."

She took another sip. "When I woke up and you weren't in bed with me, I assumed you had left. After all, I'm sure your executive duties keep you busy."

"They do. And I called this morning to see if I had any meetings. The few I did have I asked my secretary to reschedule for me. Thought this was where I should be." He paused a beat.

"Why are you looking at me like that?"

"Because most men wouldn't do that."

"They wouldn't?" he asked innocently. "Sounds like you speak from experience."

"More experience than I care to admit."

"I've got breakfast started. I hope you don't mind. I've grated the potatoes for hash browns, and they're soaking in cold water now. And I've got the eggs whisked waiting patiently on the sink for an omelet.

"But all that can wait. A good omelet requires the eggs to be at room temperature before you pour them into the pan, and the longer the potatoes soak, the better they'll be."

He took the cup from her and said, "I think we have a little more time to ourselves, as long as you don't have to be at the coffee shop anytime soon."

She shook her head. "Got Mel working my shift."

Mel practically demanded she work my shift "just in case" the spark between them would ignite an extended visit. What a good friend she is.

"Then we have no problems."

"Who am I to protest?" she asked.

He set the cup on the nightstand and kissed her deeply. They fell back on the pillows.

Yes, she thought, everything else can wait.

Chapter 8

"Charlee Lightheart, you're not supposed to be here today." Mel greeted her from behind the counter. "I gave you the day off," she said as she wagged her finger.

"I'll deal with that last sentence later." Charlee joined her. "I completely forgot about the fundraiser Diane Montage was holding today. I had to come. I didn't want you to think I abandoned you."

"Everyone's seated and eating. Jessica is taking good care of them." Mel paused and stared at Charlee.

"What?" Charlee poured herself a cup of coffee.

"You know what." Mel grabbed herself a cup as well. "Let's talk. I want details."

Charlee laughed. "How did I know that was coming? Can I, at least for the moment, get away with saying it was an amazingly awesome experience. I think I should go say hi to Diane and her group."

"That's your way of getting out of telling me anything."

Charlee looked over at the banquet area, a small room added to the original shop. The owners before her had it built and used it as a bar. Charlee decided it would be perfect for larger gatherings.

"Okay, Diane and her guests look like they're busy. Let's sit down at the end of the counter."

Charlee gave her friend as many details as she was

comfortable sharing. She knew Mel would have no trouble filling in the blanks with her imagination.

"I did take a quick pic of the lilies before I left the house." Charlee took her phone out of her jeans pocket.

"Gorgeous." Mel leaned over and gave her a hug. "You deserve this."

"I don't know." Charlee sighed. "It feels too good to be true. He's so out of my league it's crazy."

She stood. "Let me go over and talk to our guests. Diane said this event was to raise money for a boy with brain cancer." She downed the last of her coffee. "I can't imagine what the family is going through. And the medical bills they have."

"I'll get their proceeds first." Mel jumped from the stool. "You can give them to Diane now."

Charlee nodded, and Mel ran upstairs to the office. She was back in no time and handed her a thick envelope. "I did exactly as you asked."

"You always do when it comes to these events. Are you coming with me? I know how much you love this moment."

"Can I?" Mel broke into a huge grin. "It's so cool how generous you are. I happen to know you lose money on these events. If I were your business manager—"

"You're not my business manager. Let's go."

"Diane, is everyone enjoying themselves?" Charlee asked above the din of some 25 people in the room. She thought the answer was obvious.

Diane had been talking to a woman Charlee recognized. She was a regular customer. "Hi, Karen. I didn't mean to interrupt."

"What a nice surprise. Mel told me you took the

day off," Diane said. Charlee hoped that Mel hadn't told them why.

"I had to come in and say hi."

Charlee scanned the tables. She saw empty platters that had held spaghetti and chicken. For these events, she always served family style to lessen the work on her staff.

"Everything was delicious. And Mel and Jessica took good care of us. Even Marco came out to make sure we were okay."

Charlee smiled. "Marco's my best cook. But don't let him know that. I don't want his head to get any bigger than it already is."

"There is one small problem though, Charlee." Diane said softly.

"What is it? The food was good, wasn't it?" Charlee couldn't believe after all the compliments she had screwed something up.

"The food was delicious." Diane took Charlee's arm and led her to a relatively quiet area behind the bar where a dozen baskets were set for a raffle. Mel followed.

"We advertised a spaghetti dinner. I wasn't counting on the chicken when we calculated the costs of the tickets."

"Is that all you're worried about?" Charlee held the woman's shoulder. "I hope you don't mind. I threw that in as an extra. I was hoping that would loosen up your guests' wallets for those raffle items you have. By the way, is there still time for me to buy tickets?"

"Don't worry, boss," Mel said. "I took care of that for you. You've got a couple in for each item."

"Here's your profits, too. I hope this helps."

Diane took the envelope and thanked Charlee. Then she noticed the amount written on it. "Oh, no. There must be some mistake. This is the sum of the tickets without subtracting the cost of the food."

Charlee didn't even have to look at Mel. She knew this was the moment Mel broke into a big smile. Her assistant would probably tell her later she had tears in her eyes. She shook her head. "I don't charge for food or for my staff."

Now the shop owner thought Diane would cry, but she continued to explain. "There's always a great need for money in situations like this. I feel honored to be able to do my part. Once the attendees know how much was raised, I hope they'll be inspired to donate even more."

"Oh, Charlee, I don't know how to thank you." Diane gave her a long, tight hug. She stepped back. "And Mel, thank you for everything you've done to make us feel at home here." She gave her a long hug as well, then ran off toward the group.

"Quiet, everyone, I have some wonderful news."

Charlee looked at her assistant. "It's time we leave."

Mel nodded, and they went into the main area of the coffee shop. Jessica was stationed at the cash register. A short line had formed.

"Here, let me help you." Mel hurried to her side. Charlee picked up the coffee pot and checked on the customers.

They didn't get a chance to reunite at the counter for nearly an hour. Only a few people were left in the banquet room. Charlee stared in that direction.

"Doesn't it feel as if we're doing an awful lot of

fundraisers lately? This town seems to have more than its share of devastating diseases."

"Yeah, I was thinking the same thing. You don't think people are taking advantage of you?"

"No. These are all legit needs. I'm just wondering why living in Prague is hazardous to your health."

Chapter 9

That night, Charlee sat on in her living room and stared at the television set. She had armed herself with a soda, a bowl of popcorn, and the remote control. But her mind wasn't on the television. It wasn't even on the successful fundraiser or anything about the coffee shop. It was on Riley, and their date last night that extended into the morning.

She was ecstatic when he texted her during the day. He thanked her for a lovely evening. She returned his message between customers, especially mindful to thank him for the breakfast. And she mentioned how good he looked in the Kiss the Cook apron.

His last text at about two o'clock promised he'd talk to her after he had finished with a conference. He even made several yukky emojis to show his displeasure with the meeting. He hadn't. She knew he was a busy man. She tried to take it in stride, but she had been involved in bad relationships before. Men always said they'd call, they'd visit. But they seldom did. Last night went so well, how could this be history repeating itself?

The doorbell startled her and knocked her out of her doubts. "It's too much to hope for," she said, as she went for the door. She looked through the peephole first, then laughed. She quickly opened the door.

Riley started with an apology. "I know. I know. I

told you I'd talk to you after my meeting." He glanced at his watch. "Technically, this is after my meeting. Just a bit later than I had planned on." He held a bottle of wine in one hand and raised it. "Care for a glass?"

"Of course, come in." She stepped aside. She closed the door after him. "Let's get that opened." She turned on a heel.

"Not so fast." He took her hand and pulled her toward him. "I believe this is the apology I owe you." He embraced her and kissed her. Her knees grew weak. "Now, that's a proper act of contrition," he said. "Let's get this thing open."

She led him through the living room and hoped he didn't notice how wobbly she was. She figured he hadn't when he asked, "Watching anything good on TV?"

"No, it was just on to keep me company."

He laughed. "Good, then my timing is perfect. I can keep you company now."

She pulled a corkscrew out of a kitchen drawer and handed it to Riley. Then she retrieved two glasses from the cabinet. He poured the wine and led her to the couch. As they settled in, he wrapped an arm around her; she snuggled close to him. It felt so right.

"So how was your day?" he asked as if they had been together forever.

"It was good. Wait on tables. Pour coffee. Serve food. Make conversation." She paused. "The Zen of coffee-shop ownership." She wasn't sure how much of her day he wanted to hear about. She thought she should keep it simple.

He nodded and then she asked, "So what did you do all day?" She looked up at his amber eyes.

"Are you implying I do nothing at work?" He pulled her closer.

"Not at all." She panicked. "I hope I didn't give you that idea."

"No, I'm just teasing." He took a sip of wine. "Though most people do think that. But my dad taught us kids the value of hard work."

There are kids? She never thought about other Brocktons before. But why should she?

"You have brothers and sisters?" she asked, intrigued.

"One brother, Quinn." He talked about his brother briefly. Though he said few words, she knew those words were evident of the love he had for his brother.

With only a little nudge from her, Riley explained the structure of the business. "To answer your first question, I basically buy and sell companies all day." He told her he recently moved back home from New York City. She knew by the way he dressed he was big bucks. But now she knew he was big city, too. What was she getting into?

"I came home because I got tired of the fakeness of the people," he said, as if reading her mind. "I don't want to talk about New York, I'd rather talk about you. Tell me about yourself."

Charlee told him that her parents had grown up in Prague and she was born in town. But they moved when she was five. "They didn't move far. Just a couple hours away to Bell Wyck, Ohio."

"So, did you go to the University of Northern Ohio?" he asked.

"No, I wanted to." She paused. "But my mom died when I was a senior in high school. I'm an only child.

Dad's arthritis got worse. He had a hard time doing for himself. Even tying his shoes was rough. His fingers couldn't do that detailed of an activity." Riley held her even closer.

"I chose just to work and stay home with Dad. He missed Mom. He was lonely."

He knitted his brow, as if he were thinking about what she had said. "I'm sorry you missed out on your schooling."

She smiled slightly. "I'm not. That time I had with Dad in his last years was so valuable. I'll never regret my decision."

Riley poured her another glass of wine, and they talked a little longer about family. He talked how his brother, Quinn, and he were often mistaken for twins. "But he always has a way of saying something pointed that keeps me in my place that I'm still his kid brother."

They sat there for several minutes in a contented silence. Riley moved a bit. "I hate to do this." He kissed the top of her head. "I have a morning meeting I need to prepare for."

She felt a pang of disappointment, but she understood. He wrapped his arms around her and kissed her. Her knees went weak; her spine tingled with electricity.

He stood, and when he did, brought her with him. They stood in front of the couch held together, she thought, by that unseen magnetism. Finally, he held her at arm's length. They headed for the door, his arm wrapped around her shoulder, hers around his waist.

"I hate to leave like this," he said.

She laughed, despite her sadness at seeing him go so soon. "I hate for you to leave like this."

He gave her one last quick kiss as he opened the door. "I'll see you tomorrow morning when I come in for coffee and muffins." And he left.

She stood, her back against the door, as she thought she was the luckiest person in Prague. No, all the world.

Chapter 10

Riley smiled as he heard the small bell on the coffee shop door tinkle as he walked in. He was eager to see Charlee again—even if only the length of the time it took to make lattes and bag muffins. When he dressed in his best black designer suit, he told himself it was for the negotiations that would take up most of his morning. That was a convenient excuse. He had Charlee on his mind.

Hell, she was on his mind from the moment he left her house last night to the time he fell asleep. He wasn't one to remember dreams, but if he had any, he was sure she was in them.

As he walked the short distance to the counter, his expectations grew. Until he noticed who was at the cash register.

"Good morning, Mr. Brockton," a woman who wasn't Charlee said, a bit too brightly.

He was at a loss for words. "I thought…" his words trailed off.

"Charlee's here." He felt relieved.

"It's not that—"

"Oh, don't worry. I'm not offended. Let me get her."

She hurried into the kitchen, and within seconds Charlee appeared, her golden hair tied back in a ponytail and her apron tied around her slim waist, accentuating her hips.

"You really did come," she said. Her smile melted his heart.

"You thought I would be a no-show?"

Her cheeks reddened. "I would never stand you up." He winked at her.

The woman who greeted him followed Charlee out of the kitchen, and said, "I'll get your order, Mr. Brockton, so you two can talk for a while." Riley noticed she too had blushed.

"Where are my manners?" Charlee said. "This is Mel."

"Hi, Mel." He shook her hand. "And please, call me Riley."

He then gave her his order of three lattes and three coffee cake muffins, and Mel got busy.

Riley started to say something when Mel let out a curse word. "Sorry," she said softly. "I'm frustrated, Charlee. The evening crew didn't clean the steam wand again. It's clogged."

"This is going to take at least ten minutes, Riley. Could we deliver the coffee to you?" Mel asked.

He heard voices and glanced behind him. At least a half-dozen people were behind him.

"Why do these things always happen at the worst times?" Charlee asked. Mel shrugged. Then she said to Riley, "This is our morning to-go rush."

He glanced back. "We've got this. Let me behind the counter."

"We?" Charlee asked, and began to protest. But he had already taken off his jacket and laid it on an empty stool.

"Yes, we. I can unclog that. It looks like it's going

to take the two of you to take care of your customers." While he talked, Mel had already let him behind the counter, and he was in the process of sizing up the situation.

"I need lemons and hot water." Mel went off to retrieve them. Charlee, though, simply stared at him. He nodded toward the queue of people. "They're waiting. If anyone wants a latte or cappuccino, tell them I'll be done soon."

He watched her interact with the customers as Mel brought his supplies. She thanked him and hastily moved to the cash register to help.

All he heard for a few minutes was the whoosh of the pressure going through the wand as he alternated turning it on for several seconds, then turning it off. On one of the off cycles, he heard a woman say, "That's a handsome employee there, Charlee. Is he new?"

Immediately another agreed and commented, "Well-dressed, too. Now I know why coffee prices are so high. Got to keep the employees dressed in style."

He heard nothing more for several minutes as he focused on his task. Then he felt someone tap his shoulder. "Riley, your phone is ringing." Charlee stood next to him holding his jacket. He looked up, saw only a few customers left, and smiled. "I better take that. Renee is probably wondering where I am."

"Brockton... Really, I'm that late? I'll be there in about fifteen minutes. I'm just about done here." He smiled up at Charlee, nodded, and gave her a thumbs up. "What am I doing? Well, I'll save that story for when I see you, Renee." He held the phone away from his ear, then said to Charlee, "My visitors are a bit miffed I'm late."

He turned his attention back to his caller. "Yeah, I know they're upset. I think they're more upset they have to meet me in Prague rather than New York City. But I have faith you'll keep them calm with your charm." He clicked the phone off and returned it to his jacket pocket.

"Your meeting. I forgot all about it. I'm so sorry."

"Do I look worried about being late for a meeting?" When he didn't get a response, he answered the question himself. "No, I'm not. These people weren't happy to begin with to come out to Ohio. And they want something from me. So, they'll wait."

He turned to Mel, who had just waited on the last few customers in line. "It's ready to use. Make my order last." He didn't know how many had to wait for the wand to get cleaned, but he hoped they weren't inconvenienced. "And tell them their coffee's on me."

He enjoyed the look of amazement on Charlee and Mel's faces. Charlee started to protest, "You don't have to do this. It was our mistake."

"I know. But it did take me a little longer than I expected. I'm a little rusty. I'll just sit at the end of the counter until you get caught up." He pointed to an empty seat. "And by the way, make that five lattes now. I think I'll bring a peace offering." He paused. "Not that I have to, but…"

Mel told Charlee to sit with him; she had everything under control. And it looked like it. The only customers left were the ones who waited for their lattes. And they looked content.

"Care to tell me where you learned how to unclog an espresso machine?" she asked once she sat next to him.

He gave her a peck on the cheek. "My dad. His first job was as a coffee salesman. After ten years of selling, he bought the company." Riley smiled as he remembered how his father continued to buy companies after that. "And then another company and another. But back to the point. My brother Quinn and I used to tag along with him at the coffee company. You'd be surprised how often he was asked to clean those things. We learned just by watching him. And then...he would put us to work."

Charlee nodded, apparently satisfied with his explanation. "Then I have your dad to thank in addition to you. It would have taken us twice as long if one of us had to clean that." There was a moment of silence, and he wanted nothing more than to embrace and kiss her.

"Here are the lattes, Riley," Mel said. "And I've included extra muffins, too, just in case you want to make a larger peace offering."

He stood and put on his jacket. "Duty calls." He kissed Charlee and gathered up the cardboard container of four lattes in one hand and the bag and the fifth coffee in the other. "I'll text you later." And he kissed her again.

As he walked out the door, he felt confident not only in the outcome of the meeting, but in his new relationship with Charlee, his lioness.

****

Charlee watched as Riley exited and, as luck would have it, someone entered at the same time and opened the door for him. She could see him nod in appreciation.

"That was a surprise," Mel said. "That's about all I can say."

Charlee laughed. "I know. Who would have a thought a billionaire could do anything manual like that?"

She sighed and wondered what other surprises he held. Then she realized she had just met him; he probably had many. She looked forward to learning them all.

"It's time to get ready for our lunch crowd." Mel's comment knocked her out of her reverie. She checked on the kitchen while Mel retrieved the lunch menus. She went through the motions of helping Mel bus the few tables, but her mind was on Riley. Even when she checked on the kitchen crew, she thought about him and his promise to text.

Perhaps, she shouldn't say promised; mentioned would be a better word. After all, she thought, Riley was a busy man. And she knew firsthand how time gets the better of you. Then the lunch rush began.

She barely had time to think about Riley for an hour and a half with the steady pace of orders. Finally, the café grew quieter and there were more tables to clean than guests left. She dutifully got an empty tub from the kitchen and headed for the dining area. She knelt on the booth bench and started when her cell phone chirped.

She sucked in a deep breath and pulled the phone out of her back jeans pocket. It was Riley. So far, he was two for two following through. At that moment, Mel stopped by. "By that smile on your face, I'd say Riley texted you."

"He did. He wants to know if he can stop by tonight."

"That's great. When is he coming over? Do you

need to leave early?"

"I haven't even answered him yet." Charlee put the phone in her pocket and started to put several glasses and cups in the tub.

"Stop." Mel grabbed them from her. "If you haven't answered him yet, then why are you busing this table?"

"I don't want it to seem like I'm waiting for him to text. I thought I'd wait a while." She reached for a plate, but Mel stopped her.

"The man was here this morning and cleaned our espresso machine. He deserves an answer." Her friend grabbed the now-full tub. "And besides, we both know you were waiting for him to text." She pivoted and, as she walked away, commanded, "Text him, now."

Chapter 11

"Get your butt out here at once!" With that, Mel sprinted from the front of the coffee shop to the kitchen where Charlee was cutting strawberries for the strawberry shortcake dessert she had advertised. She had discovered it was Riley's favorite.

Charlee's eyes grew wide with panic. She was just putting down the knife and taking off the gloves when Mel burst through the swing door.

"What's wrong?" Charlee asked. "Is the shop on fire?"

"No. But, Ms. I-don't-watch-the-news Lightheart, you really need to see the next story on Chanel 5's noon news show."

Mel pulled her out of the kitchen while she protested. "Why would I possibly want to see this, whatever it is?"

"Because it answers the question you asked the other day." Mel pushed her into a seat at the front counter where she had a clear view of the television. Once she was seated, Mel ran to get them both coffee.

Mel placed the coffee down in front of her. "For an intelligent woman, you sure are unaware of what's going on in the world."

"What question—?"

"Sshh! This is it."

"Once again Prague City Council voted against

54

placing a city-wide moratorium on hydraulic fracturing on the ballot, despite the growing pressure from the Citizens Against Fracking group and area University of Northern Ohio geology and environmental professors."

Lawrence Montgomery, the Chanel 5 TV anchor, explained fracking had become a booming business in the once economically distressed city. Standing next to him was Jeremy Zorkawsky of the University of Northern Ohio geology department. He asked the professor to explain the drilling process. "In simplest layman's terms, hydraulic fracturing is a method to extract natural gas from the earth. Instead of boring vertically down to the natural gas sites, fracking employs horizontal drilling."

"You mean drilling sideways? Is that even possible?" Montgomery asked.

"Certainly. They're doing it, despite the irreparable damage it's doing to the earth. This form of drilling stimulates the gas by fracturing deep rock formations with a highly pressurized liquid. These holes then provide an exit for the gas."

"That sounds harmless," Montgomery said.

"Hardly," the geologist said. "By allowing those rock formations to move and slide, you're setting yourself for the possibility of earthquakes. After all, what is an earthquake but two plates of the earth moving in different directions?"

"What has this—?" Charlee began.

Mel shushed her again. "Listen and you'll learn the cause of the rash of fundraisers."

"You mean you think the spurt of earthquakes northeast Ohio has experienced of late is due to the fracking?" Montgomery asked.

"Of course, the EPA will tell you otherwise, but I would stake my life on it."

Dr. Zorkawsky paused. "The EPA would like nothing better but to discount the earthquakes and ignore the damage fracking is doing to the residents of this community."

Montgomery looked at the camera. "Recently, several concerned citizens have formed a group to protest the drilling." The camera pulled long and showed a woman standing on opposite side of him.

"With me right now is Karen Manning, one of the members of the Citizens Against Fracking. Mrs. Manning, what are the group's concerns?"

"She was here at yesterday's event," Charlee whispered.

"First and foremost, the health of our families. The air is unfit to breathe. The water is undrinkable. And the rate of major illnesses among the families is astronomical."

"What kind of illness are we talking about?"

"Anything from chronic colds to brain tumors." She recounted the several types of cancer some residents who lived near the well had developed.

Montgomery nodded. "I understand there are issues with your water supply as well."

"What water?" Karen let out a snicker. "Our water is chunky and gray. Definitely not fit to drink."

The anchor thanked Karen and then signed off.

Mel let out a burst of air and said, "That's what's been causing all the fundraisers."

Charlee sat stunned for a moment. "I can't believe that fracking company can be so callous."

"My God, Charlee, what the hell are you thinking?

Did you think that the pharmaceutical company that made your dad's arthritis drugs was callous?"

"Of course, they were and still are," she cried. "They killed my dad."

She grew silent and stared into her coffee. Mel was about to say something when it finally clicked. "That company is an arrogant giant, just like the drug companies."

****

Riley frowned as he clicked off the television in Quinn's office following Montgomery's interview.

"They give the entire industrial system a bad name," Riley said with a flash of anger. "It's the twenty-first century, for God's sake. The era of the robber barons is long past."

Quinn nodded his agreement. "It's hard to believe there are still companies that allow their greed for profits to override the health of people and the environment. It's a damn shame."

"I'm pleased Brockton Enterprises has a good reputation. I know I'm not about to do anything to mar it," Riley said.

Just then the phone rang. It was Renee. "Sorry to interrupt, gentlemen, but there is a phone call for Riley. Something about his procuring a 'green' portfolio."

Chapter 12

One month.

An unbelievable month.

No, wait. Charlee decided it was an *amazingly awesome* month.

Well, to be honest, it hadn't quite been a month, but almost.

Rewind back to the day they met. That was the day she decreed, buoyed by a self-help book, something amazingly awesome would happen. She couldn't even begin to envision that her awesome day would be life-changing. The day she met Riley, sparks flew and became the catalyst for the most momentous romantic relationship she ever experienced.

If anyone suspected every so often she pinched herself to make sure it wasn't a dream, they would laugh at her. But after years of crappy and misguided entanglements, it seemed like she was living someone else's life.

She couldn't celebrate her one-month anniversary until tomorrow, and she thought it best not to mention it to Riley. Men usually didn't remember or recognize the importance of such a small steppingstone.

But the anniversary was uppermost in her mind as she floated around the coffee shop that morning. She smiled when she saw two of her favorite regulars, Ed and Fred walk in.

Those weren't their real names, but that's what she dubbed them on their first visit. One rarely came in without the other. To tell the truth, she didn't know their real names. For the longest time, she kept their monikers to herself. After she let the names slip one day, she discovered they enjoyed them—and undoubtedly the attention. So, the nicknames stuck.

One was tall, about six feet and bald except for a wisp of gray hair around the lower part of his head. What hair he lacked on his head he made up for with his beard. Snow white and hanging to the center of his torso. The other was about four inches shorter, had hair down to his shoulders which he always kept in a neat ponytail.

"Same booth as usual?" she asked them. Silly question. Of course, they were going to sit in "their" booth.

"Coffee?" she asked. Another silly question. She knew they had never deviated from their routine in the five years she'd owned the coffee shop. First the coffee. Ed took his black. Fred with cream and sugar. Then the muffins. Always coffee cake muffins. Every morning, she set two aside for them, just like clockwork.

As *That Coffee Shop's* signature variety, they were the first to sell out. She ensured Ed and Fred always got theirs. And, if by some fluke they didn't want them, she knew she would have no trouble selling them later in the day. But to this day, that fluke never occurred.

She left them at their booth and went to get two cups and the pot of coffee. She returned, poured their coffee, and turned to prepare their muffins.

"Before you go running off again, Charlee girl," Ed said, "sit with us a quick spell. We have a question or two to ask you."

"We've heard a few rumors. And want to know if they're true."

"Depends on what you've heard," she said easily. She could just imagine what they were about to ask. If it were anyone else, anger would be welling up in her. She would be prepared to say, "None of your business." But these two elderly gentlemen had good intentions and always looked out for her welfare. Something like uncles. And when you didn't have any family around, she thought, their concern was sweet.

She put the pot down on the table behind her and sat with them.

"Now, what's the rumor you've heard?"

Apparently, there were some topics even these two frank—that should be blunt—gentlemen found difficult to broach, as they looked at each other trying to get the other to speak.

"Okay, I'll ask," Fred said before he shot his pal a dirty look. "The word on the street is that you're dating that Brockton boy, what's his face. The one who had been staying in New York City."

She winced. She wondered how old a person had to be in order to be considered and called an adult in some people's eyes. They always called her "Charlee girl" and now Riley was "that Brockton boy." She bit her tongue and let the reference pass.

"It's good to know the word on the street is spot on," she said. "As a matter of fact, I am, and his name is Riley."

There, she said it. It was the first time she had said it to any of her customers, even though she knew many of them had figured it out by now. It was, after all, a small town. She wondered how quickly the "word on the street" would spread once the pair left the coffee shop.

"You best be careful," Ed said, sitting up a bit straighter, evidently so he would appear to have a bit more authority than what he did—which was zilch. "You know all the rumors about that family, don't you?"

Charlee took a deep breath. This is one of the reasons she had told so few people about it. For each person she would tell, she knew they would warn her against it and cite some rumor.

Fred cleared his throat. "The following interrogation is brought to you by Ed. His questions and concerns do not reflect my own personal views. I say more power to you, girl. As long as you're happy."

The pair had her baffled and nervous. "Just tell me what the rumor is."

"That they're nothing but a bunch of lion shifters," Ed said, his voice quivering a bit as if he had just heard Pearl Harbor had been bombed.

Fred threw up his hands. "Remember, I have nothing to do with this." He took a sip of his coffee.

She laughed. "I have heard those rumors. But I can't help you with clearing up that scuttlebutt. I really don't know."

"What do you mean you don't know?" he said, almost in a panic. "That's something you really need to find out for yourself if it's true."

She glanced at Fred who looked as if he were trying his best not to smile.

"Ed," she said as she patted his hand, "if I ever leave Riley alone in the living room and return to find a lion sitting on my couch, you'll be the first to know."

"Are you taking this question seriously, Charlee?" he asked. "I hear those Brocktons are lion shifters, and every time one of them throws a party they go out and roam the city as a pair of lions."

"This is what I have to put up with, Charlee girl," Fred laughed.

"There's nothing funny about this, Fred. We're talking about her future."

Fred took a deep breath.

"Everyone knows that the accusation of that family being lion shifters has been hanging over them for years. No, for generations," he said. "And everyone knows that the chances of that are about the same as the royal family over in England being those alien, reptilian shifters. Give it up already."

"But that's not what—"

"Don't be ridiculous, Ed," Fred said. "You know as well as I do that there ain't no shapeshifting lions in these parts of the state. They all cleared out ages ago. And it's a damned shame, too. They were a good lot of people. Some of my dad's best friends were lion shifters, he used to tell me.

"Now, what we do have are Bigfoot—families and families of Bigfoot. That's what you should be worrying about. You never know where they'll pop up next."

"I can't argue with that one," Ed conceded.

"I'll get your muffins now, gentlemen," she said as she stood. She reached for the coffee pot and refilled Fred's cup. Ed hadn't touched his. "If you think of any more rumors you'd like me to try to verify, just let me know."

As she walked away, she smiled. The two were still bickering.

When she approached the counter area, Mel glided up to her, deftly took the pot out of her hands, and was about to turn on her heel when she stopped and whispered, "Everything all right over there?" she asked.

"Yeah, I'll tell you all about it when we meet up behind the counter."

Mel nodded and took off.

Even though she and Riley hadn't spoken about the subject yet, it was clear in her mind that it was one that needed to be clarified. They both should know where they stood on certain topics. A generation ago, the ultimate clarification centered on whether the couple found themselves on the same page about having children. Now, the topics for some couples are "lion shifters." If the rumors she heard were, indeed true, she wondered why Riley hadn't yet mentioned it. If the family were, she would understand. No big deal.

Every family had secrets. Even hers. She couldn't chastise him for not mentioning his past when she hadn't brought up the skeletons in her own family closet. Secrets that could be as potentially explosive. She knew it was doubtful if she could keep her own a secret forever. She also knew the longer she procrastinated explaining it, the less likely he'd accept it. She was doing herself no favors by delaying the revelation.

As she grabbed the muffins she reserved for Ed and Fred from their hiding place, she chuckled. Perhaps Riley would be accepting of her family history, she thought, especially considering the rumors about his family.

She placed the muffins in the microwave and then walked over to grab two small containers of butter. Just like Ed and Fred liked.

She smiled as she delivered the treats to their table and looked over to their coffee. "Looks like Mel took care of you two," she said and walked away, surprised that they were willing to let go of the previous conversation so easily.

When Mel finished the rounds of checking on her customers, she joined her behind the counter and asked about Ed and Fred. When she heard about their concern and their argument, she said, "That's sweet, actually."

"I know. That's why I didn't get upset. They know I have no family in the area and are just looking out for me in the only way they know how. I really do appreciate it."

She leaned back on the counter with her elbows resting on the countertop.

Mel took the quiet moment to ask, "So what plans do you have for your one-month anniversary?"

"Holy Heavens! None," she answered quickly. "I haven't mentioned it to Riley."

"Why not?"

"Because it seems so trivial. Men have a tough enough time remembering a wedding anniversary or a birthday. Why put him on the spot for a measly month milestone?"

"I suppose you're right," Mel said.

"And if I don't expect him to remember, then I'm not disappointed when he doesn't and I don't get anything. He's visiting tomorrow evening. Seems like a great way to celebrate our anniversary without making a big deal about it."

"So, you do have plans," Mel countered.

"You got me there," she confessed.

Just at that point the bell at the door rang. She turned around to see four women walk in. She took a double take because she had never seen all four of them together. She knew each of them separately and even hosted fundraisers for two of them. She had no idea that they knew each other. But, then again, why not? This was, after all, a relatively small town.

As she watched them, they appeared to walk with a purpose, they looked as if they were nearly marching.

"Hello, ladies," she called to them even before they reached the counter. Three of the four went to find a table as Karen Manning strode up to the counter. She was the woman Charlee had seen on the news report not too long ago. Not only was she a regular customer, but a neighbor of sorts. She lived several blocks down from Charlee. They greeted each.

"Four regular coffees," Karen said. "I'm treating some of my neighbors today."

"Of course."

Mel immediately began to pour the coffee, and Karen took the opportunity to speak to Charlee.

"Do you have a few moments to sit with us? We have something to ask you, Charlee."

Talk about a panic attack. From the way they had marched in, she wondered if they had a grievance with the coffee shop. She hadn't heard of anyone being unhappy either with the service or the food. But who knew?

She turned to Mel before answering. "Go ahead," her friend said, "I'll be fine. And I'll bring their coffee out. How about you Charlee, should I bring out a cup for you as well?"

She indicated yes as she walked with Karen toward the table.

After Mel had served the coffee, placed a carafe in the middle of the table, she passed menus around. "Just in case any of you get hungry for lunch."

Everyone took a sip of coffee. She felt that even though they wanted to talk to her, they didn't know how to bring up the topic.

"I didn't realize you knew each other," she said, trying to break the tension.

"We became friends after we saw we all had a common concern," Karen said. She was probably in her mid-forties if Charlee had to guess. She wore her shoulder-length brown hair well.

Karen—in fact, all of these women—had frequented the coffee shop since the day she opened it. While she waited for them to find the right words to say what was on their minds, she took a moment to be grateful for their patronage.

Then in an instant, Karen just dove into the topic and explained what they needed. When she finished, you could hear a pin drop. The conversation bounced squarely into Charlee's lap, and she had no idea how to answer them.

Chapter 13

"Let me get this straight."

Charlee squinted as she tilted her head and eyed up the group. Their eyes were trained on her. *Nothing like a lightning bolt hitting me out of the blue.* As she surveyed each of the women, she knew they were serious.

Yet she still couldn't believe the question. She thought she heard the words correctly; they couldn't possibly mean what they just asked her. Her mind wasn't processing what she thought her ears had heard.

"If I didn't know any better," she said, "I could have sworn you just asked me to run for city council."

"That's exactly what we did ask," one of the ladies, Jayne Canfield, said.

"And what you want is someone to stand up to the hydraulic fracturing drilling industry, correct?"

"All of us live near fracking wells, Charlee," Karen explained, "and not only is it ruining the value of our homes, but more importantly, we're now very concerned about our health. Even though the EPA claims our water is safe to drink, the geology professors at the University of Northern Ohio believe otherwise. Some of the houses have chunky gray water. Not fit to even take a bath in."

She paused to take a sip of coffee. She recalled Karen saying that on the news. "That's why we formed

Citizens Against Fracking. Right now, city council is divided four to three in favor of fracking. If we could get you to see its dangers, you could upset our incumbent councilman, Myron Whiffler, who favors the fracking. Then the balance on the council would be tipped in our favor and we could at least get the issue on the ballot for the people to vote on a moratorium on drilling."

"Why me? There are plenty of other people in our neighborhood who know the issues better than me. I don't even listen to the news or read the newspaper. Why not one of you?"

Jennifer, who she took to be the youngest of the group in her early thirties, had been quiet throughout the meeting, spoke. "We don't want them. Besides, none of us has the name recognition you do. Don't worry about not knowing the issues. You can learn the issues. We all know you well enough that we know that you have the fortitude to stand up for your convictions."

The others readily agreed. "Besides that," Karen said, "you're compassionate. How many times have we come in and asked you to host benefit dinners or lunches here? You've never once denied us the use of your coffee shop as a venue for a civic event like that."

"Not only that," Jennifer continued, "you refused to let us pay for anything. A spaghetti dinner? No problem. We're always ready to buy the supplies or wait for you to take what the event cost to host in the way of at least menu items. Instead, you assume the entire cost and give us the profits in their entirety."

Karen agreed. "The last time we held a benefit dinner you wouldn't let us pay for anything. At the end of the evening, we received every penny of what we took in. You didn't have to do that."

Embarrassed by what she felt was excessive praise, she tried to downplay her actions. "I was taught—and I firmly believe—that we should all give back to the community what has been given to us. I've been blessed with this successful coffee shop. It's only fair that its existence does more than just make me money. In fact, from the opening day, I wanted it to be a place where the community could come together and feel unity. I was lucky enough to learn a few simple rules in life."

She paused, taking a breath.

"Trust me, my motives aren't purely altruistic. My dad taught me many things about generosity. One of them is you reap what you sow. Whatever I donate to your cause—whether it's food or labor—comes back to me in the form of increased business. Who can say no to that?"

She bit her lip and returned to the topic. "How can you be so sure I'd be against fracking. You haven't asked me yet my stand on that."

"Before you make up your mind," Karen said, "please meet a few of the families affected. See and hear for yourself the conditions these families are currently living with. Their lives have been torn apart. It's not just about the noise and the intrusion of the fracking well. It's about their health. Especially the health of their children. No one should have to live under these conditions. If you don't agree that fracking is a threat to not just our corner of the neighborhood, but our city and—I know this sounds hokey—the good of our environment in general—then you can turn us down. But I think once you see the conditions, your hesitancy will disappear."

She relented, partially because she knew these women wouldn't give up until she had agreed. They were determined and passionate. And while she certainly admired their courage, their fight wasn't hers. She wasn't, couldn't, work up the zeal for the anti-fracking movement. Not to be that involved. The fight against the pharmaceutical companies had drained her.

Nevertheless, she made arrangements to see for herself the conditions near the drilling before she decided.

She told herself she would keep an open mind, but she felt she would have to tell the ladies she couldn't do it. Her goal at this point was merely to find a polite way to decline their invitation. Perhaps she could suggest a person she trusted who could fire himself up to go to fight for them.

****

The following morning Charlee's first thought was of her date that evening with Riley. It had been several days since she had even seen him, even though they talked daily. Still, it wasn't the same as being with him, taking in his masculine scent, sitting next to him on her couch, raking her hands through his deliciously silky soft hair.

No, talking on the phone couldn't even compare to making passionate love in bed, experiencing the tingling sensation as he explored her naked body.

She anticipated all of that during her shower that morning. After all, it was the one-month anniversary of their relationship. Basking in a month-long anniversary may seem silly and even immature to some, but to her, it was more than just a mile marker. It was an achievement she hadn't experienced in a long time.

As she got out of the shower and dried herself, she thought, *let's just say I must have had a lapse or two in the last several men I chose to date*. Every one of them couldn't hold a candle compared to Riley. She swore every time they made love, she died in his arms, losing herself in the pure sexual sensations of his animal magnetism and his irresistible electrifying field of sensuality.

She hiked her jeans up over her hips and zipped them when she remembered she had promised Karen and the others that she would visit their end of the neighborhood today after her shift. She groaned and questioned her judgment, but she knew she had no choice but to follow through with it.

She appreciated the ladies' confidence in her, but she feared it was misplaced. She couldn't see herself getting fired up enough to do justice to their cause. After their meeting yesterday, she researched the topic a bit. If the conditions near their homes were even remotely as deplorable as the stories she had read online, then the women needed someone with more clout, time, and energy than she could devote to the cause.

She only had to convince the group of that.

Chapter 14

Charlee pulled into the driveway. She didn't need to double check the address. If the people gathered in the yard didn't tip her off, the flaming well not far from the homes was a sure bet she had found the place.

The yard resembled a mini-protest event. At least a dozen women and several men stood in front of the house and marched around anti-fracking signs.

"Don't frack with Mother Nature." "No Frickin' Frackin'."

She took a deep breath as she shut the ignition off and opened the car door. That's the instant the rotten-egg odor smacked her senses. The odor, the fumes tore through her nose, stung her eyes causing them to immediately tear uncontrollably. She wiped her eyes with the balls of the palms of her hands. Charlee choked back an involuntary cough as Karen greeted her at the car door.

"The smell is a bit overwhelming at first," Karen said, apologetically. "I probably should have warned you of how bad the stench is. But I was afraid you wouldn't believe; you'd think I was exaggerating to get you out here."

As Charlee recovered from the initial slap to her senses, Karen escorted her to the group. It was obvious Karen was in her element, and she had the admiration and trust of her neighbors. Just as she had at the coffee shop, this woman took charge of the meeting immediately. Charlee thought Karen should run for city council. She appeared not only to have the sincere conviction, but also the energy, and the compassion to be the voice and face of their movement.

She took a good look around at the small group. "Marco?" she blurted out. "I didn't know you lived over here," she said, stunned to see her best cook.

He walked up to her. "When they told me you were willing to consider helping us, I can't tell you how happy I was."

If there were anything similar to chef's blood or chef's DNA, Marco had it. Responsible for many of the coffee shop's most popular sandwiches, he never tired of developing new taste treats.

"Wait a minute," she said, raising an eyebrow. "You didn't have anything to do with my being asked to check out these conditions?"

Marco laughed. 'I'll never tell," he said. "But I'm glad you're here. If anyone can help us, it's you."

Too many people in this small group seem to have a very extraordinary level of belief in me. I'm a bit uncomfortable with the high expectations. And I haven't even viewed the damage or agreed to do anything yet.

"That flaming well over there"—she pointed to the structure that looked like something more suited for a Grade B science fiction movie than your average back yard—"is uncomfortably close to your houses."

Her hosts laughed. "Yeah, we kinda thought that, too," Karen said.

"You always had the eye for the obvious," Marco told her playfully. "And by the way, it's approximately seven-hundred fifty yards from us. As bad as that is, about another 500 yards on the other side of the well sits a playground. And not far beyond the playground is the Prague Elementary School."

No scientific research had to tell her the smell was noxious. Nothing the fracking industry argued could convince her otherwise. It was tough enough for adults, but there were so many children affected.

That meant that even when the children were in school, they were undoubtedly breathing in what had to be health-damaging fumes and all the potential health threats that went with it. The kids couldn't get away from it. Not much of a childhood.

When she asked about the quality of the air, Karen said the company hacks, as she called them, contended that while not pleasant, the fumes posed no immediate health threat. Of course, not one of the residents believed it. "We needed a second opinion," Karen said. "That's why we enlisted the help of Dr. Zorkawsky."

"Actually," Marco added, "we didn't stop there. If they had a Ph.D. behind their name, we called on them for help."

These individuals were resourceful when it concerned the health of their children. They asked chemists, biologists, and geologists to investigate. The experts took the challenge and discovered that the air posed an immediate danger to their health, including shortness of breath, asthma, and in the worst-case scenario, given enough time, lung damage.

"That was a far cry from what the company told us," Marco said, who was invited to accompany her and several other residents throughout a tour of the houses.

"I know what you're thinking," Karen said quickly. "You're wondering why we're all still living here. Why we just don't move."

She hadn't wondered that, at least not up to that point. But she intuitively knew. She tried to envision a real estate agent finding overlooked features of the home location. "And in addition to poisoned water and a polluted air, you have an unimpeded view of this fracking well constantly lit for your enjoyment."

"Aside from the fact that these are our homes, we couldn't afford to move even if we wanted to. The price of real estate on this street has plummeted so badly that we couldn't sell without losing money." She paused a beat. "But who in their right mind would even buy these homes?"

"And the kicker is," Marco said, "that housing prices and even rent is going up everywhere else in the city due to the fracking."

"Excuse me?" Charlee didn't follow the logic.

"So many workers from the well are from out of town," he explained. "Their company pays for their expenses, including their living costs. The area landlords have raised the cost of rent because the company is willing to pay higher rent."

She had to agree—clearly, they were stuck. Karen knocked on a door of the neighbor, one of the few who weren't out waiting for her. "This is Jayne's home, and she has a unique story to tell."

The door opened, and the woman gave the group a big smile. "Hi, Charlee, good to see you again," she said. "Thank you so much for visiting and inspecting our problems."

"I thought maybe we could show Charlee the foundation of your home," Karen suggested. "Your house, for whatever reason, has sustained the most damage."

Karen, Marco, and Jayne led her to the basement where a deep crack existed in one of the walls. "The result of one too many earthquakes," Jayne said.

"I never thought that I would have to worry about earthquakes in Ohio. Tornadoes, yes. Earthquakes, no." Jayne shook her head in amazement.

Karen jumped in immediately. "In the last twelve months, we've had at least twelve earthquakes of varying magnitudes."

Charlee let out a low whistle. "I didn't realize we've had that many. I felt the one New Year's Eve while I was at the coffee shop, but I don't particularly remember sensing the others."

"We checked with the geologists at the university several months ago," Karen said. "It seemed only natural since they were helping us on every other level. If you're concerned about the accuracy of our statements, we can consult with them. They'll not only confirm the number, but they can show substantial evidence that the earthquakes were due to the nature of hydraulic fracturing."

Karen continued to explain the cause of the quakes in simple terms. "As I understand it, the quakes occur when the water sucked up from the wells is then poured back underground. It causes the faults in the area to get wet and become slippery, which makes the perfect conditions for the quakes."

She turned to Marco. "Did I get that right?" she asked him. "You seemed to grasp that issue much better than I did."

"Basically, that's how I understand it," he answered. "But of course, the representatives who come from the company deny this. They call it all a 'coincidence.' "

"What's the name of this company?" Charlee asked.

"The firm we're dealing with is Natural East Energy," Marco said. "But it's owned by a larger corporation, and we can't seem to learn what that is."

"That's totally irresponsible," she exclaimed, her ire rising. "Not only is this company destroying the health of innocent people. That's a sin. But they're also destroying the earth."

She wondered if hiding the true owners of the company was standard operating procedure for fracking companies. If you couldn't find the ultimate culprit, you can't cut off the head of the monster, so to speak. It's like playing whack-a-mole. As much as you take the rubber mallet and hit those moles, they keep popping up.

The ultimate goal of this strategy, as she understood it, was to create smaller subsidiary companies, sacrifice them—and their employees for that matter—and then simply either create or purchase a new one. She couldn't believe she was delving into this problem that deeply. *I came just to satisfy the group's insistence. I won't, I can't get involved. This is not my fight.*

Yet the anger gnawed at her conscience. Ever since the death of her father, she felt compelled to take some step, however small, to right the wrongs she witnessed.

Charlee, Marco, and Jayne headed up from the basement where they had been holding the discussion. That's when she noticed a large water cooler like those found in offices in the kitchen.

"Let me guess," she said. "Your water is undrinkable."

"Badabing! You got that exactly right. Not only can't we drink it, but it's horrible to look at," Marco said.

Without being asked, Jayne padded into the kitchen, took out a glass, and ran tap water into it. The liquid in the container looked nothing like water. It was brownish and held chunks of crud in it. Jayne handed it to her, and she couldn't help but put it up to her nose. She choked back a cough.

"Yeah, pretty bad," Jayne said.

She owed it to the women to give them an answer as soon as possible. If she didn't run for city council, they needed to find someone who could stand up to the fracking "forces that be."

"I know we're asking a lot of you, Charlee," Karen said. "But is it okay if we visit you at the coffee shop tomorrow just to get an idea of where you stand in your thought processes?"

"Of course," she said, as she climbed into her car and waved at the small group of residents.

Can you say the word pressure?

Chapter 15

"9-1-1. Stop in the coffee shop before you head for home."

Normally, Charlee didn't check her text messages while she drove. But when stopped at a red light, she took a sneak peek at her phone. The message, from Mel, definitely spelled emergency.

Immediately, her mind raced through the worst-case scenario. It would be just like Mel to try to keep her calm as long as possible. The coffee shop could be burning to the ground, and her text would probably say "Bring marshmallows." Perhaps it wasn't an emergency. *What could be wrong?*

Her thoughts were interrupted by the long and angry car horn that blared from behind. She looked up, tossed her phone back on the passenger seat, and drove through the green light. She wondered how patient the driver had been before he laid on the horn.

She rushed to the coffee shop and burst through the back door. "What's wrong?" She nearly shouted the words. Ann, walking out of the kitchen with a tray of food, smiled innocently at her and asked sweetly, "Why, Charlee, what gives you the idea something is wrong?" Then she walked behind her, not waiting for an answer on her way to serve the food.

Mel popped up from behind the counter and asked nearly the same thing. "You're acting like something horrendous has just occurred."

"If I am, it's because you sent me a 9-1-1 distress call. Care to defend that?"

Jeff came out of the kitchen. "Told you she wouldn't it take it well."

"Stay right here for a moment, Jeff," Mel instructed him. "She doesn't know why I sent it yet."

"As far as I can see your main goal, aside to age me ten years, was to be a smart aleck. I thought maybe the place was on fire."

"Good grief, no. I would have at least given you some subtle heads up if the coffee shop was burning. Something like 'bring marshmallows.' "

"Not funny. Now why did you drag me back here?" At this point in her rampage, she wasn't about to tell her she had planned to stop by anyway.

Mel appeared not in the least bit affected by her panic. "I'll be right back," she said, holding up her index finger, and then dropped down behind the counter again.

She was just about to have a meltdown when Mel popped right back up like a beach ball in the ocean. She held a vase of Stargazer lilies. "These came for you shortly after you left today. I wanted to make sure you stopped by to pick them up and see who they're from."

"We're all curious," Ann said as she walked behind Charlee again on her way to the kitchen.

Every muscle in her body relaxed. The entire staff on duty seemed to be behind this conspiratorial text. While it did nearly give her a heart attack, the worst that came out of it was they fooled her.

"Are you guys finished having fun at my expense?" she asked. As hard as she tried to sound upset, she knew that instant had passed and looked at the humor behind the text.

"Not yet," Jeff volunteered. "There's still one last pesky shred of information we want to know. Who sent you the flowers? The card's in the envelope, and it's sealed. Whoever sent them knew you had a nosey crew."

She knew instantly who sent them and why.

Oh, my God. One month ago, today. She had been consumed with the fracking problems of her neighbors and had completely forgotten about their anniversary. She couldn't believe that what she had just seen took her mind off of, even for a minute, her relationship with Riley.

She still had a quiet dinner at home with Riley—and all the benefits that went with that—to look forward to. Thank goodness. At that moment she realized she needed his advice on her decision. She would talk to him tonight.

She walked up to the counter and plucked the card out of its holder. She tore open the envelope and smiled as she read it to herself. "Happy One Month Anniversary, Darling. Why don't we go out to dinner tonight? I know the perfect place."

Nobody had said a word, but she sensed all eyes were on her, waiting for an answer. Like they didn't know.

"Yes. Yes. If you must know, the lilies are from Riley."

The little group of employees applauded, and Mel asked, "So, he's remembered the one-month anniversary that you thought he would ignore?"

****

Riley paced Quinn's office while his brother sat behind his desk, his legs extended and set comfortably on his desk.

"You could do that in your own office and wear your own carpet out," Quinn suggested, a slight smile on his face.

"What is that supposed to mean?" he asked, suddenly thrust from his thoughts into the real world again.

"It means why don't you just sit down and relax already? You've must have paced a good three miles already. I swear you're more nervous now than you were on your first date with Charlee."

"Fine. Fine. I'll sit down. But you're absolutely right. I should have told her long ago about being a lion shifter. It just doesn't seem fair to either of us to talk about it tonight—our anniversary."

"You're the only person I know, Riley," Quinn said, "who actually celebrates a month-long romance. Most people don't pay much attention to it."

"When you've had relationships like mine, you learn if one lasts even this long, you need to celebrate it and be grateful for it."

"Remember when I dated Eli? You hounded me into telling her about our background. You wondered how I could wait so long to bring the subject up. I wish I could say I get pleasure from doing the same to you today. But the truth is, bro, I don't."

"I'm not exactly sure I believe that, but I appreciate the thought," he said. "And I deserved everything you shot at me earlier today. I'm stalling, frightened that if she knew, she would break off our relationship. And I really care about Charlee. I love her, Quinn."

"I know you do, Riley. I've never seen you act like this with any other woman. You might as well find out how much she loves you. Eli stuck with me when she discovered our family secret. If Charlee is even half the woman my wife is, I'm sure she'll stay with you. She may be angry for a bit, and she may even not talk to you for a while. But in the end—the Brockton charm wins them over. It happens every time."

"Not this time, bro. I'm pretty sure nothing is going to save me from the fury of Charlee. I'm trying my best to make it the perfect date, so when I tell her tonight, it softens the blow some. But I know her well enough she's still going to be teed off."

He paused a beat and allowed the silence to fill the room. When he did speak again, it was almost a whisper. "I just hope I haven't waited so long that she totally casts me off."

"That's highly unlikely," Quinn said.

Chapter 16

Riley took a deep breath and checked his watch before he knocked on the door. Normally, he felt much more at ease striding up to Charlee's front porch. He wouldn't call it self-confidence because that would imply that there would be some type of ego involved. No, walking into Charlee's home was more akin to coming home. He knew that inside these walls, he could be himself, safe from any criticism.

She never judged him, never tried to get him to do something he didn't want to, and she never tried to manipulate him into giving her presents or money.

If he felt that way, he wondered, then why was he so concerned with her reaction to his lion-shifting background? Just as with everything else, logic seemed to dictate that she would accept his shifting background as well. He blew out a deep breath, checked his watch for a second time, and knocked at the door.

She answered it in a matter of seconds. He took one look at her and found it difficult to breathe. Her freshly washed hair held the intoxicating lavender scent that healed his primal urges. Her glowing—yes, glowing—blonde hair radiated an aura around her head. An angel's halo. That's what he thought the first time he saw it.

She smiled broadly when she saw him. Like she was sincerely happy to see him. None of the New York

City's pasted-on smiles of the women who chased billionaires. You'd think that after all the time the two of them spent together, he would become accustomed to this type of greeting. But every time he saw it, he marveled as if he were seeing it for the first time.

"So where are we going?" she asked as she locked the door. "You do know I had a quiet evening at home planned."

"I know you did. I think you'll forgive me for disrupting your plans." He took her hand. "Our destination is a surprise. I hope you'll like it."

He knew that she appreciated his attention to detail. That was why he chose the same restaurant where they held their first date and made sure everything was perfect. He went to great lengths to reserve the same table.

The server approached their table with the menus.

"I understand the same restaurant," Charlee said, "and the same table. But how in the world did you swing getting the same server to take care of us tonight?"

He laughed. For a moment, he thought about taking credit for it with a sly answer. He knew that she wouldn't buy it. "I wish I could claim that little miracle, but that is purely a coincidence."

"No, Mr. Brockton, actually it wasn't. My manager called me this afternoon and asked if I would mind working tonight. He said you had requested that everything be exactly as it was last month, and he thought this would top off your evening."

****

"It was the perfect evening." Charlee snuggled closer to him as he led her up the few steps of her front porch, her head pleasingly nestled in the crook of his shoulder.

"It was," he agreed. He watched as she unlocked the front door. She led him into the living room.

Riley closed the door behind them and locked it. He turned toward her, held her arms, and gazed into her eyes, as if he were sizing her up for the very first time. He loved every little thing about her. His desire, his yearning to make love to her, had not diminished one bit since the first day they met.

He had no idea how he had made it through the meal. Early in the evening, he had lost track of how many times he thought about skipping dinner and taking her straight home. But he knew that would not be the romantic thing to do.

The one thought that didn't bother him all evening, though, and only now crept back in, was his secret. He knew he had to say something. He promised himself he wouldn't completely ruin the evening. He would wait until they shared her bed and each had been satisfied beyond belief.

And he was prepared to make that happen.

"Before you even ask," he whispered in her ear, "the only nightcap I want is you."

He placed an arm around Charlee's waist and tugged her toward him. Their lips drew closer together nearly touching each other's as their bodies were melding. His torso rubbing her breasts, her leg wrapping around his thigh.

He couldn't imagine that there would be a time that he would tire of the sweet blend of fragrances that created her appeal to him, his yearning for her. With his hand firmly wrapped around the back of her neck, his lips sought hers as if it was their first encounter. She obediently, willingly, allowed him in as he explored her mouth.

She moved her hand to his butt and squeezed. He couldn't help himself. His lower body moved ever more closely to hers, confirming, if he had any doubt at all, his delight in her intentions, in her desire to take care of him even as he yearned to take care of her.

Standing as close as any two people could brought out the animal in him, but tonight of all nights he intended to make love slowly, promising himself that she would be satisfied with every nuance of the process. He stepped away from her for an instant, took her hand and intertwined his fingers, and whispered, "Let's continue this in your bedroom."

Her hair fell over an eye. It made her more seductive and sensual than he had even remembered. He led them into the bedroom, where they hurriedly unclothed each other and fell into bed.

He lay on top of her. She raked both her hands through his hair, before she fondled his chest. The slow, gentle action of the woman he loved made him moan.

As she moved her hands down his torso, his body arched slightly. She took her one hand and began to rub his organ rhythmically. Within a short while his entire body joined in moving to the rhythm, and the blood flowed ever faster to his groin.

In response, he found her sweet spot and caressed it to set a similar rocking sensation within her. As this sensation spread throughout her body, she moaned softly.

"Please, now," she said softly, nearly breathlessly. Without a word, he guided himself into her, and they both found indescribable bliss.

He rolled over and tugged her close to him. She nestled her head into the crook of his shoulder. Bending his head slightly, he whispered in her ear, "Happy anniversary, Darling."

"Yes, it is," she responded without hesitation. She paused a beat while she positioned her leg over his, then said, "Happy anniversary to you, too, Sweetheart."

They lay there for a few moments, their breathing the only sounds that could be heard. She wrapped her arm around his torso and closed her eyes.

****

Riley, however, couldn't close his eyes, let alone fall asleep. He needed to tell his lioness that...well, that she was his lioness. His soulmate. That involved a minor technicality, though. He had to get to the part about his lion-shifting family. He knew for a fact that several years ago the lion shifter rumor churned around his brother Quinn. But he didn't know how much Charlee knew of those rumors or if she had even heard them.

She had to have a hint of the gossip. She owned Prague's busiest coffee shop. She must have heard at least one of her customers talking about it.

A rogue freelance journalist and blogger tried every trick in the book to confirm that fact from Quinn several years ago. When he refused to answer her, she interrogated Renee and eventually cornered his future fiancée and now wife, Eli.

She wasn't able to get any type of substantial confirmation from anyone, so she finally abandoned the topic. But that didn't mean the woman wasn't still out there lurking, eager to raise the topic again. In fact, he'd been lucky so far; she hadn't come snooping around yet.

Before he could take this relationship any farther, he had to come clean with Charlee. He had already procrastinated too long. At this point, she may not be frightened off by the idea of loving a lion shifter. It's possible she would huff off because he waited so long to tell her. And who could blame her?

He was doing her a disservice by withholding this vital part of his history. It was the essence of what he and his family were. She had a right to know. He chastised himself for not being upfront with her. But he vowed he would tell her before the night was over, regardless of the cost to him.

For a moment, he considered waking her but dismissed the idea. Charlee looked so peaceful, so angelic.

****

When Charlee opened her eyes again, she felt Riley's protective arms wrapped round her entire body. His chin rested comfortably on the top of her head. She nearly convinced herself he was asleep.

"Well, hi there." His voice was sweet, melodious, mesmerizing.

She realized that she was lying in the arms of her best friend. And as much she hated to break the continuity of the romantic moment, she was in desperate need of some advice. Who better to ask than her best friend? She had never fully decided what she would tell her neighbors tomorrow concerning her run for city council. My God, even the mention of it sounded preposterous to her.

She almost prayed he would find the idea just as

ridiculous, that he would advise her not to get entangled in local politics. Her experience told her local politics usually involved some form of collusion or corruption. And with Prague's tightly knit web of families, she thought it would be inevitable.

Even though her parents had lived in Prague for years, they weren't one of the founding families. That branded Charlee as an outsider, an individual who had little right to meddle in the city's political business. It didn't matter that for the last five years she had proved herself to be an excellent businesswoman who contributed to the town's economy. Lucky for her, she cared nothing about politics. Up until now.

Despite how the women of her neighborhood saw her, she knew in some ways she would remain a second-class citizen. She certainly wasn't councilwoman material in many people's eyes. What about her relationship with Riley? A populist candidate with a billionaire boyfriend.

She knew, though, Riley would understand the timing of the question. Not only would he understand, she thought he would be flattered she asked for his advice.

She propped herself up on one arm and faced him. He was everything every woman could possibly ask for in a true love. Kind, generous, loving, and as she began to learn, he displayed all of these traits daily.

Yes, he was the exact person she needed to consult. She trusted his judgment implicitly.

"Riley," she began gently enough, not wanting to disturb the moment, but knowing she could never be mentally at ease until she talked this issue out with him.

"What, darling?"

"I need to ask you a very important question, and I hate to do it now, but I can't get the issue out of mind. These thoughts have haunted me for a while, and I know you're the only one who could answer it."

She expected perhaps a hint of irritation to cross his face because she was disturbing a romantic, sensual moment. But she was unprepared for the look of horror that crossed his face. His eyes widened, almost as large as a feral animal's. She knew she had made a tremendous miscalculation.

He didn't even know what she was going to ask him yet. How could he possibly be so upset?

Chapter 17

Oh my God, Riley thought, *she's heard the rumors. Maybe she even knows.* He tried to knock the latter thought out of his mind. *Of course, she doesn't know, not with any amount of certainty, that is. No one outside of the family actually knows for sure.*

Momentarily paralyzed by her advancing the topic, he recovered as quickly as he as he could, but he knew it wasn't soon enough. She probably read the answer on his face.

He didn't realize the lion-shifter issue had been on her mind. He wondered for how long. Now, not only was he cornered into fessing up that he was a lion shifter, he also had to explain why he hadn't discussed the subject earlier with her. Boy, this could really get messy in a heartbeat.

Of course, if that were to be the extent of it, a messy, complicated discussion would be one thing he could handle. But his mind shot immediately to her walking away never to return. He wasn't ready for that. He felt he had been backed into a corner.

"I wish I could say I can explain it all to you,'" he began, trying his best to keep calm. "But it's an issue that isn't easily raised in a relationship. It's not that I was trying to purposely hide anything from you. You have to believe me."

He could tell by her reaction—she knitted her brow

and tilted her head—that she didn't believe him. "Quinn warned me. Told me not to wait to bring the topic up. But I refused to listen."

She went to say something, but he continued. He sighed loudly. A sigh that sounded more like a growl. She jumped back a bit when she heard it.

He knew the relationship was doomed. Perhaps it had been doomed from the start. But there was no way he could ever make this up to her. No way could he ever repair this. Not by a long shot.

"Charlee, you deserve someone so much better than me," he said. "I think it's best, at least for the time being, that we stop seeing each other. I need to sort all this out. And I can't ask you to wait around while I'm playing out some scene from a Tennessee Williams play.

"You know I love you. But not revealing my true identity up front is inexcusable. I'm sorry I disappointed you, left you in the dark about my ancestry. I don't expect you to ever forgive me. But please try to understand I didn't do it purposely.

"I need to leave now."

He hurriedly got dressed, gave her a quick kiss on her forehead, and left.

****

What the hell just happened?

She knew he was gone; she heard the door slam.

He wouldn't even allow her to speak, to ask his opinion. She sat up in bed. She reviewed his actions several times in her mind. Certainly, he couldn't possibly know what she planned to ask him. She knew for a fact she had never told him about it.

His words bounced around in her mind. What did

he say? What was he talking about? All she could remember was the part about him leaving.

She took a deep breath and tried to work through his reaction a bit more logically. Why would he react so strongly? Nothing made sense. She felt as if all of her energy had been zapped from her body. It had been a long, overwhelming day for her. It started with the incomprehensible request to help a group of residents living under inhumane conditions due to fracking.

If he weren't on the same page as her, if he weren't talking about her need to make a decision on running for office, then what the hell was he talking about? Could somebody else have said something? Why the hell did he leave like that?

Once she got over the initial shock of his sudden and unexplained departure, she was angry. Furious even. Her history with men wasn't good. So, was this just a repetition of past relationships? If it was, why did she let it blindside her?

She looked at the time on her cell phone. "I might as well get ready for the day. If I stay in bed any longer, I'm just going to start crying." Then she realized the tears already streamed down her face.

"That's it." She threw off the covers, swung her feet down to the floor, and stood. She was shocked and angry with Riley, but when she opened the window blinds, her thoughts flew to her other dilemma. Citizens Against Fracking. The view from her window didn't include an "eternal" flame from a well. She opened the window and smelled the clean, fresh, crisp air. There were no noxious fumes. The group wanted an answer. They deserved one. How could she decide anything in this state? She wiped tears from her cheeks with the back of her hands.

Suddenly, the decision was clear. Riley didn't think enough of her to hear her out. She didn't get a chance to ask his advice. She couldn't even begin to fathom what his problem was. But she knew what her neighbors' problem was. Even though she told herself the fracking issue wasn't her fight, the fact remained the health and safety of her friends and neighbors were threatened. She thought she should do more than just host fundraisers.

And without Riley to think about—"Because, let's face it," she said as she stared out her window, "apparently we aren't a couple any longer."—she knew what she had to do. She would do it through tears; she would do it with a broken heart. But she had to do it.

Excitement welled up inside her. Well, as much excitement as she could muster considering her personal circumstances.

It reminded her of the fight she took on with the drug company. Only this time it wasn't just in honor of her father. This time she had a chance to save lives.

She didn't need Riley's input. All she needed to do was get the buy-in of her employees.

I wonder how hard that will be?

Chapter 18

Charlee wasted no time. Mel barely got herself behind the counter the following morning before she shoved the keys to the office into her hands. "Find the list of employees' phone numbers." She rarely barked orders, but at that moment, she came close to it.

"Tell them they need to be here at 10:30 sharp for an emergency employee meeting. No excuses. If they have to bring their kids, so be it. If Jessica is watching Aunt Lilac, have her bring her, too. I expect everyone to attend."

Mel started for the office. "For God's sake, tell them they absolutely need to be on time."

"Could I ask—" Mel began, before turning back toward the office.

"No. Not right now. Just make sure every single employee is here. If they have any questions, tell them to call me." She paused and rethought her answer. "No, wait. Better yet. Tell them to get their butts in here and all of their questions will be answered soon enough."

****

Charlee watched as the clock inched slowly toward 10:30 and her employees were gathering, just as she had requested. A trickle of persons, at first, one and two at a time, then as the hands of her coffee-cup clock closed in on the meeting time, they entered at a faster rate. Jessica Madison even brought her Aunt Lilac, just as she was invited to.

She ran up to Jessica's aunt. "Sorry to make you leave your farmhouse, Aunt Lilac." She gave the older woman a quick hug and a kiss on the cheek. "Did you want a cup of your favorite caramel latte?"

"That would be delightful, dear, thank you. I figured it had to be important if you let me tag along with Jessica."

Charlee turned to Mel. "Already on it. One caramel latte for Aunt Lilac."

"Mel and Marco are going to handle the floor and the kitchen while we meet," Charlee told the group. "I've already informed them of what this meeting is all about." Then she wasted no time in telling her employees that she had been asked to run for city council and why.

She explained to them the conditions she saw families were living in. She talked about her hesitancy in getting involved. The potential that not only she, but the coffee shop itself, could be a target of derision and protests.

"I don't know the extent of this company's power," Charlee told them, "but I have to at least consider the possibility that they may shut us down. And then there's the worst-case scenario—which is a long shot—but you need to know there may be physical danger. All of this would not only affect me, but it could impact your lives as well." She paused a moment and took stock of their faces. "You see, I can't make the final decision without consulting you.

"While the visit I had yesterday touched my heart and stirred up my sense of justice, my employees, each and every one of you and your families, are my first and foremost responsibility. I have to take into consideration the option that the 'powers that be' may retaliate."

Charlee waited for a moment, so her employees could absorb it all.

"Let me be very clear," she continued, not in the least bit concerned about her repeating herself, "my decision to run may not only create real consequences for me, but the consequences may very well trickle down touching your personal lives as well."

The employees sat there evidently stunned at what they had just heard. Her muscles tensed as the silence continued for several moments. The ordinary noises of the coffee shop filled in the void all too loudly. The laughter of the few customers seemed to echo throughout the shop. Customers' conversations converged into one unintelligible tangle of words; silverware clanged against plates and grated her nerves.

Of course, she knew the topic of the meeting had to have stunned her employees. Of all the reasons for an emergency meeting, their employer considering a run for city council was surely the last on their list, if it were on their list at all. She had to admit it wasn't on her bucket list before yesterday.

Jeff broke the stunned silence. "I'll go back and relieve Marco," he announced. "I think you need to hear his story."

The cooks changed positions, and Marco spoke to the group. He explained his family lived chillingly close to the well. He described the fire spewing out of it day and night. It was everything that Charlee had seen.

"But please," he said, "don't make any decision about your families' financial future based on my personal story."

Again, silence overcame the group. It didn't last long though. Aunt Lilac let out a big sigh and stood up. "What the…"

She dropped the f-bomb. All eyes turned toward her. The attention she got seemingly surprised her. "What? Sometimes you need to say what the…

"There are times when you must let go of security and do exactly what is right. I don't think there's a person in this group who can argue that standing up with Marco and his family and our neighbors on the other side of town is wrong. If we don't stand up now for our friends and neighbors and for Mother Nature, when will we? The truth is we may never get another chance. I, for one, will support you, Charlee, should you decide to run. I'll be here helping in any way I can."

She looked down at Jessica. She stood up next to her aunt. "I'm with Aunt Lilac. Charlee should run. Anyone else with us?"

In one motion, every employee stood and applauded. The several customers in the shop stared at them momentarily. "It looks like we're all ready to stand with you and fight," Jessica said.

"And we sure can't let some corporation bigwig in New York City rob us of our quality of life. They don't know who they're fooling with," Aunt Lilac said.

Chapter 19

Another Lion Sighted Roaming the Area.

"Front page news," Quinn told his brother the morning after he had walked out on Charlee. He tossed the *Prague Bugle* to him.

"I'm sorry. I didn't mean to stir up this stupid lion-shifting controversy again."

Riley read the article in the *Prague Bugle* out loud:

For the second time in a little more than one month, the Prague Police Department found itself deluged with calls about an African lion roaming the streets.

The calls started at midnight, according to Officer Jonathan Harris, who took the calls. Individuals were still reporting the large African cat as late as 2:30 a.m. as several women walked out of a local bar.

While the police officers took reports on every sighting, they didn't find any lions prowling the city. The police department also checked with all regional zoos, wildlife refuge centers, and any visiting circuses.

No one reported a missing lion.

Quinn chuckled. "I'm not in the least bit upset about the publicity, I'm more concerned about what happened to you. I thought you were out on your anniversary date with Charlee."

"Before I even tell you the story," Riley said, "I owe you an apology."

"You do?" Quinn's voice shot up an octave at the same time he raised his eyebrows. The characteristic Brockton lopsided smile crossed his face.

"For how I judged you when you didn't tell Eli about being a lion-shifter. How cowardly, I thought. You needed to tell her she was your lioness." He paused. "I discovered that admitting who you are isn't easy. Sometimes, it's downright difficult. Sometimes, it's easier to take the path of least resistance. Like I tried to do."

"So, what happened?"

"Charlee brought the subject up," he said, "or I thought she did. She said she had something important to ask me. Naturally, I thought it was about the shifting. But when I left her house, shifted, and roamed the city, I realized she never mentioned the topic by name. And to be honest, I didn't give her a chance to ask before I walked out on her."

"What?" Quinn asked.

"Yeah, not smart, I know." Riley paused a beat. "The more I roamed, the more I scrutinized my actions. Looking back, it's altogether possible she was going to bring up a different subject." He made a guttural sound that he knew sounded more like a growl than the sigh he intended it to be.

"All I know is I didn't give her the courtesy to ask the question. In fact, I presumed she already knew the answer. That's why I left."

Riley took a gulp of the office coffee. He gagged and nearly spit it out. "This is the crap we serve here? Not only did I lose my lioness, I've lost the best coffee I ever tasted in my life." He paused. "And before you even ask me, no, I'm not going in there on the pretense of buying coffee. My gut tells me there's no way I can win Charlee back. Even if I groveled on my knees and begged forgiveness, I'd be wasting my time. It would be nothing but a futile experiment in humiliation."

As he talked about what happened, he clearly saw what a fool he had been. Between now and the time he had walked to clear his head, he questioned more and more if Charlee was going to bring up lion shifters. It's altogether possible she had something else that weighed on her mind.

"I would love to say I told you so," Quinn said. "But I just can't."

"And now I know just how tough fessing up can be." He paused a bit, took another sip of coffee, and gagged again. "Gotta get better coffee in here if I'm condemned to drink this crap."

"It's good to see you still have some humor left in," Quinn said.

"No humor. Just honesty."

Riley continued to spew his thoughts; they'd been dammed up in his mind overnight. "I probably blindsided her," he said, only casually aware that his brother was listening.

He paused a beat, finished his coffee, and tossed the empty cup into the wastebasket on the far side of Quinn's desk.

"I've mucked up big time, Quinn. I can't see anything that would possibly convince her to talk to me again, let alone revive our relationship."

He tossed the newspaper in the basket after the cup, never reading any farther than the front page.

Chapter 20

"Frankly, Mel, I can't see what could convince him to talk to me again, let alone reignite our relationship," Charlee said. "If I knew what I did to cause him just to get up and walk out like that, I may have more hope in getting back together. But how do you mend a relationship when you don't know what caused it to fall apart—in a matter of minutes. Besides, I don't even know if I want to get back with him. He's such a jerk."

"All I know," Mel said, "is that you decided to run for city council, and instead of being pumped about it and planning your attack like I thought you'd be doing, you're looking like you lost your best friend. I knew something was wrong."

"I have lost my best friend." She pulled a book out of her purse. "You see this?" She waved a book. "This is a bunch of bull." The book was titled *Something Amazingly Awesome is Going to Happen to You Today*, by I. M. Glad. It was the book she had been reading when Riley walked into the coffee shop for the first time.

She slammed it into the wastebasket behind the counter. The book crashed with such a force that the used coffee grounds in the wastebasket flew up onto the floor around the basket.

"Darn," she said, "somehow I should have known that would have happened."

Mel simply shook her head. "I'll clean it up in a bit, Charlee."

She took a deep breath and counted to ten. She didn't want to wallow in her depressive state much longer. She didn't want to give Riley that much control over her emotions. She knew when she met him, he was out of her league. This only proved it. The faster she could put the whole ugly episode behind her the quicker the pain would heal.

"I'll feel better tomorrow. That's when I'll check out what I need to do to get my name on the ballot. I sure hope I'm right."

"If that man can't see that you're the best thing that has happened to him, then he doesn't deserve you," Mel said as she retrieved the broom.

She laughed. "Now you sound like someone's mother. I think that line is ingrained in the DNA of every mother the moment she's born."

"Didn't you know that there's a hormone in the woman's body that switches on an entire set of 'Mom phrases' the moment she conceives. Of course, I haven't had a baby yet. I'm just practicing."

Charlee laughed again. She felt a bit better, but she still wondered if she would ever see Riley again, regardless of what her blind anger told her at the moment. No, she didn't think they would ever get together again. But she had to admit that she was curious to know why he left so suddenly without giving her a decent explanation. She figured he owed her that much.

She did her best to try to move beyond this nightmare, but it was difficult. She moped around the coffee shop. She pasted on a smile when she waited on her customers. She prayed that Mel didn't catch her unusual interest in the small bell that indicated customers entering. Every time it tinkled, she would stop whatever she was doing hoping that it was Riley and he wanted to talk. She wasn't sure she would believe him or even take him back, but the least he could do, she thought, was try to win her back.

Memories of him haunted her day at work. The moment he walked into her house. The site of him in only the "Kiss the Cook" apron, which became his customary morning garb. The way he sprawled out on the couch. She swore she could nearly taste him when she went to bed at night.

His shampoo and body wash. His lips. My God, she suddenly realized he had his own unique packaged scent. If only the world knew, women would be clamoring to buy it as a cologne. Clearly, Riley was never fully out of her mind.

"What are you two doing back?" Charlee couldn't hide her surprise at seeing Ed and Fred make an extraordinary afternoon visit.

"We saw you in action this morning, Charlee girl," Fred said lightly, "and had to congratulate you."

While that sounded like a plausible story, Charlee noticed Ed's body language said something different. She cast a quick glance at Fred, who shrugged.

"I'll be right back with your coffee."

After she poured their coffee. She placed the pot at another table and joined them.

"What's the matter guys?" she asked.

"Now, I'm not saying your boyfriend—"

"My former boyfriend for all intents and purposes," she interrupted Ed.

"But did you see the newspaper this morning?"

"Of course, I saw the lion sighting. Are you trying to tell me that was Riley?

"I'm not talking about the front page, Charlee girl," Ed continued. She thought he sounded a little impatient, if not irritated.

"I'm talking about the story on page three. The story about the history of lion shifting in the city."

"Now, you should know better, both of you," she said. She stole a glance at Fred, as well. "I don't read the news." She paused a beat before asking, "Why should I care about this?"

Then again, my parents were frank in discussing the issue in our house.

She had a feeling this would be an involved conversation and sat with them. She glanced at Mel, who nodded and mouthed, "I've got it covered."

"Ed, you know it's a ludicrous interpretation of lion-shifter history." Fred said. "The article is nothing but a hate-mongering rendition of the true story. It's obvious because Gretchen Carlyle wrote it. She's always trying to dig up dirt on the Brocktons." He looked at Charlee and said, "I'm surprised she hasn't cornered you yet with her questions."

"What's wrong with her version?" She couldn't see how anyone could alter history that dramatically that it gave a whole different tone to the facts.

Fred chuckled. "She made the migration of the shifters in the 1890s sound as if they were here to find fresh meat. She painted their settling as if they were hostile forces. The truth of the matter is that the families were the kindest and friendliest folks around. They wanted nothing more than to be an active, productive part of Prague."

"That's what my dad always said."

"Your dad was right," Fred said. "They were among the pillars of the community."

Ed groaned. "I wouldn't go that far."

Fred shot him a look. "That's because you're letting one incident skew your view of them."

"My dad told me something serious happened, but he never went into any details."

"The year was 1968. It was a tumultuous year nationwide to begin with," Fred said. "With the deaths of Martin Luther King, Jr., Bobby Kennedy, and the riots at the Democratic convention that year, people's nerves were pretty taut.

"City council proposed an ordinance that would curtail the rights of lion shifters. A few muckety-mucks seemed to have a problem with them." He paused. "The only problem was that these individuals were successful businessmen. They felt threatened.

"When the proposed ordinance was read at the meeting, a member of one of the families shifted and lunged for the councilman who sponsored the bill," Ed explained.

"Oh my God! I can't believe that actually happened."

Fred nodded. "Believe it, Charlee girl, because it did."

Ed took a long draw from his coffee, then carefully placed it on the table. "They were able to pull him off the councilman. Mostly, the other shifter families restrained him. In fact, the councilman was the granddad of that Myron Whiffler guy who you're going to be running against."

"Was the man hurt?"

"A few surface scratches, that's all," Fred said. "Of course, the media made out like he was mauled within inches of his life."

Ed began to speak. "But that shows—"

"Don't go there," Fred warned him. Ed sighed and leaned against the back of the booth.

She let out a short moan and asked, "What about the bill? Did it pass?"

"You bet your hat and suitcase it passed," Ed said.

"It can't be still on the books, can it? And even if it is, how can you tell whether the person is a lion shifter or not?"

"It was easy at first because all the lion shifter families were known. Then families legally changed the last names of their children so they would avoid any discrimination and hatred," Ed said.

"Yeah, there was a group of residents who were so anti-shifters they used any resources they could to keep the families out of here," Fred said. "Even violence."

"Are these laws still standing today?" she asked.

"No, but they stayed in force until the year 2000, when they were finally rescinded. While you can erase laws from the books, it's harder to erase the attitude from people's hearts.

"All we're saying, Charlee girl, is that you may get some of the old-fashioned anti-shifting feelings when you run. You're linked pretty tight with that Brockton boy," Ed said. "You should think twice about it."

"I was," Charlee said. "Past tense. But thank you." Even though they were no longer a couple, she knew Prague residents would still associate her with Riley.

She stood up to leave, turned, and almost collided

with a tall, blonde-haired woman. "I'm sorry, I didn't see you there." She started to walk around her when the woman stepped in front of her.

"I'd like to talk to you, Ms. Lightheart. You are Charlee Lightheart, aren't you?"

"Y-y-yes, I am. And you are?" She knew she didn't sound friendly but when a person blocks your path, cordiality gets tossed out the window.

"I'm Gretchen Carlyle." She forced a business card into her hand. "I'm a freelance writer."

"Aren't you the writer who wrote the lion-shifting history for today's *Bugle*?"

"Yes, I am. So, you read the article."

"No, I didn't." She watched as the big smile on her face was replaced with a look of annoyance.

"But a couple of my customers told me about it."

"I'm sure they enjoyed my insight."

"That's not the word I would use. Why do you want to talk to me?"

Against her better judgment, she offered Carlyle a seat at the counter. She also asked if she would like a cup of coffee. *Darn it, she accepted it.*

After the two of them were settled with their coffee at the counter, Carlyle got down to brass tacks. "I'm not going to beat around the bush. I'm here to ask you what you would know about Riley Brockton and his brother, Quinn."

She squinched her face. "I beg your pardon?"

"You should know better than anyone else. Are the Brocktons lion shifters? The residents have a right to know."

"Are you crazy? Is this really a news story?"

"Of course, it is. If you had read my article, then

you know how dangerous they can be. If it wasn't for the swift work of the security personnel, Myron Whiffler might have been mauled to death."

"What does that have to do with Riley and Quinn? The incident you're talking about happened more than a half century ago."

"Lion shifters are lion shifters," Carlyle huffed. "Just like a leopard's spots never change, the lion shifters' manes stay the same. After all, lion shifters are primal animals. They're beasts pure and simple."

"That's it! I've heard enough hate talk from you. You need to go, immediately."

Carlyle seemed unfazed by the outburst. "Then are you saying you know that the Brocktons are lion shifters?"

"I'm saying whether they are or not is nobody's business."

"You've been dating Riley for nearly a month now. You surely know the truth."

"What I'm saying is I have no comment because it's nobody's business. I don't know if they're shifters, but if I did I sure as hell wouldn't tell you."

The loud argument caught the attention of most of the customers. "Now, if you would please go now, you're disturbing my customers."

Carlyle picked up her messenger bag and stuffed her notebook in it. "Well, I've never been treated so rudely in my life."

"I find that hard to believe."

She started to leave when she pivoted on her heel. "You haven't heard the last of me. I don't take kindly to the way I've been treated here. You'll be sorry. Very sorry."

Chapter 21

As Carlyle exited the shop, she practically ran into a group of women coming in. "Watch where you're going," she said and pushed through the group.

"What's wrong with her?" Karen asked.

Charlee rushed up to them to apologize for the reporter's actions. "Her day didn't go as planned."

"I'm surprised to see you here so early," Charlee said.

"I'm sorry if it feels like we're pressuring you," Karen Manning said, "but we're here to get a feel for your thinking."

At first, she panicked. This was it. She was really going to do it. Once she told them, there was no turning back. She fought down the fear and cordially invited the women to sit down. Mel pulled two tables together and told Charlee she would bring coffee and menus. *Subtext: Sit with them and do not work.*

She engaged in small talk while they drank coffee and ordered. After all the preliminaries were completed, Karen brought up the subject. "Have you made a decision about the council seat?"

The moment had come. The fracking industry had not been her battle, true. The pharmaceutical companies were. But she couldn't turn a blind eye to the cause. People were suffering, acquiring terminal diseases, and living with the pollution fracking created. She knew she should be more excited, but considering her estrangement from Riley, she couldn't muster her usual enthusiasm. She was ready, nevertheless, to throw herself into the fray.

"Yes."

"Okay," Karen said, "so you've decided. Are you going to tell us your decision?"

"Yes."

The group groaned. She wore a smile. At that moment, Mel came with the food. "Your boss here is being enigmatic," Karen said.

"She's playing hard to get. If she's playing games with you, I'll tell you myself. She's going to run."

The women applauded and yelled, which drew the attention of all the customers. Fred yelled, "It's official. Charlee girl is running. Hip Hip Hooray!" Corny as the chant was the entire shop repeated it. "Hip Hip Hooray!"

After the congratulatory choruses died down, she decided she needed to know something about the situation.

"Right now," Karen said, "as you know, the seven-member board is loaded toward the pro-frackers: four to three. When you get in, you'll tip the balance to our favor."

"*When* I win?"

"You'll win, don't worry."

She wasn't really worried—*yet*.

Her next question was about her opponent, Myron Whiffler. Myron Whiffler III to be precise.

"Tell me about Whiffler. All I know about him is that he is pro-fracking. You do realize your recruit doesn't follow the news."

The group laughed. "No problem," Karen said, "we'll give you a crash course on Prague City Council 101."

"The first thing you need to know is that Whiffler believes that he has a right to that seat, given that his father and grandfather held it before him. Because of this, he may get nasty," Jayne said.

"She's right," Karen said. "I've already heard rumors that if anyone dares challenge his seat, he plans to pull out all the stops."

"What exactly does that mean?"

"Who knows? I've got to be honest with you, though. He may go after your relationship with Riley."

Karen paused a beat. "I hope that doesn't give you second thoughts."

Former relationship with Riley, she thought. "It only makes me more determined to beat his butt." She cupped her hands around her mug. "There's one thing I really don't understand. Why is he so gung-ho on this fracking thing?"

Karen took sip of coffee. "He claims the booming economy is more than worth any alleged damage done to the earth. He doesn't even recognize the harm it's doing to our health.

"Lots of people favor it, but they don't live with it and don't know what we go through. You'd think that our own councilman would take that into consideration."

****

Charlee was busing tables shortly after the group left when Mel came up to her.

"I hate to see you so depressed."

"I'm not depressed. What makes you think I'm

depressed?"

"For one thing you're not smiling. You're trying to show enthusiasm about being a candidate, but you're not fooling me. And I know what it is."

Mel began clearing the table with her and put several glasses into the bus tub.

"I don't normally give out advice, and I've never given you any, but if I were you, I'd walk into Brockton Enterprises and find out from Riley himself why he left. I'm not saying that will lead the two of you to getting back together, but at least you'll know why he walked."

She paused a moment. "Heck, you may hear his reasoning and slap him across the face. God knows he deserves it. But then you'll at least know what was bothering him. Not to mention the letting off of steam of slapping the SOB."

****

That night in the bathtub, Charlee sipped on her wine and stared at the lone candle that lit the room. She seldom drank, especially at home, but decided she needed more than a warm bath. After several sips, her mind wandered to how her life got so mucked up that she found herself in this situation. She was thinking about the advice Mel gave. It seemed like a good idea, but she wasn't sure she could get up the nerve to do it.

Then her mind jumped to the morning history lesson with Ed and Fred and her encounter with Carlyle. *That's it! Riley's a lion shifter! Of course! It's so obvious.*

She quickly reviewed some of the words Riley had used that night. She was so stunned she hadn't processed them at the time. He said something about discovering his "true identity." Then he rambled about

"I shouldn't have left you in the dark about my ancestry."

Suddenly everything became clear.

Lion shifter.

"Oh my God. That has to be it," she said. "He thought I was going to confront him on the rumors about his family's history. What if he were a lion shifter and he didn't know how to tell me?"

She jumped out of the bathtub, blew out the candle, and got dressed. Her mind raced a mile a minute. There was no use trying to relax in the tub. She realized she needed to find out the truth. But it was only fair, then, that she tell him about her family history.

For the first time since Riley left, she felt excited about facing tomorrow.

Chapter 22

What am I doing here?

Charlee stood in the lobby of the Brockton Enterprises offices, waiting for the receptionist to finish her telephone conversation.

She hung up the phone and turned her attention to Charlee.

"Would it be possible to meet with Riley Brockton, please?" She suddenly felt like a child, asking permission from the mother of her best friend if she could come out to play.

To make matters worse, she stood there with four cups of coffee and a bag of muffins. As she talked, she clutched the white sack with the muffins ever more tightly until her knuckles were as white as the bag. It seemed like a good idea when she flew out of the coffee shop the instant Mel walked in this morning. She not only left Mel bewildered by her action, but she left her alone at the restaurant.

"Do you have an appointment?" Renee asked.

"No, I don't, but I was hoping he'd have to time to see me. I'm Charlee Lightheart."

"That's who I thought you were," the receptionist said, dropping the professional tone she originally used.

"Oh?"

"I'm so glad to see you."

"You are?"

"I know it's really none of my business," Renee said in a stage whisper, "but Riley's been a bear to work with since you two broke up."

"But it's only been a couple of days."

"That's a couple of days too many."

A short silence followed, but Renee was quick to fill it.

"I sure hope some of those goodies you hold in your hands aren't just for Riley."

"No, ma'am," she said, as she placed them on the desk. "It's his usual order of coffees plus one for me and the muffins, plus a few extra. I thought maybe if nothing else, I could bribe you to let me see him."

"We do miss your coffee and muffins."

Just then the Brockton brothers came from seemingly out of nowhere.

"What's this about a disturbance out here, Renee, I don't see any disturbance," Riley said. Then stopped short when he saw her. She took a double take.

Riley had told her that he and his brother looked alike, but she wasn't prepared for the amazing similar characteristics. They could have been twins. Riley was several inches shorter than his brother, and his hair was a shade lighter.

"I saw you walk in with the reserves of food," the receptionist said to Charlee, "and hoped you were who I thought. Even before you approached the desk, I was working on getting Riley to see you. Sometimes it takes just a bit of imagination…and a lot of deception."

"I don't think this is a good idea," Riley said. He ran a hand through his hair.

Second thoughts flooded her mind. *What am I trying to prove? But I've come too far to turn around and run now.* She believed that confronting him would ease her mind, even if it didn't reunite them. So far, though, it didn't sound like he wanted anything to do with her. And that was good, she told herself, because she didn't want anything to do with him. Or so her rational-self told her.

"I thought the meeting would be best held in the conference room," the receptionist indicated to Quinn. It took a few moments for Charlee to process they were talking about Riley and her.

"Excellent idea, Renee," and he took a coffee off the desk and shoved it toward his brother. "Take this with you." He walked toward the conference room and motioned to his brother to follow him while Renee nodded to Charlee to follow the brothers.

She grabbed her coffee and hurriedly followed them the length of the luxurious lobby, their long legs able to make the short trip faster. She did have a chance to admire the quality paintings of the big African cats on the walls, with an occasional painting of a giraffe or an elephant.

"Here you go, guys," Quinn said. "Charlee, just so you know, this is a soundproof room. Feel free to give Riley an earful."

"By the way, it's very nice to meet you," he added, giving her a grin that was nearly as lopsided his brother's.

Once the door was shut, Riley stiffly offered her a seat. She sat down and tried to decide the best way to start the conversation. She was so excited the night before, after she figured out what she thought Riley wanted to talk about, she hadn't even planned what she would say to him.

Now she didn't feel quite so excited. She doubted her initial enthusiasm and swore at herself for not thinking it through a bit more. Regardless, she was here, and she had no choice.

Usually, she could read Riley's moods. But this time she couldn't. She had no idea the type of reception her words would get. It was obvious, though, from his brother's and Renee's reaction that he might be open to at least talking a bit.

"Riley," she began. It sounded to her as if her voice quivered. Silence. She didn't know how to even begin to say it without the fear of teeing him off.

"I'm sure you didn't come here just to sit in silence," he said, without looking up at her.

His voice carried a rough, almost nasty growl that she had never heard before. She was tempted to bolt. Instead, she closed her eyes, took a deep breath, and worked past it. *Not the time to be sensitive, Charlee. Just spit it out any way you can.*

She took her own advice.

"I'm not going to beat around the bush. I was not only stunned when you walked out on me but deeply hurt."

"If you came here to give me a lecture," he said, "save your breath. Quinn and Renee have been lecturing me daily. I get it. I mucked up, bigtime." He said all of that while staring at his coffee cup.

"No, I didn't come to lecture you, I came to find out what you thought I was going to ask you that night. Because I'm betting it's not at all what I had planned to."

He mumbled something she couldn't make out. Having gotten a few words out, though, she felt braver.

"You believed I was going to ask either to confirm or deny the rumors about your family being lion shifters. Am I correct?" She had to figure out a way for him to open up.

He pushed his chair back from the table, stood up, and paced his side of the conference table. She waited as long as she could. She was about to continue when Riley stopped and turned on a heel.

"You're right. My family—I am a lion shifter. I put off telling you because I was terrified that you'd run off. I didn't want to ruin my relationship with you. I've made mistakes before in relationships. I thought I had met my lioness, but...well, let's just say a lion's instincts are sometimes wrong. But with you I couldn't be more sure of myself. So, I was walking on eggshells, trying not to muck up that something special I thought we had.

"But, by not telling you sooner, I accomplished nothing more than our breakup anyway.

"All of my instincts, my intuition, my inner lion, all tell me you're my lioness—you're my soulmate."

She was tempted to interrupt him but decided not to. He was finally opening up. She didn't want anything to shut him down,

"If you're not a lion shifter, the concept of lioness is strange. More than one shifter has lost his lioness because she didn't know how serious of a bond they had. It's not a pickup line or something we say lightly to flatter someone. It's—"

Finally, she could keep quiet no longer. Riley had crossed the line from confession to self-flagellation. She couldn't take him beating up on himself anymore. Especially in the light of her background, such self-torture was unnecessary.

"Riley, stop right there. First, my question that night had nothing to do with your shapeshifting. But thank you so much for telling me about it, even belatedly."

"You're not going to hightail it out of here now that you know?"

"I'm still here, aren't I?"

She took a deep breath. "I thought this would be a lot easier now that I know you shift. But somehow it isn't. There's no other way to tell you this. I, too, come from a lineage of shifters."

He had continued pacing but came to such an abrupt stop he nearly fell over. "What do you mean?" he asked. "What are you talking about?"

She gazed into his eyes and suddenly found the courage to continue talking. The hard, icy edge that enveloped him when they first walked into the conference room had melted.

"My family, going as far back in my history as I can remember, are shifters. I know what it's like to keep secrets from the public. Believe me, my parents impressed upon me at an early age that I don't tell anyone outside our family about it.

"When I was really young, like three and four, it was easy for my mom to dismiss my stories to others by invoking the overactive imagination of a toddler. She would say anything to excuse or discredit my story. Too much television. I spent too much time watching my brothers and father playing video games. I'm sure you know all the excuses yourself."

For the first time since they entered the conference room, Riley smiled—that adorable, lopsided Brockton smile. This visit, she thought, could stab my heart again if they couldn't get back together. She found it hard to believe, but that darned smile was associated with so many memories. Could she live with them as just memories? She would have to if he couldn't or wouldn't mend this fence.

"So, you shift?"

"No, darn it."

"I don't understand, you just said—"

"I know. And every other member of my family does. But you're familiar with how all males shift for the first time around puberty?"

He had been at the other end of the conference room but strode over to sit across from her. He nodded.

"Then you must know that puberty isn't the shifting marker for females like it is for you guys."

He shook his head. "No, I don't know anything of female shifters. I didn't have any sisters. My mother, of course, shifted long before us boys showed up. And, of course, no one in town talked of shifting. Quinn and I didn't even know if we had lion shifters as friends. It wasn't spoken of when we were growing up."

She thought of the conversation with Fred and Ed. She wasn't surprised Riley didn't know. "If it's going to happen for a woman, it may occur close to puberty, but sometimes the first shift is delayed. And then, it's different for every female. It could be some crisis that triggers it, or it might be some exciting news. Some people even think it might be related to hormones.

"As you can imagine, if the first time can occur at any time, it may happen when you least expect it, which, for some women, means in public. Try explaining that to your neighbor. One minute you're in their living room sipping tea with them, the next minute there's a lioness lying on their floor.

"But I personally haven't shifted yet, and it's doubtful that I will. Most women my age have already experienced their initial shifting."

He laughed.

"What's so funny?" she said, trying her best to sound defensive. Though she was just glad to see his mood lift a bit even if it was at her expense.

"Most women your age," he said, "makes you sound so old."

"I am for any initial shifting process, that's for sure."

"I'm so sorry that I underestimated your capacity to understand this," he said.

They both grew silent. Though no words passed between them, she knew this silence was the first step to healing and restoring their bond.

He finally broke the silence. He knitted his brow, cocked his head, and asked, "So if you weren't going to ask me that, what was on your mind that night?"

"I wanted your advice. No, I needed it. I had to make the decision whether to run for city council."

"And obviously, you decided."

"Oh, so even though you haven't come to visit me at the coffee shop," she chided him, "you have been following me in the news."

"I know you'll make a fantastic council member. If anyone can help ban fracking in this town, it's you."

"As a business executive you don't mind that your soulmate, as you call me, is battling the 'forces of fracking.' "

"I think it's high time someone stands up to that

company. I'm very proud of you."

He let a long, low sigh, slightly guttural, sounding close to a growl.

"I can't tell you how I've missed you and how many times I've tried to will myself to walk into the coffee shop. But I feared that I not only would embarrass myself, but I would alienate you. I assumed you'd never want to talk to me again."

He took her hands in his across the desk and said in almost a whisper, "I love you. I can't live without you."

Charlee closed her eyes; she rejoiced in the familiar touch of his large, paw-like hands, and replied quickly, "You underestimate what you mean to me. I love you, too, Riley. I really do."

A few seconds later, she opened her eyes. She was shocked to see that Riley was no longer sitting across from her. But she felt something pressing against her legs. She looked under the table and saw the amber eyes of a lion gazing up at her.

Chapter 23

Charlee plopped herself on the seat at the counter of the coffee shop. The lunch rush seemed to be over, although lately they'd been getting hit a second time, about half an hour after the first rush.

She had no idea why, but then she chalked it up to the whims of the public, and she knew deciphering that was impossible.

Pulling her cell phone out of her pocket, she immediately flipped to her calendar app. For the thousandth time, or so it seemed, she counted the months between her officially becoming a candidate for city council and the election date.

She always came up with the same answer.

Four months.

Four months to educate the city on the evils of fracking. She thought that would be more than enough time. If she couldn't make a case in that amount of time, then she wasn't worthy to have the trust of the Citizens Against Fracking, let alone to hold the office of councilperson. It didn't take long for her to see that her thinking had been short-sighted.

She had arranged a press conference during her first month of campaigning. Still not used to the "power" that she held, she was shocked when the press and other media outlets within a radius of about fifty miles actually showed up. Even private citizens came.

She knew she had the perfect backdrop for the conference.

"Karen, do me a favor and stand right here for a few moments, please," Charlee said after she wandered aimlessly through the residents' yards. Karen dutifully and unquestioningly stood still while she roamed around a bit more.

"Charlee, I hate to break your concentration, but what exactly are you doing?"

"I'm new at this, but I figure the largest impact we could make would be if you and I stood so the media had the best view possible of the well at all times. I think you're in that sweet spot right now."

She chuckled at Karen's apparent bewilderment. "You see, we'll stand there with our backs to the well. The television stations and photographers and videographers can't capture our images without the well blazing behind us. There's no way they could ignore those sharp, ragged flames. They really do look like something more befitting a movie than real life."

"Okay, so why are you still doing an imitation of a free-range chicken?"

"The stink. I'm trying to find the perfect part of the yard that has the most noxious fumes. Then, I'm going to see if we can find some type of compromise. I want those media people to have the best vantage point of the well. And if I find the most horrible smelling spot, they'll find it difficult to ask questions without coughing. Now there's a scenario you couldn't write into any movie script."

During this discussion, she had randomly roamed the yards, holding her head up high at times, bending down to check out the smell a little lower. She wasn't sure how the physics of smell worked. So, she wasn't taking any chances.

"Yep," Karen observed, "a free-range chicken."

Charlee was nervous enough that she couldn't ignore the comment and began to squawk. "Brocc! Brocc!" She folded her arms, hands in her underarms, and began flapping her "wings." Then she began digging in dirt with her feet. "Brocc! Brocc!"

Karen couldn't resist as she, too, took up the improvisational chicken impersonation. The two women bobbed their heads and weaved around each other dancing together like a chicken minuet. The pair was abruptly interrupted when Marco ran into the yard, nearly in a panic.

"What in the blue blazes are the two of you doing?"

By this time, Karen was giggling uncontrollably. "Why we're doing our best chicken impressions." She could barely get the words out around the giggles.

"So, that's what you call it?" Marco asked.

Charlee suspected she should be a bit more repentant and far more embarrassed, but she couldn't bring herself to feel either emotion. "It was triggered by a comment, but continued because I'm nervous," she confessed. "Brocc! Brocc!" she quietly added.

She pulled herself up to standing and got back to deciding where it smelled the worst. She explained to Marco her reasoning for this strict stage blocking.

"Smart woman," her cook said. "I knew we asked you to run for a reason."

"Running is one thing, winning is a completely different matter."

"I'm amazed at how easy it is to call a press

conference and actually have the media attend. I've had several news outlets tell me they're planning on being here."

"Thank you, Charlee. I've been trying to do the same thing for I can't tell you how long, and I only get the brush off."

She tried to do her best Bogart impression. "Stick with me, sweetheart. We're going places."

"And you think that was a Bogart?"

"You recognized it, didn't you?"

Karen couldn't argue with that.

As the time crept closer for the start of the press conference, the media arrived. She was astounded. She didn't realize there were that many news outlets in the area. But when you count local websites, radio stations, and self-proclaimed blogging journalists, there were quite a few. Even private citizens attended. Finally, the issue was going to receive the publicity and attention it deserved.

****

"Thank you all for coming today," Charlee began. "Any of you who have interviewed me or read anything about me, know that my reason for running for the fifth ward city council seat is to be able to improve the deplorable living situation for our neighbors which was dropped on them through no fault of their own."

She paused and took a deep breath. "Prague is not a large town. Natural East Energy is doing this without regard to the health and safety of our citizens. What prevents them from drilling even more wells in other parts of the town? Nothing. There is no one who listens to us. The company is so spineless we can't even find out who owns them. We're dealing with low-level drones. They repeat the same lines and ignore the hazards this activity causes.

"For those of you who believe this fire, the noxious odor wafting ominously over this neighborhood, and the polluted, unusable drinking water could never occur in your back yard, you're only fooling yourself. There's no guarantee this is the only drilling site they have in mind.

"As you know, the reason you're here is to inspect a few houses that have sustained serious foundation problems because of the excess of earthquakes and to see first-hand this so called 'water' coming from their taps.

"And so, in order for you to get the most complete tour, I'm turning the rest of this conference over to Karen Manning, president of Citizens Against Fracking. Of course, I'll be right with you for any follow-up questions, but believe me, Karen is the technical expert here."

"Are there any questions before we begin the tour?"

A hand raised and a voice said, "I have a question, Ms. Lightheart."

She looked into the small crowd and saw the voice belonged to none other than Gretchen Carlyle. *I already threw her out of the coffee shop, what could she possible want from me now?"*

Before Charlee could even acknowledge her, she blurted out, "Isn't your crusade against the fracking industry in direct conflict with your dating Riley Brockton, the biggest industrial businessman in town. Surely, he must own a hydraulic fracturing company. Or two?"

"This event is not about me." She gritted her teeth. She wanted to yell: *It's none of your damned business.* She thought better of it and contained those emotions. "If there are no other questions, then let's proceed with the tour."

Karen led them into her house first and talked about the "deadly" water. "Not surprisingly, the company hasn't owned up that fracking has caused this, but when you dump your wastewater wherever you can, this should come as no surprise."

The flashes of all the cameras went off as Karen held up the glass. It was just as Charlee remembered it: gray and chunky. *Very appetizing.* She imagined how the *Bugle* would place the story on the front page along with this photo and others the journalists would take at the other homes.

Yeah, it was about time the media took the issue of fracking seriously.

****

Charlee held her breath the following morning. She unlocked the coffee shop's front door and picked up the *Prague Bugle.* She was sure that the fracking press conference would be displayed prominently—front page, above the fold of the newspaper.

"No, not again!" She moaned. She went inside feeling defeated.

"I'm probably the only politician alive who would moan at coverage like this," she said out loud to no one at all. Then she began laughing at her pitiful reaction to the story.

"What's so funny?"

She jumped. "You startled me."

It was Marco. "What are you doing here so early?"

she asked. "I thought you weren't scheduled until 10 or something like that?"

"I had a feeling that you might need an extra cook this morning," he said. "The neighborhood is coming over for breakfast to read the news coverage and check out the internet coverage of yesterday. There are quite a few of them."

"They're going to be disappointed and probably be teed off at me."

Marco leaned against the counter as she took a seat so she could scrutinize the articles a bit more.

"See," she said, "I have to admit the tour of the conditions did make the front page, but it's below the fold. It really should have been the newspaper's main headline. But there's an accompanying article devoted just to me. How disgusting."

"You are the person running for city council," he said, as if she didn't know it. "And the voters—well, this may come as a surprise, Charlee—but they need to get to know you a little."

"It's not as if I don't talk about the issues—and not just fracking," she confessed to Marco. "I try to make a stark contrast between Whiffler and me."

"And believe me you do." Marco laughed. "It's refreshing to see someone so committed to keeping her word. You're trying so hard to get your message—our message—out that somewhere you think any article about you detracts from the fracking issue."

"But it does," she protested. "I want people to get mad as hell about the fracking, not all lovey-dovey about me."

"Trust me, Citizens Against Fracking feels all lovey-dovey about you if that's any consolation," he offered.

Just then the bell on the door tinkled. "They're here," Marco sang.

"Do they look friendly?"

"They look very friendly. Why shouldn't they?"

"I feel like this is an ambush," she said.

The women moved a few tables together even before she greeted them with menus and silverware.

As she approached them, the group broke into applause and cheers. She stopped suddenly and then looked behind her.

Before she had a chance to say anything, Karen gushed, "You're magic!"

The others agreed. Jayne volunteered, "We've been trying to get front page coverage forever. We've called press conference after press conference with little response from the media. And with just one call, look at what you were able to do." She waved her copy of the newspaper in the air.

"It doesn't bother you that the newspaper wrote this large article about me when, in all honesty, they could have devoted that much more space to the appalling conditions you have to live with?"

"Charlee think of it this way. You're running for council. Sure, it's important that we get the fracking issue out there. But if you can't get elected then the balance of the council doesn't change. Which means..."

"That you can't get the anti-fracking moratorium on the ballot." Charlee finished.

"Exactly."

"As far as I'm concerned," Karen said, "we're doing great. We have the media at least willing to talk a bit at the movement and my God, the *Bugle* loves you.

As long as they keep writing about you, that newspaper is helping the fracking cause. I feel nothing but good coming out of this entire situation."

She wished she could feel the same confidence. If everything were going so well, why did she have so many misgivings and a sense of impending doom?

Chapter 24

Charlee convinced herself that the local media's mantra was "Issues? What issues?"

One night, after a satisfying visit of pure sensual bliss with Riley, she cuddled up into the crook of his shoulder. He had asked about the progress of her campaign. She looked into his eyes as she snuggled closer to him. She couldn't imagine being anywhere else in the world.

"I'm totally frustrated, to be honest," she said, as she wrapped an arm around him. "And more than that I have an unfounded constant anxiety that something horrible is about to happen. I'm hoping it is unfounded."

"Why? You and your campaign are on the front page of the *Prague Bugle* nearly every day. Just this week they showed you touring the homes and surrounding areas where the majority of the fracking is occurring."

"That's true. The photos were great, and I'm grateful for all of it, don't get me wrong. But the article was, to say the least, more focused on me than the issues. And then to top things off, the reporter wrote a separate article about this 'young upstart.' That's what she called me. I'm still not sure if that's a good thing or a bad thing. The reporter seemed surprised that a coffee shop owner would run for office, let alone know anything about the issues."

"Welcome to my world," he said good-naturedly. Then he got a bit more serious. "I know firsthand how frustrating that can be. When I speak to the press about a new acquisition or a charity event, the reporters can't stay focused on what I'm saying. They're much more concerned about promoting my reputation as a playboy. In every article they have to refer to me as the 'billionaire playboy,' whether there's a shred of evidence for the description or not."

"I didn't jump into the campaign without giving it a lot of thought," Charlee said. "Nor did I run in order to get free publicity for the coffee shop. In fact, I'm risking the financial future of my employees should the corporation behind the fracking decide to retaliate. I have no illusions. I know whatever corporation is behind the Natural East Energy Company is powerful.

"The mere fact that the group's lawyers can't find the parent company behind it tells me something bigger than what we see at the surface is stirring. I know this sounds paranoid, but I'm afraid they—whoever they may be—could shut my little business down in a heartbeat. And my employees would all be out of their paychecks, their means of feeding their families."

"And how about you?" Riley asked. "Aren't you worried about your financial future? What happens when you don't have your income from the coffee shop?"

"Nothing. Nothing happens."

"I don't understand."

She positioned herself on the bed so she was lying on her side, one arm propped up her head so she could look directly at him.

"This isn't something I tell many people. In fact, I don't think I've told anyone this before except for Mel. So, please don't tell anybody." She paused, took a deep breath to inhale the scent she loved from being so close to him before she continued.

"I already figure you're going to tell your brother," she said as she tilted her head and sighed.

"No."

"Don't play innocent with me. I could tell how close you two are the moment I saw you together. Hell, it's probably going to come out sooner or later—especially with that Carlyle woman nosing around everything. So, it's better I tell you this now. I'm not sure if it would affect the campaign. It shouldn't. But then, this is a small town. I'm not sure how the *Bugle* and the other media would play this."

"Wow! Now you have my full attention." He pushed a strand of hair behind her ear, making sure his thumb brushed her cheek. She measured her words as she drank in the touch of his hand.

"Relax. It's nothing that exciting. It's just that about ten years ago, my father died of a heart attack. It was during the period when all the research and scientific studies were being released about prescription arthritis drugs. Every television news outlet was abuzz with the dangers of them. Dangers they had kept from everyone, not just the patients. Even the doctors prescribing these drugs weren't aware of the serious side effects they caused. These drugs caused my father's heart attack."

"A lot of people have heart attacks, Charlee."

"I know, but not everyone took these medications in the humongous quantities my father did. The moment I saw the amount and the different kinds of drugs he took, I flipped.

"I immediately called the doctor. He assured me my father's regime was well within the safety limits. Besides, he said, the bizarre cocktail of drugs reduced my father's pain significantly. The doctor then turned the tables on me and tried to make me feel like a bad daughter. He asked if I wanted my father to suffer daily.

"That was before the studies. When all the news came out that questioned the safety of these drugs, I called the doctor again. This time he got irate and accused me of questioning his decisions."

Riley stroked her hair. "Of course, that was exactly what you were doing. And that was a good thing."

"Long story short," she said, "when he had his series of heart attacks, I brought in the bag of arthritis prescription painkillers my dad was taking. But I couldn't get anyone to listen to me."

He nodded, signaling her to continue. "Once Dad died, I knew I had to do something so no other person would be harmed by this cocktail of drugs again. So, I found a great lawyer who agreed to take the case."

She took a deep breath. "Bottom line. The court saw the overwhelming evidence. Between the drug companies' negligence and their cover-up of the scientific data which explicitly showed the dangers, they determined I was due compensation."

"Did you sue your father's doctor for malpractice, too?"

"No, my attorney wanted me to, but I didn't see what that would do. I personally talked to my dad's doctor before the case went to court and told him my reasoning."

"What did you tell him?"

"I knew that it wasn't his fault. The drug companies deceived everyone from the consumers to the doctors. Why take his ability to heal people because the drug companies were greedy and unwilling to admit their mistakes.

"I was totally shocked at the amount they awarded me. I didn't care about the money. My purpose in suing was to bring the drug companies to justice. I didn't want another person to live through what my father did. And I didn't want another adult child to feel as if they were helpless and stood by while their parents were used as guinea pigs."

She swept one of her bare legs over his thighs before continuing. She had no intention of telling him all this tonight. It just seemed to flow out from nowhere. She thought at various spots she should end her story, but his eyes were fixed on her face in a concerned gaze, encouraging her to discuss the entire story. *I wonder if he knows how much it hurts just to talk about this.*

"And here's the most important piece of the puzzle. I made sure that I put enough money in the bank that I could live on, bought the coffee house, and then invested the rest.

"Technically, I don't need to work. Every night before I fall asleep, I renew my promise that I will help anyone who needs it. Especially if it involves people who had contracted a disease or an illness."

He nodded. "So, that explains your generosity with your fundraisers."

She smiled in agreement.

"And your running for city council is just one more

way you're trying to save the lives of people from greedy corporations?"

"Exactly."

A brief silence followed before she blurted, "Oh my God! I didn't mean to imply that your companies were greedy and you're—"

He placed his finger on her lips and said quietly, "I never thought you implied that for a minute. Quinn and I make sure all the companies we own and all that we acquire have impeccable credentials. If we sniff out anything that hints at being unethical or injurious to the public, we deal with it swiftly to correct the situation. I guess you could call us 'New Age' investors."

Chapter 25

"Of course, I would love to answer a few questions," Charlee said into her cell phone as she refilled Ed and Fred's coffee cups. "Can you give me just a minute to get to a location that's just a bit quieter?"

Her two regulars smiled and winked at her, giving her their tacit approval as if they were proud parents. As she walked toward the counter, she passed the pot off to Mel and pointed to the phone. This had become such a regular scene that her second-in-command knew exactly what she meant.

She walked outside and sat on the chair she had set up several days before when the calls began to pour in. She tried at first to count and keep track of all the different media outlets that asked her to comment on either the election, the fracking issue, or both. But she soon lost count.

Of course, the local newspapers, bloggers, and web sites reported on her candidacy. What she could never have predicted was that her run for city council would become a national focal point, a symbol of potential triumph for anti-fracking forces across the country. It never occurred to Charlee that media pundits would label her campaign as a possible tipping point for thousands of others who faced the same problem.

She had made a promise to herself after her dad

died, she would never let another person die from a company's greed if it were within her power. She didn't realize, though, in her attempt to keep that vow, how far-reaching her actions would be.

She finished up her conversation and walked back into the coffee shop, shoving her cell phone into the back pocket of her jeans.

"Well?" Mel asked. "Who was it this time?"

"A reporter from Sydney, Australia."

"You're kidding me. Come on, tell me, who wanted to interview you this time?"

"I'm not kidding you. It really was a reporter from Australia who had a totally amazing accent."

She got no farther in the conversation when the phone rang again.

But this caller wasn't interested in an interview.

"If you know what's good for you, your coffee shop, and your employees, you'd drop out of the race right now."

Her hand shook from the evil sound of the voice; she double checked the caller ID. She had automatically picked it up. The call was labeled "private."

The voice, clearly digitally altered, continued, "If you persist in staying in this campaign, you'll be sorry. You don't think for a minute you and your band of silly anti-frackers can stop a big corporation, do you? You'd be wise to quit now."

"Who are you? Why are you doing this?" She had recovered a bit, but the words still stung. She prayed her voice wasn't quivering. She didn't want to give the SOB the pleasure of knowing she was scared.

"If you don't withdraw your candidacy, you'll discover exactly why. Not only will I make sure you suffer, but your precious coffee shop, and your employees will too. You can take that to the bank."

She clicked the disconnect button quickly and then looked around and hoped no one actually saw her actions. Especially Mel, who could read her like a book.

That's when she noticed her hands were shaking.

It took no time at all for Mel to be-bop over and place a pot on the burner.

"And which media was that? *The New York Times, Washington Post*? You're becoming quite a celebrity in…"

Her voice trailed off.

"Charlee?" Mel lowered her voice, and her tone grew serious. "Who were you talking to? You look like you've just seen the ghost of Abraham Lincoln."

"I don't know who I was talking to," she said. "The person didn't identify himself."

"How could you take part in an interview when you don't know who you're talking to?"

"It wasn't an interview; it was a threat."

She related the details of the call to her.

"You know there's only one thing to do," Mel said.

"What's that?"

"Report it to the police."

Charlee protested. "I can't do that."

"Why not?"

"I don't want this to be publicized in the local media."

"Why not?"

She hesitated to answer as she shifted her weight from one foot to another. She took several steps toward the coffee pots, picked up a cup, and poured herself some.

"You're stalling."

"I know I am."

Mel laughed. "If you think I'm going to drop this, you're wrong."

"I don't want it publicized because I don't want Riley to know."

"Don't you think that if he's dating a candidate for city council, he has the right know if you're getting death threats?"

"Who's getting death threats?" a voice from seemingly out of nowhere asked. Riley was approaching the counter and evidently overheard Mel.

She narrowed her eyes as she glared at her friend.

"No one is getting death threats," Charlee said. "Mel tends to blow things out of proportion."

"And you, Charlee Lightheart," Riley said, "usually downplay things. So, fess up. What kind of threat did you get?"

"Look what you did, now, Mel?" she whined. She knew that she couldn't keep it from him now. She wouldn't consider that withholding information from him would be the same as lying. But since he was directly asking her, she had to answer him. She was a firm believer that you never lied to those who loved and cared for you. Besides, Mel was standing right beside her.

By this time, he was already settling down in a seat at the counter. "Should I get your usual?" Mel asked when she realized this was going to be a war of wills.

He nodded. "I'm ready to listen," he said. Charlee felt his eyes on her.

She hesitantly recounted the call. "Quite frankly," she confessed, "it did shock the socks off of me."

"I know you don't want to hear this, sweetheart," he said slowly. He touched her shoulder. "You need to report it to the police."

"You know as well as I do," she argued, trying not to sound too agitated with him, "that they can't do a darn thing unless someone carried that threat out. Right now, it ranks up there with a poorly designed and not very funny prank call."

"And you know as well as I do," he shot back, "that it will be easier should someone carry through on that threat if the police have already started building a case against him.

"You know I'm right. If this would have happened to someone you love," he said, looking down at his latte, when he said the word "love," "you would be dishing out the same advice."

She knew that he loved her. She understood the concept of lioness. But she melted at the sound of it, nevertheless. He had never used it with such a depth of feeling. It felt like he had just included her in his family.

"Charlee," he said. Her thoughts came back to the ugly present moment. "Did you hear me?"

"Okay," she sighed, "I'll call the police and report it."

"When?"

"Excuse me?"

"When? When are you going to report it to the police?"

"Later."

"Don't buy it," he said calmly, as he leaned back in his seat. If she didn't know better, she would have sworn he was deliberately holding back a smile.

"Why don't you do it right now?" he suggested, "I'll stick around and provide you with moral support. And I doubt that the newspaper will pick it up without any substance or action toward the threat."

Finally, she relented. "Fine, anything to get this incident behind me."

Chapter 26

"Who is this? What do you want?"

The voice on the other end of Charlee's cell phone sounded like the same, hideous, digitally altered one that called her before. It had been more than two weeks since the original call, and she was just now getting over the incident. She had just stopped shaking with terror every time her ringtone played.

"You don't listen very well. I've already advised you that it would be in your best interest to drop out of the race. It seems you're still giving interviews to every Tom, Dick, and Harry that ask. You'd do well to heed my advice. Or else."

"Or else what?" Despite her growing fear, she tried to sound defiant.

"Continue with your silly, futile fight, and you'll find out soon enough. Somehow, I don't believe you're smart enough, though, to take my advice. Maybe you should run to your billionaire boyfriend to get a second opinion if mine isn't good enough."

And with that, the voice disconnected the call.

She plopped on her bed. It was too early in the morning to deal with this. She had just exited the shower and dressed and was waiting for Riley to finish showering.

"Dammit!" she cried out, letting her frustration out.

In that instant, Riley walked out of the bathroom

and into the bedroom. He shook his head vigorously to get the last bit of water out of his hair. Droplets of water splattered everywhere.

"What's wrong, baby?" he asked. His long strides filled the short distance from the threshold of the bathroom to her bed. He slowly sat down next to her, his head bent in an attempt to keep his eyes focused on her face. He rubbed her back gently while he waited for her to answer.

His touch. His caring touch.

That was the last straw. She released the tears that had been welling up inside her and flung her body against his. She tried to tell him, but through the sobs and the tears she was sure it would be difficult for him to understand her.

Somehow, though, he did. "Same voice?" he asked.

She nodded as she grabbed a tissue on the nightstand and wiped her cheeks. "Yeah, I recognized it immediately."

"You know what you have to do next, don't you?"

"Yeah, I know. Can I wait till I get to the coffee shop?"

"Of course."

****

The following day the threatening phone calls made the headlines. She read the story, then tossed the paper aside, determined to ignore it. That didn't mean that she could get the incident out of her mind.

She looked up and surveyed her coffee shop. The small bell announced an incoming customer.

She glanced at her watch. Right on time, as usual.

Ed and Fred.

She grabbed two cups and a coffee pot and met

them at their table.

"So, Charlee girl," Ed said, "I see they won't leave you alone."

"Who do you mean 'they'?"

"Both the person making the calls and the *Bugle*."

"Do you have any idea who's badgering you?"

"No, I don't. I've been trying to dig into who is the ultimate owner of the fracking company; perhaps it's somebody from the subsidiary doing the drilling here, getting nervous I might find out who owns them."

Fred took a sip of coffee. "It's hard to believe in this day and age of all this internet news, you can't get a simple answer to a simple question. Who owns this company?"

He paused and looked up at her. In that moment, he reminded her of the way her dad would look when he was about to say how proud he was of her.

"I hope you don't drop out of the race because of this," Fred said. "I don't know if you realize it, but you've become something of a folk hero around town."

"Oh, come on. I don't believe it for a minute. I would believe that I've been a thorn in the side of the residents."

"Why would you say that?"

"Because I feel like the majority of the residents would just rather ignore the fracking issue. They believe I'm stirring up trouble where there is none. They're riding high on the burgeoning economic conditions. Of course, those are people who don't have to live with the noise, the odors, and the chronic health problems."

"I think you've misread them." Fred opened a packet of sugar and dumped it in his coffee. "The people I talk to are thrilled someone is finally taking a stance against the corporate powers. Someone who is looking out for the interests of the little guy. Despite what you hear, we're all pretty scared that one day we'll wake up to find one of those wells in our backyard."

"Yup," Ed said, who had been quiet until now. "That's the word on the street."

She finally sat down. "Frankly, I have thought of quitting. I don't want to come to work to find my shop destroyed. Worse yet, I'm afraid they'll hurt my employees. I'm worried about their safety."

"The impression I get from your employees is that even if you tried to withdraw from the race, they wouldn't let you," Fred said. "You're underestimating your efforts. Everyone is proud of you—employees and customers. I know me and Ed are. Everyone would walk to hell and back with you."

She laughed. She knew they were exaggerating, but it did buoy her spirits. "And how do you know this? Don't tell me that's the 'word on the street'?"

"Prague has a lot of streets. There are a lot of words out there."

She excused herself to retrieve their muffins, hidden from view from everyone to ensure no one would sell the last two.

She went into the kitchen to warm them in the microwave. That's when they cornered her.

The employees on duty, led by Mel, surrounded her. "I've called everyone this morning, Charlee," she said. "And asked everyone privately so they wouldn't feel pressured."

"What did you ask them?"

"Whether you should withdraw from the race."

"Why would you do that?" Charlee asked. It had been a long couple of days—a couple long weeks—for Mel to be playing mind games with her. "I don't recall telling you I was giving up."

"No, but I read your face and body language this morning. You're worried. And not about yourself. You're worried about us."

Mel paused as Charlee pulled the muffins out of the microwave.

Marco took the muffins from her hands. "You two keep talking, I'll make sure Ed and Fred get these."

"Don't forget their butter," she reminded him. Mel led her to an empty table in the café.

She talked softly. "The bottom line is simple, Charlee. We all, down to a person—even Aunt Lilac—want you to stay in. At the very least don't drop out because you're worried about us. We're all behind you one-hundred percent.

"If you truly fear for your life, though, that's a decision that only you can make. And if you drop out because you feel you're being threatened, well, we understand that too."

She had a difficult time focusing her eyes. The tears welled up in her quicker than she anticipated. She knew her attempts at hiding her emotions were futile. Luckily, Mel didn't call her out. These people, her employees, and dear friends, were all standing by her.

Today she realized that what she had around her right now was a true family.

Chapter 27

The lights were brighter than she expected.
And they were distracting.

Charlee tried not to show her nervousness, especially when Whiffler, behind the podium to her left, appeared to be calm and professional.

The media had arranged this debate between the two fifth ward candidates. She remembered when Channel 5 had asked her if she would be willing to debate her opponent live.

She also distinctly remembered answering enthusiastically. "Of course, I'd love the opportunity." Perhaps looking back at that, she spoke a bit too hastily.

Even with her second thoughts, she knew this debate would draw a large audience. It was the most effective and profitable venue she could ask for to educate the residents on fracking's hazards. The potential impact of this appearance was priceless as far as Charlee was concerned.

Two weeks and counting till the election. She had to convince the voters of Prague, and not just the fifth ward, but the entire city, of the severity of the situation. The polls showed she and Whiffler were practically in a dead heat. For every resident sympathetic to the adverse conditions that were a natural consequence of the drilling, there was one who saw the activity as the savior to Prague's previously disastrous economy.

A voice interrupted her thoughts. "And we'll be live in five…four…three…two…one…"

The moderator, Lawrence Montgomery, introduced the two candidates…and they were off.

Montgomery tossed the first question to Whiffler. It was about fracking. He made a sane and logical argument about what he called the stunning improvement in the economy since the company began drilling.

"It's true. The industry has attracted workers into Prague on a temporary basis. But even this has boosted the city's economy. These fracking employees stay in local motels and hotels. They rent apartments and houses. They eat at local restaurants. In fact, new restaurants are popping up, and they're flourishing. It's quite a change from previously. Prior to the arrival of these employees, there were few small businesses able to stay afloat. Now, according to the chamber of commerce, our economy is doubling. It's thriving like we haven't seen in a generation."

While Whiffler answered the question, Charlee saw Riley approach the anti-fracking group. He knew he was going to be late; they had said they would save him a seat. The group was in the front row, several of them with protest signs. She watched as he sat down next to Karen who immediately handed him her sign as she dug in her purse. Charlee smiled at the irony of it—business exec holding an anti-business message.

At that moment a flash went off as well as the *click* of a camera. A photographer snapped of photo of Riley and the sign.

"Ms. Lightheart." Charlee's full attention swung back to the debate. Now it was her turn to state her case. She emphasized the "boom and bust" cycle of the industry. "And yes, those individuals are guests in our community and renting homes. But Mr. Whiffler declined to tell you that the company they're working for are reimbursing those costs, priced be damned.

"This has caused housing rental rates to soar and price long-time residents out of the market. Families with deep roots in Prague can't afford the current housing costs."

"Woohoo!" Charlee heard Karen's voice in the group as they cheered her. She glanced at them and saw Riley's smile. It buoyed her.

"Ms. Lightheart, you get the first opportunity to answer the next question. You're obviously running on an anti-fracking platform. What evidence do you have that proves your—"

Charlee was puzzled as the moderator suddenly grabbed the table he was sitting at. Then, she felt the floor move. It rocked again.

An audience member shouted, "Earthquake!" Charlee held onto the podium, knowing that in the long run that wasn't the most brilliant of moves. But she had little choice. She swiftly scanned the building; she couldn't see anything else that even would remotely provide her protection.

She glanced over at Whiffler, who appeared panicked. At first, he stood there paralyzed gripping his podium, a grim look on his face. She watched him run to the moderator's table and sought refuge underneath it. He nearly pushed Montgomery, who had already dove there, out of the way.

She gritted her teeth; she knew the quake wouldn't last forever. She had no choice but to ride it out where she stood.

When it ended, she saw Riley check on the members of the group. Then he ran up to see if she was safe. She assured him she was.

Chaos erupted for a few minutes. Audience members were talking among themselves. The moderator, though, was one of the last to recover. He and Whiffler were still tucked under the table long after the audience had come to terms with the quake. "Come on, guys," an audience member called out. "It's all safe." Then he hopped onto the stage and dragged Montgomery out. Charlee recognized him as Jeremy Zorkawsky, one of the local geologists who worked with the group. It took a pale Whiffler a few moments longer to come out of hiding.

Jeremy whispered in the moderator's ear. Montgomery shook his head and then announced, in a quivering voice, "Dr. Zorkawsky tells me his sources have confirmed that was an earthquake we have just felt, and it ranked 4.0 on the Richter scale." A low buzz filled the studio.

"He also tells me that this is the sixteenth earthquake in this region in as many months, and they are convinced they're linked to the fracking."

"Charlee, would you like to comment?" Montgomery said, taking a deep breath. In the few moments the camera scanned to her, someone had brought the moderator a glass of water and he drank it down like a parched man in the middle of the Mojave Desert.

She answered quickly, "There's nothing more to say when a geologist and his expert sources declare what we just experienced was an earthquake that can be linked to the fracking activity. In my opinion when you have an expert opinion, you at least give some consideration to what he says."

****

Riley and Charlee drove back to her house. "Are you too tired," he asked her, "for me to spend the night?"

She laughed. "So, I'll take that as a no?"

"I'm never too tired to spend time with you."

"That's good, because all during that debate I was imagining what we would do when we got to your place."

"And here, I thought the serious look you were giving me during the debate related to the issues."

"The only issue I had on my mind was seeing you naked tonight and what I planned we could do when we got home."

"I love it when a plan comes together," she said. "What did you decide we could be doing?"

Keeping his eyes on the road, he reached for her hand, pressed their palms together, intertwined their fingers, and with his thumb caressed the top of her hand. "We would start by gently caressing each other. I know I would start with a breast.

"I'm not sure where you would start," he said, "but just choosing a part of my body—any part—and visualizing you caressing it stirs me to excitement."

She couldn't resist interrupting him. "Do you want me to tell you where I would start?"

"No, not in the least," he replied in a gravelly whisper. "I'd much rather be surprised."

Then he continued. "After I've satisfied you by stimulating those gorgeous breasts, then I would bring my attention down some."

"You don't say?" she said, her voice breaking.

Riley let go of Charlee's hand and placed his palm on her thigh and reached as far as he could to place it between her legs.

"Clothing is a bit constricting when you detail these sorts of actions," he said flashing that boyish lopsided smile. "But I'm sure you're getting the idea."

She raised her butt slightly when his paw-like hand fell naturally between her thighs. "I can see by your reaction your body has already discovered my intentions."

They strode into the house. Riley quickly locked the door behind him, took her hand, and made a beeline for the bedroom and made good on every one of his promises and then some.

Chapter 28

Earthquake Rocks Prague
Is God Endorsing Charlee?

"Did you see this morning's paper, Charlee girl?" Ed asked. "You have the Big Guy's backing, huh?"

She laughed as she poured their coffee.

"Yeah, right."

"Whether God endorsed you or not, that earthquake, according to the paper, seems to have knocked the undecided voters off the fence. And they seemed to have fallen into your camp," Fred said.

"I hope so, but you know what Yogi Barra said."

"It ain't over until it's over," the three of them said together. The men held up their cups as if toasting the quote.

Business was brisk that day. She couldn't help but wonder if the events from the night before played any part in it. Certainly, just about everyone she waited on commented on the timing of the earthquake; it seemed as if it were the topic of conversation at every table. Then again, how could it not be?

Charlee had been so busy she didn't see the key members of Citizens Against Fracking walk in.

"Charlee, you were so professional last night and so effective. You can't help but win the election," Karen said. She thought that despite all the hours Karen had been investing in this group, she looked vibrant and energized. It just goes to show you that following your passion only fuels you to accomplish more than you thought possible.

The women had pulled tables together and sat down. Mel hurried over with coffee and menus. She motioned Charlee to sit down with them. "Don't let me interrupt your conversation," Charlee said, but Karen grabbed an extra chair.

"Sit right here."

She looked at Mel, who nodded. "Thanks, Mel. I owe you one."

"You owe me more than one. But we'll discuss that after you're a councilperson."

"I'm in trouble, now," she replied, more for the benefit of the group than for Mel.

She let out a long sigh. "If I do win, we all know it was the because of the earthquake. You'd have thought a Hollywood director said, 'Cue the quake.' "

Jennifer agreed. "All that was needed was background music, and it would have made a great scene in a movie."

"I'm sure you have the election all wrapped up," Karen said.

"I'm not so sure," Charlee said, "but if I do, we all know it's only the first step of the overall plan. The next steps would be getting a proposition for the city-wide vote of anti-fracking on the ballot and then getting it passed. In so many ways, we've only just begun."

"There's one other thing that bothers me," she confessed, "nobody seems to know who ultimately owns that Natural East Energy Company. Oddly, the only employees the company sends out are second level executives. They swear up and down that the corporation is self-sustaining and not owned by a larger corporation, but everything on the web says otherwise."

Karen agreed. "Even our lawyers can't dig behind that. What does that tell you about this industry? All they've been able to discover is a corporation registered in the state of Delaware that turns out to be merely a shell. Nothing behind the paperwork."

"Sooner or later, we'll discover the responsible party. We all just have to be patient and keep digging," Jennifer added.

Charlee stood up to get back to work. She turned on a heel, only to nearly crash into Riley. "Hi, darling," he said and gave her a quick peck on the check. They had all but given up keeping their relationship out of the media's eye.

"Ooh," the ladies gasped as they feigned surprise.

They went out to local restaurants, Riley visited her at work, and did everything else "normal" couples would do in public. They even tolerated what seemed to be an inordinate number of local photographers attempting to snap a candid moment or two between them.

Each of them, though, made a vow that they wouldn't comment on the record to any reporter or blogger about the other. They hoped that the strategy would discourage the press and they would be less of a topic of area gossip.

Charlee knew that her candidacy heightened the attention. But she was no fool; she knew this was her new normal.

Chapter 29

Two days till the election, Charlee thought. She couldn't believe how quickly the time had flown. She sat home alone in front of the television, remote control on the arm of the couch with a bowl of popcorn on her lap, and a drink on the end table. She was keenly aware Riley wasn't next to her.

Her arms ached to touch him. Her body, even in his absence, burned with desire. But he had an important meeting the following day. He told her he was considering buying a portfolio. That's all he said, but she could tell he had been brooding over it. He was at his home, or knowing Riley, his office all night, trying to "make sense of it all," as he described it.

He wouldn't go into much detail about the transaction, but that didn't mean a thing. He seldom talked in depth about how he spent his day at work. "It's all so boring," he told her.

"Then why are you still doing it?" she asked him once. She recalled his hesitancy to admit it and how he blushed before he answered.

"This is going to sound like a naïve, even hokey answer. But this is truly what keeps me going."

"Annnd...?"

"When I make a deal it's always with the goal of improving the company's profits and the promise of the majority of the shareholders that we boost the employees' pay and benefits. I try very hard to make sure what I'm doing brings them a better life—even if it's only an incremental improvement."

It was at that moment that she realized that he was no ordinary capitalist billionaire.

No ordinary man.

Though she hated to see him put himself through that worry, she understood his need to be certain. One evening alone was a small price to pay.

In her solitude, she discovered thoughts of the election consumed her. She wasn't sure what frightened her most, winning or losing.

Losing meant that there would be no hope of improving her friends' living conditions. But if she won, then she would be responsible for those improvements. She hoped she could live up to, not only the expectations of Citizens Against Fracking, but everyone else who would vote for her. And this time, she prayed no one died before justice could be served.

She had been wrestling with her emotions and, in her weaker moments, second-guessing herself throughout the campaign. Those threatening phone calls didn't help. Sure, she told Mel and Riley she didn't want to make a big deal out of them. Yet she found it hard to dismiss them. She was relieved there were no more. Apparently, the caller tired of playing the game. She was certainly tired of having to play along.

But her intuition told her no one went to the trouble he did just to drop the entire topic after two calls. As the election drew closer, she grew more nervous. She feared that he—whoever he was—might decide to introduce a new level of play. She didn't know if he still had a surprise for her these last two days. The worst part of the entire ordeal, though, was not knowing the rules. Not knowing where the next step in this prank phone call game would lead.

She placed her glass and the popcorn bowl on the kitchen table on her way to bed. She thought about how her life would change if she won the election.

Charlee realized she had no concept of how a councilwoman behaved, how she should conduct herself. There were many more issues she would have to educate herself on. She had a cursory knowledge of some of them. Honestly, though, all anyone wanted to talk about was fracking. And she had no idea what went into creating and passing laws.

She climbed into bed, a thousand thoughts flying around her head bumping into each other. She wondered what she would do if she could hit the rewind button on her life. *Would I refuse the offer of running for council, knowing what I know today? No, I knew there might be retaliation. I warned my employees about it. I would have run regardless. Buck up.*

She thought about the delicate nature of the universe and how it only took one decision to make a forever change in her life—and others around her.

She collapsed into bed, unaware until that moment, the extent of her exhaustion—physical and mental. Her muscles welcomed the opportunity to relax. *Now, if I could only turn my mind off.*

She dreamt she won the election. Seated at a council meeting, she argued for quick action on the moratorium before anyone died. The alarm they heard, she told them, was a death. She woke up, shaken from the dream. It took her a moment to realize her own phone alarm was beeping.

"A dream," she said, thankfully. "Is it really time to get up?" She automatically hit the snooze button.

But that didn't stop the alarm. She opened one eye and looked at the phone. It was a call. At three a.m.

Her thoughts flew to Riley. "Oh, no, something's happened to him." Her heart shot like a bullet to her stomach; she felt her dinner hurl upwards. She swallowed hard, as she wondered what the bad news was.

"Riley, what's wrong?" she questioned the moment she connected the call.

Silence.

Silence that only made her stomach churn louder and her hand shake. Silence that told her Riley was not on the other end of the connection.

"No, not Riley, sweetheart. Sorry to disappoint the star-crossed lover. Not your dream man, but your worst nightmare."

The electronically altered voice sent shivers throughout her body.

"Do you still want to know who owns the fracking company?" the voice questioned her.

She nodded, then realized he couldn't see her. At least she prayed he couldn't. Quietly she said yes.

"Then, meet me at the corner of Third and Commerce in half an hour. If you don't, I'll come knocking at your door, and you won't like how that option ends. And by the way, neither will your boyfriend, Brockton. I can destroy both of your lives with a flick of my wrist. As easy as flicking a pesky fly off my arm."

He paused a moment, as if he were thinking about what he had just said. "I'd probably be doing Prague a great service. But I think I would much rather play with you, and like that fly, before I do anything rash, just pick the wings off of you.

"Half an hour. I expect you to be there."

Tears filled her eyes. She wanted nothing more than to ignore the call. But if she did, he'd come to visit her, or so he claimed. Even if he didn't visit her, she'd be terrified to fall back to sleep. And she knew better than to call the police. That would only tee him off all the more.

Then anger rose from within her. "God bless it. I'm tired of this. How dare that man, whoever he is, try to terrorize me."

"He can only do that if I let him." The full truth of the statement hit her. "Hell, that's the truth." She started to dress. "I refuse to let him intimidate me or terrorize me. It stops right now." She hiked a pair of jeans up above her hips and zipped them. "If he has the name of the parent company, I'll go meet him." She picked up the phone from the bed. "But I won't go in stupidly."

She went to the living room and rattled through her purse. "There you are, baby," she said to her can of mace. "I've never used you, but tonight just might be the night." She flung the purse over her shoulder, surprised by the amount of adrenaline she had. She was headed toward the door when a thought struck her. "A little extra insurance, that's what Dad always said." She hustled to her home office and pulled out her father's hunting knife. "Just in case."

Charlee was satisfied she did everything within her power to ensure she could protect herself.

As she drove to the spot, she ran through the plan, just in case she needed it. She'd spray him with mace first and run if she could, if not, she'd pull out the knife. She felt surprisingly confident.

By the time she reached the location, there was already a black SUV, headlights on, engine running in the public parking lot close to the street. *Of course, a black SUV*, she thought. *What else do bad guys drive?*

Charlee watched as a large man got out of the back seat of the vehicle and walked toward her car. Her window was rolled down slightly, and he spoke through that. "My boss wants to talk to you in his vehicle." He tried to open her car door, but it was locked.

The hairs on Charlee's neck tingled, but she was determined this guy—whoever he was—wouldn't terrorize her any longer.

She had already transferred her mace from her purse to her pocket; she double-checked to make sure it was still there. Then she grabbed her purse which held the hunting knife. She unlocked her door and followed the man.

Once he ushered her into the back seat, she saw two figures in the front. The driver remained silent, but the passenger spoke. She instantly recognized his voice as her anonymous caller.

"Look," he said, in the same hideous digitally altered voice, "I can't do much physical harm to you tonight." He kept his face forward, not looking at her when he spoke. "It's too close to the election. Even if you were to just magically disappear, the cops would be all over the case, determined to find who did it. Now, do you want to know who owns the fracking company or not?"

"Who the hell are you?" she asked, ignoring his question. She leaned forward as far as she could to grab his shoulder. She needed to know who sat there. He wore a black trench coat. A large black hat blocked her view of his face.

The moment she leaned, though, the man next to her pulled her back—roughly.

Then she felt the vehicle move. Her companion in the back seat kept his hand on her shoulder, presumably so she couldn't discover the identity of the passenger.

The fact that the SUV was now in motion unsettled her. And yes, she admitted to herself, she was frightened. But that didn't translate into her giving into her fear. I can't let him win, she thought. He won't terrorize me.

"Let's get this over with," she said, as she pulled all the inner strength she could muster. "Who owns the fracking company?"

A derisive laugh emitted from the man. "I'm afraid I can't tell you that yet. But I knew that was the only bait I could use to get you out here and talk to you. I want you to drop out of the race. You need to back out. And you need to do it first thing tomorrow morning." He paused a beat.

"I've even written a statement for you, explaining your withdrawal."

As he talked, she concentrated on recognizing his voice. The man next to her still kept a firm grip on her; she couldn't identify him by sight.

The man in the passenger seat handed an envelope to her companion, who took it with his free hand. She flinched when he stuffed it into her coat pocket.

"I'm tired of playing games with you. You need to back off and keep the balance of the council as it is. Do you understand me?"

"Yeah, I understand English," she said, as she swallowed hard. "But it ain't gonna happen." Her courage welled up inside her as she recalled the weeks she spent—no, wasted—fearful of the anonymous calls.

"Listen, you arrogant SOB, I don't know who you are, or for that matter who you think you are. But I refuse to take your suggestion."

"You haven't any idea who I am, do you?"

"No, because you're too cowardly to even show your face. All I know is that I'm not about to drop out of the race, and nothing you do can make me do it."

"That's a short-sighted attitude, now, Charlee. Within the next couple of days, you'll come to regret it. I guarantee it."

"Sorry, but within the next couple of days the election will be over. So, I'm not too alarmed by your idle threats." She could feel her heart beat as furiously as a racehorse trying to get out of the gate at the beginning of a race.

The vehicle came to an abrupt halt. The man next to her opened the door and exited first before he grabbed her arm and forcefully pulled her out.

She quickly pulled the envelope out of her pocket and shoved it in that man's face.

"Tell your boss, whoever the hell he is, I don't need his damned script. I'm not some participant in his reality TV show." The vehicle lurched forward as the man in the back seat closed the door, leaving her...

Well, she wasn't quite sure where was. It certainly wasn't at the same location where they—whoever they were—picked her up. There was no parking lot, no streetlight. But they must have had some ilk of compassion because there was an all-night diner and, she checked her pockets, she still had her cell phone.

She slowly walked up the three steps to the 1950s era diner and opened the door. It was old, but clean, and as one might guess at about 4:30 in the morning, there was only one person on duty and no customers. She ordered a cup of coffee and sat for a moment trying to decide who to call for help.

Calling the police first was out of the question. She had a feeling she would eventually have to do it, but she didn't want it to be her first call. She thought about Mel, but did she really want to deal with her chastising her like a mother hen? And while she wanted to call Riley, she knew he would make a really big fuss over her.

Oh, hell. Now, that the episode was over and her adrenaline began to fail, she knew she needed him. But she made her point—if only to herself. She wasn't going to be terrorized. Yeah, she thought reluctantly, it was a close call.

She knew it was selfish of her to seek Riley as a place of refuge at this moment. He faced a big decision at work in the morning. Holy crap—in a few hours. And he would, no doubt, lecture her sternly. But that was okay. His soothing voice, his gentle touch, his familiar arms around her body. She decided she would call him.

She hit his speed dial number; he immediately answered. "What is it, Charlee?" His voice pierced her ears. His panicked tone came through loud and clear. She was pretty confident even the cook heard him, and he was in the kitchen.

"It's nothing really," she heard herself say and winced, "except that I could use a ride home."

"A ride home? Where in the world are you? More importantly than that, what the hell are you doing there?"

At this point, the cook came out from the kitchen and told her the address. "I didn't mean to eavesdrop," he said. "But I could hear him all the way out there even without straining."

"Please, Riley, just come and get me, and I'll tell you everything."

"You're damned right you will."

"Well, that went fairly well," she said to the cook, after she disconnected the call.

"Sounds like you had quite a night," he said quietly, as if he didn't want to intrude but felt like he should say something.

"Yeah, and it's not going to end anytime soon, I'm betting."

"Care for a bowl of chicken noodle soup?" he asked. "My grandmother used to say it was good for the soul. I can't offer you much, but food, as you can see, is my stock in trade."

"Actually, chicken noodle is my favorite. Although that thing about it being good for the soul. It didn't work out so good for the chicken."

The cook went into the kitchen and came back with the soup.

"Be careful, it's hot."

She was grateful for the soup as well as the man's respect for her privacy. She hadn't finished the bowl when she heard the screech of brakes, a car door slam, and the diner's door open.

Her back was to the door; quite frankly she was afraid to turn around to look into Riley's eyes.

The moment he sat next to her, she embraced him tightly and sobbed. Her dammed up emotions erupted once she touched him, once she felt his physical and inner strength. She recounted her ordeal in one long breath. Once done, she collapsed into his arms and sobbed quietly.

Chapter 30

"Would you be my second set of eyes on this proposal, bro?" Riley asked later that morning.

He tossed it on his brother's desk as he sat down in a receiving chair. "Everything appears to be in order, and as it stands it would be an excellent investment in 'green' companies."

"Then, what's bothering you? I thought you'd be in a great mood, considering how Charlee's debate went a couple of evenings ago."

He finally smiled. "Yeah, that was pretty awesome, if not a bit scary. For a moment, I thought I was dating Moses. Instead of parting the Red Sea, she created an earthquake.

"But it's what happened last night that has me concerned. I really fear for her safety."

Quinn met Riley's eyes.

"Wow. What happened? I'm here to listen."

Riley leaned forward in his chair. "She called me last night," he said. "Actually, it was early this morning, closer to 4:30, and she was near hysterical, I could tell from her voice, even though she tried hard not to show it." He paused for a moment and smiled. "That's the way she is, you know," he said. "The more she tries to show me she's calm and cool on the exterior, the more frightened she is on the inside."

Riley told him the story, punctuated with asides on

the color of Charlee's hair and the fragrance of her shampoo.

"Thanks for listening, bro."

"Don't you think Charlee needs police protection?" Quinn leaned forward. "This sounds like these threats are escalating."

"Of course, I think so. But Charlee doesn't. I can't talk her into it. Believe me, I've tried."

Riley deliberately looked down at the folder in his hand. "My worrying about Charlee isn't going to change her mind. I can use my time more effectively by stewing over this acquisition. Something doesn't sit right with me. It's that one company—Amalgamated American Green. It claims to be a green company, but my gut says otherwise.

"Mike and I have discussed it. He says it's making money hand-over-fist. The firm supposedly uses cutting edge technology to lower fuel costs. Not only that, but the huge profits from this nebulous-sounding firm keep the other companies they own afloat."

"I trust Mike Morris with my life, Riley," Quinn said. "If he says that, it sounds like a solid investment. The Morris family—"

"Yeah, yeah," Riley interrupted, "they've been our corporate attorneys forever." Riley handed his brother the folder. "Here, take a look."

"So, they're offering you fifty-one percent of the business?" Quinn raised his eyebrows when he read that. "Why? That would mean you, or Brockton Enterprises, would have the last say on any decision."

"Yeah, that seemed strange to me too. I never really requested that. When I asked Mike, he said the current owner wanted to free up more of his time to devote to other projects and perhaps take on a few more scattered businesses of his own."

"Well, that sounds reasonable," Quinn said.

"Yeah, I guess. But my gut still says something's wrong."

While Quinn read over the papers, Riley paced, stared out the office window for a moment, and paced a bit more. Between what his intuition told him about Amalgamated American Green and his overwhelming sense of anguish about Charlee, he thought his head would explode.

"Mike tells me I'm foolish to be so concerned. It does look like it's a great opportunity. And you know Dad's old line."

Quinn laughed. "Strike while the iron's hot." Riley nodded.

"Bro, you've got a lot going on in your life. I think maybe your gut is overreacting. I've read it, and if it were me, I'd jump at it. It's that good of a deal."

"Thanks, Quinn." Riley leaned back in the chair. "Mike and the attorney for these guys"—he waved the folder—"will be here any minute for a few final negotiations."

He smiled and extended his hand over Quinn's desk. "Thanks for the encouragement." They shook hands. "Maybe you're right. I could be overthinking this. You've just verified Mike's assessment of the situation." He sat down in the receiving chair. "There's just way too much going on." While he thought he might not be able to trust his own intuition at the moment, he knew that his brother and his lawyer would never give him bad advice. That was good enough for him. He took a deep breath. "Okay, I'm going to take the plunge. I'm going to buy it."

"Good call," Quinn said.

"I'm sorry to interrupt, gentlemen," Renee said as she knocked and opened the door, "Mike's here and a Mr. Clayton Nelson for you. I've led them to the conference room."

"Perfect. Thank you, Renee. I'll be right with them."

He picked the folder off his brother's desk and smiled. He headed for the door when he turned around, almost as an afterthought, and said, "Thanks again, Quinn."

Chapter 31

"As we await the results of the fifth ward council seat, I'd like to take a moment and recap what has happened in this race."

The voice of the anchor of Chanel 5 news, Lawrence Montgomery, reverberated throughout the café election night.

The entire anti-fracking group and Charlee's campaign workers gathered. In addition, many of her regular customers were there, including Ed and Fred, ready to be among the first to congratulate her should she win.

"First off," the station's anchor said, "local politicians hadn't even foreseen Whiffler being challenged for his seat at the start of this political season. Charlee Lightheart, owner of *That Coffee Shop,* seemed to emerge out of nowhere when four months ago, she filed the necessary paperwork to run. Even at that, most people didn't pay much attention.

"But she made hydraulic drilling, better known as fracking, the centerpiece of her campaign. The city took notice. Soon, the entire country was watching Charlee. What started as a small group of mostly women protecting their families grew into a large well-oiled machine.

"This initially small crusade, in four short months, grew into a pivotal national campaign. Her stunning surprise insurgency created a political earthquake, figurately and literally, and sent aftershocks not only nationwide, but globally as well. In Prague, Ohio, we're looking at possibly what could be called a microcosm of elections to come. If Charlee wins tonight, it will give a bump to other anti-fracking groups, not only nationwide, but worldwide."

She was sitting on the leather couch in front of the television. Others were in the leather chairs, and still others had pulled up spare chairs from the tables to get a closer view of the results. Snuggled up next to Riley, her relaxed posture masked her nervous condition. She held him tight and pressed her head against his side.

There was no mistaking it. In that instant before the television anchor announced the winner, the group took a deep collective breath. While the newspersons droned on about the background of the race, he kissed her on the head and said softly, "Regardless of how this turns out, I'm so very proud of you just for being brave enough to run."

"And in the fifth ward race, local businesswoman Charlee Lightheart pulled off an unexpected victory, ousting incumbent Myron Whiffler. The final count shows that Charlee won 59 percent and Whiffler 41.

Aunt Lilac was the first to respond. "You did it, Charlee!"

The results were displayed on the shop's three television screens.

The anchor continued. "Her win now tips the balance of the composition of city council in a very meaningful way."

The crowd's thunderous response drowned out the remainder of the report, but no one cared. She had won.

They had won.

Aunt Lilac sipped her coffee and quietly said to Jessica, "Justice has won today. You don't get to see that every day."

Her friends and employees chanted, "Speech! Speech!"

All eyes turned to her—and caught her and Riley in a long, passionate kiss.

Chapter 32

Charlee fidgeted at her seat. Her throat suddenly dry, she sipped from the glass of water on the table in front of her. She had no idea she would be this nervous. She had no idea what to expect.

Welcome to my first city council meeting.

Thankfully, she didn't face this moment alone. Sure, she sat by herself as she faced the audience who came to observe. But among those observers was the Citizens Against Fracking group. Right in the front row. Along with Riley. She smiled as she recalled telling him he didn't need to attend. "I won't be able to attend them all, sweetie," he said, "but I'm sure not going to miss your first."

As he walked with her into the city's administrative offices before the start of the meeting, he had said, "I'm so proud of everything you've accomplished. Knock their socks off." He gave her a peck on the cheek before they parted.

"I'm pretty sure not much is going to happen," she said. "I think it's probably too early to start the groundwork for a proposition for a city-wide vote on fracking."

"Don't be too sure. Your addition to the council ignited momentum on the topic. Don't rule anything out tonight."

He gave her a quick kiss on the lips. "There's more

waiting for you at the front door of your home, once this meeting is over."

"There's motivation to get through the agenda quickly."

As the council's newest member, she thought she would be expected to sit quietly and observe the proceedings. That was fine by her. She was keenly aware she walked a political tightrope. Already branded an upstart by the *Prague Bugle* and considered a firebrand by the public, she had to prove she was responsible enough to execute her new position.

Because of her reputation, she planned to delay discussion on the anti-fracking moratorium bill for a couple months. She prayed she could pull both off.

The voice of Scott Hirgelt, the council president, jolted her out of her thoughts. "I'm pleased to introduce the newest member of our council, Charlee Lightheart."

"Whoop! Whoop! You go!" Members of the anti-fracking group showed their enthusiasm.

"You go, Charlee girl," declared a voice.

Of course, Ed and Fred would be here.

After the crowd quieted, the president continued.

"I'm not going to waste any time," Hirgelt said. "This council has been talking about this issue for as long as I can remember. Now that we have a new member, I thought it would the perfect time to bring the topic up again. I would like the council to vote on whether we should draft a ballot issue that would allow the citizens to decide if they want a moratorium on hydraulic drilling."

The words shocked Charlee but ignited a roar of applause among the anti-fracking group and many others in attendance. She took a good look at the audience. Prior to the announcement it was impossible to tell those individuals who were pro- or anti-fracking. With the exception, of course, of the group of her hardcore supporters.

She had just realized anti-fracking backers filled the room. She wondered how the council could be divided when it appeared clear so many residents opposed it. The sound of the gavel quieted the audience and brought her back to the present.

"I would like to place a motion on the floor," the president said, "to authorize a special election regarding a moratorium on hydraulic drilling within the city limits." He paused. "Is there a second to the motion?"

Immediately, the first ward member, Michelle Gilmore, seconded the motion.

"Those in favor of the election raise your hands." She raised her hand along with Scott, Michelle, and another member, Joshua Kowalski who she hadn't met before. The motion passed.

The audience gave the council a standing ovation. Who knew that such a simple vote of a city council meeting would be met with such enthusiasm? It was good to know that democracy was alive and well in Prague, Ohio.

"It just so happens," the city solicitor, William Nottingham, said, "that I've already written out a proposition on the off chance that this situation would occur. With your permission, Mr. President, I'd like to read this with the purpose of submission to the Board of Elections."

"Please, do so," Hirgelt said. Nottingham read the proposed ordinance.

The council president then called for a vote.

"Shall the ordinance entitled 'Ordinance Imposing a Ban on Hydraulic Fracturing Within the City Limits of Prague, Ohio' be adopted?"

If there were a play-by-play broadcast of the meeting the announcer would have said, "And the crowd went wild." Because, indeed, they did. The crowd gave the council another standing ovation. "Yeah, finally," she heard someone from the area of the anti-fracking group.

Again, Hirgelt pounded the gavel to restore order. "Mr. Solicitor, can the board vote on this proposition tonight? If we can, then we can finally get this show on the road."

The crowd fell silent, as they strained, it seemed, to listen for the answer.

"Yes, if you're pleased with the wording, of course, the Council may vote."

"Is there a council member who has issues with the wording of the proposition?"

"I believe it's well-written and straightforward. It won't confuse the voters, and we can have a clear and fair election," Gilmore said.

The others agreed. The council then voted four to three to place the ban on the ballot.

One might have thought the audience had no energy left to cheer the action. One would have been wrong. The member of Citizens Against Fracking jumped into the aisle as they cheered and embraced each other. Charlee even saw Ed and Fred dance and hug.

When the noise quieted down, a voice from the back of the room loudly said, "Bull feathers! You'll all regret your actions. Especially you, Lightheart." Myron

Whiffler stood, shook a fist at them. Then he strode out of the room.

The unexpected outburst stunned everyone. But the warning sent chills up her spine. Her legs turned to rubber. She clutched the pen in her hand until her fingernails dug into the palm of her hand. She panicked, though, when she looked at Riley.

Provoked by the menacing words, he bolted out of his chair and headed for the back of the room at breakneck speed. The room filled with nervous chatter. People craned their necks to see what Riley would do when he caught up with the man.

Charlee watched as Marco sprinted after Riley and grabbed him by the back of the collar. Riley stumbled backward, then pivoted and glared at Marco. "Let me knock that SOB's lights out. He deserves it. You know that as well as I do." Everyone listened and waited.

"Yeah, I know as well as anyone. But look, man, he's not worth it. Besides, if you're going to clean his clock, do it when there are no witnesses."

Slowly the expression on his face softened. He flashed his lopsided smile and admitted, "You're probably right on both counts. He's not really worth going to jail over, as much as I would like to get my hands on him. And when I do, it will be in a back alley when no one is around. Thanks, Marco."

They walked back to the front and took their seats. Riley made eye contact with her as if to apologize for his rash behavior.

The room slowly settled down. Scott then said, "Now on to new business."

With that announcement nearly half of the audience walked out. People who a moment ago were immersed in the potential skirmish exited as if nothing had happened. She must have looked stunned because Michelle nudged her.

"It happens all the time, you'll get used to it. Every now and then we get an issue that draws people in. We take care of it, if possible, at the outset of the meeting. Then, after everyone has expressed their opinion and we vote on the issue, they leave. We finish up the rest of the meeting as quickly as possible. Of course, the discussion normally doesn't end with potential violence."

Michelle gave a small laugh, but Charlee didn't see the humor.

Chapter 33

"Charlee Lightheart, I presume?"

Startled. Charlee turned around, nearly dropping the coffee grounds in her hands.

"Pardon me?"

"Are you Charlee Lightheart?"

She nodded. She didn't recognize the man but assumed he had seen her at press conferences or on television. She was still unaccustomed to her new-found notoriety.

"Yes. Why, yes, I am. May I help you?"

"I sure hope you can."

He paused. Charlee wasn't sure what he was waiting for. The pause turned awkward.

"Uhm, what can I do for you?"

"I was hoping you'd be a guest on my program."

Her eyes grew wide. "What program are you talking about? Some panel of people talking about fracking?"

"Something like that he," he said, "but you'll be a guest on my television show."

She laughed. "All right. Did Riley put you up to this?" She was thinking it was a cute prank, but at the moment the shop hummed with customers. She really didn't have time to play Riley's games.

The man, who had yet to introduce himself, gave her a blank stare. In that instant she attempted to size him up, do a quick first-impression character sketch. Not a businessman, she thought, his blue polo shirt and khaki slacks definitely set him in a more casual profession. Just what, she wasn't sure.

He was tall, at least six two, she figured. He wore his dark brown hair in a crew cut. But it was his nose that really caught her attention. The large, aquiline nose was beaklike. On anyone else it may have been a detriment, but it added to his good looks.

"I'm sorry," she finally asked, "am I supposed to know you?"

The man's body noticeably slumped. His easy smile faded. "You really don't know who I am?"

His reaction startled her. She didn't figure him having an ego. She was wrong.

"I'm sorry, you really don't look familiar to me."

"Maybe you'll recognize me by my profile." The man turned sideways, his beaklike nose sticking out in front of his face. She stared at him. His short-cropped hair looked like feathers.

"I'm sorry—" she began.

Then the man quickly pivoted and faced her and was about to speak, when Mel walked up. "Jared Sparrow!" she gasped.

She not only startled Charlee, but Jared as well.

"Bingo!" he said, touching his finger to his nose.

Mel told him how much she loved his show. Jared remained humble, but Charlee could tell he loved the attention. Charlee, though, felt totally lost by the conversation.

"Stop." she demanded. "What is going on here? What am I missing? How come you know this man and I don't?"

Mel burst out in laughter. She stared at her agape.

"What's so funny?" she asked defensively.

Jared also asked, but in a softer tone.

"Of course, you mean you don't know Mr. Sparrow—"

"Please call me Jared."

"Jared is the host of Prague's most popular talk show, *The View from My Perch.* "

Charlee stared at them; she had never heard of the show. Mel's laughter grew stronger. She could feel her cheeks turn red. Mel's attitude irritated her.

"We have the show on here every day," Mel told her. "Don't tell me you never noticed it?"

She sighed deeply. "No, I've never noticed it. I'm usually busy with our customers."

The statement came out harsher than she intended. She hoped that Mel and she were good enough friends that Mel didn't take offense.

"It's a great talk show," her best friend blurted out enthusiastically.

"Thank you," Jared said quietly. He pulled his wallet out of his back pocket and handed Charlee a business card.

In the middle of the card, *The View from My Perch* was printed. Below that was Jared's name. The station's phone number and Jared's cell phone number were in the lower left-hand corner.

But it was the upper right of the card that caught her attention. It was a caricature of Jared sitting in a tall director's chair looking down at the name of the show. The caricature only confirmed her first impression of a bird.

"First off, my talk show is broadcast live. We talk

about local issues in a non-hostile atmosphere. I don't attack my guests. The format is simple. Two individuals with opposing views on an issue sit in the middle of the stage. I sit stage right on what resembles a tennis umpire chair. I ask you both questions, and I give you both the chance to rebut the other. That's the first half hour. In the second half hour I throw it to the audience, and they ask questions of the guests." He paused a beat, taking a breath.

"I would love for you to appear on my show. The topic will be the proposed moratorium on fracking. You will appear opposite another councilperson who is in favor of fracking."

"Charlee, what a great opportunity this is. Think of it. You have the chance to talk about the hazards of fracking for an hour. So many people watch that show."

"Yes, I must admit people seem to like my show," Jared said.

"Jared, you're so modest," Mel said. "You know you're the number one local television personality in Prague."

The two of them stared at her expecting an answer.

"Uhm, well, I'm not sure. I'm not the only anti-fracking council member. Why don't you ask the others?" Charlee paused a beat. A smile crept over her face. "Or did you already ask them, and they declined?"

Jared reached over the counter and touched her shoulder. "No, you are my first and only choice. And you know why. You're the poster child for the anti-fracking movement."

Charlee felt two sets of eyes bore down on her. Exasperated and, quite frankly, tired of the publicity, Charlee wanted to wriggle out of the offer. But she knew her work wouldn't be complete until the moratorium passed.

"All right, I'll appear on your show."

Chapter 34

"Hello, Charlee."

She had been busy clearing a table when she heard the voice. She recognized it immediately. She looked up and saw him standing there.

Myron Whiffler—the third—as he loved to tell people. He stood in front of her for a minute, as she knelt on the bench at a booth, putting the last of the plates and cups in the bus tub.

"I bet you never thought you'd see me so soon." He flashed her a short smile, one she read as insincere, bordering on sinister even. Prickles shot up her spine. Immediately her mind shot to the council meeting several days ago.

"Can I get you a cup of coffee, Mr. Whiffler?" she asked, as her voice cracked slightly. She had never seen that glare in his eyes before. But then, during the debate and other appearances together, she never stood that close to him.

Evil. Again, that word. If evil had an aroma, he would be oozing it from every pore in his body. It was if he possessed with some evil spirit.

"No, Charlee," he said, "I didn't come here for coffee."

His voice came out as an unemotional monotone, a characteristic that she had in the past associated with sociopaths.

"But I would love to sit down here with you for a minute," he said. "It's imperative that I talk to you."

What could he possibly want to talk about? His voice, his automaton actions began to scare her. She was thankful she was in a public place and she hadn't bumped into him in a dark, back alley.

"Let's go to a clean table instead of this one." She put on a false bravado and a smile that she knew wasn't sincere at all. This is stupid, she thought as they sat. *I'm acting as if he's going to kill me or something.*

His next words did nothing to make her feel at ease. Far from it. "You've been a bad girl." He shook his head as he said it.

She felt as if he were morphing into Creepy McCreepster right before her eyes, as goosebumps shot up her spine again. She wished there were some way she could get Marco's or Jeff's attention. But unless they came out of the kitchen on a whim, it looked pretty dismal. Now that she looked around, the coffee shop was void of customers. There wasn't even anyone coming in. So much for her "public place" theory.

"Excuse me?"

She sat on her hands and tried to look as calm as possible. God knew she felt anything but calm. "I have?"

"You weren't supposed to beat me in that election." His eyes dove deep into her own, and he held his stare for what seemed like minutes. She knew it couldn't have been more than twenty seconds, if that.

"Now that I think of it," he said, still talking a slow, monotone. "You weren't supposed to be running at all. I have no idea where you came from. It was as if you popped up out of nowhere.

"I tried to warn you, Charlee. Didn't you get my messages?" His voice was mechanically, methodically even.

Charlee almost shook her head no, but then gasped. "You're the person behind the threats," she gasped.

"I was disappointed when you didn't figure it out. I thought you were a lot smarter than that. I thought your lion-shifter boyfriend would put the pieces together. Both of you, though, acted like helpless lion cubs. If you're going to take up a cause, like you have, you first need to learn how to play ball.

"You seemed to have gone into that fight just a bit naively, don't you think?"

At that moment, Charlee remembered her vow not to be intimidated or terrorized by that person. That person now sat across from her. She gained her composure.

"Let me ask you something." She folded her hands and sat straighter. Since Whiffler was in a talkative mood, she'd draw all the information she could from him.

"Why do you support the fracking cause so fiercely? Sure, Prague has a strong economy now, but don't you care about your constituents' health?"

"You really are naïve, aren't you?" he asked. His laughter cut her to the core as sharply as if he had a knife.

Her eyes lit up. She had been laser focused on the election; she hadn't stopped to consider his motives for his stance.

"You were on the take."

"Now, I wouldn't put it that way. You make it sound like the plot of a crime novel." He smiled again.

It looked more like a snarl.

"I'd like to think I cooperated with the company to make the hydraulic drilling industry palatable to people, even for them to see it as a naturally clean and safe fuel." He paused a beat.

"Until you decided to listen to those women, I was doing a pretty good job. I was able to keep that small group opposed to it look like out-of-control fanatics."

"Why are you telling me all of this? You must know I'll be on Sparrow's talk show tomorrow."

"Indeed, I do, and I plan to be in the studio audience. And if you breathe one word of any of this, you'll be sorry. Actually, you may want to plan on not being there at all. It hurt when you cut off my income from the fracking company. I was getting paid nicely to support it as a councilman. Now, I'm not going to benefit from that income. But not to worry. I'll be fine. And just because I'm not a council member anymore, doesn't mean I'm impotent. The icing on the cake is to see your face tomorrow when I release…well, what kind of surprise would it be if I told you about it?"

She swallowed hard, not sure what information he possessed that would upset her. Hadn't the man done enough damage? She considered he may be bluffing. As he leaned in closer to her, though, his scowl and his piercing stare told her he had some dirt, and he planned to use it.

"Good day, Ms. Lightheart," Whiffler said as he rose from the table. "I look forward to seeing you at *The View from My Perch*."

She sat there a few moments after he left and tried to catch her breath. While he sat across from her and poured out his anger, she had, at some point, slowed her breathing involuntarily until it had reached a shallow, ineffective rate.

She pulled in a breath as she directed the air she sucked in to travel directly to her head, to push her mind in gear. She did this several times before Mel walked over.

"Charlee, are you okay? I saw Whiffler out here with you. I didn't want to come out and do anything in the dining room while you two were talking. What in the word did you two discuss?"

Charlee sucked another large gasp of air into her lungs before she answered. Then, in what she could only assume was a state of shock, she detailed the conversation.

Mel let out a low, long whistle. "I knew he was up to something. How else could he possibly ignore the conditions of his constituents?

"I don't know why I'm so surprised. After all, this is the same man who exploded at the council meeting." Charlee paused and stared off for a moment. "And Karen did tell me when I agreed to run that he had planned to pull out all the stops. I'm getting a better idea of what he meant by that."

She walked over to pour herself a cup of coffee. "We still don't know everything, yet. He's promised more surprises at the talk show tomorrow."

"Maybe you should cancel. Let Jared know what happened. You simply can't appear on his show now."

"No, now more than ever I have to go. I can't let him think he frightens me. I'm done being scared. I need to know what he has up his sleeve." She was surprised at Mel's about-face on her appearance on Sparrow's show.

"My job isn't finished. We may have the fracking moratorium on the ballot, but we still need the popular vote to get it enacted. I just can't walk away from a job half done."

"You're right, of course. I just hate for you to put yourself out there. On live television," Mel said.

Chapter 35

"What in the world am I doing here?" Charlee said out loud as she waited for *The View from my Perch* to begin.

"Pardon me?" her sparring partner for the hour, Bruce Throttlebottom, asked her. He was one of the council members who supported hydraulic drilling. He leaned in closer over the occasional table that separated them. It held a pitcher of water and two glasses.

"I'm just a bit nervous." She hoped that was all that sinking feeling in the pit of her stomach symbolized. When she first sat down, she had gripped the arms of her chair tightly and had not yet let go.

She held on despite the fact that her knuckles were white and every muscle in her arms hurt. They had been tense for what felt like an eternity. In reality, it couldn't have been more than ten minutes. She assumed the body posture of a person with a phobia of flying freaking out while waiting on the tarmac.

"Easy-peasy," Throttlebottom said. His voice was kind and even rather soothing. "Jared may have an unconventional format, but he doesn't grill his guests. Believe it or not, his main interest is to highlight important local issues. And he entertains at the same time. That's why his show is popular and has elevated him to something of a local icon."

Hmm. Wonder what else I'm missing? She believed

she was the only person in the town who had never heard of this show. Poor Jared. No wonder he was incredulous when she said she had never seen him before.

She tried to take her mind off Whiffler's threats, but it was impossible. She scanned the audience. The seating was arranged in auditorium style, with a stepped aisle that separated the right and left halves.

It appeared the audience was divided in two. She recognized nearly everyone seated on her side. She only recognized one person immediately on Throttlebottom's side. Myron Whiffler sat in the third row.

When she first noticed him, he was talking to—of all people—Gretchen Carlyle. She held several folders stuffed with papers and newspapers. Some of the ends stuck out the manila sleeves.

What do those two have in store for me? She didn't realize his threat would come with a mound of paperwork.

He finished his conversation and then looked directly at Charlee. He flashed his evil smile. She refused to smile back and did her best to ignore the fact he seemed determined to keep her on pins and needles.

Then she remembered her vow. *He may think he's in charge,* she thought. *But he's mistaken.* She decided if he—and Carlyle—would shovel dirt at her, she would throw twice as much back at him.

She quickly sized up what he had told her in the coffee shop. She had told no one about this but Mel. She hadn't even confided in Riley. A thundering voice knocked her out of her thoughts.

"And now give a warm welcome to your host,

Jared Sparrow."

Jared entered from stage right and sprinted to center stage with the casual jog of nearly all talk show hosts. He was dressed for his role. He wore khaki slacks and a black-and-white-striped referee shirt. He also sported a pair of half glasses for reading. What completed the costume, though, was the referee whistle which hung from his neck.

The crowd exploded into applause and cheers as soon as they saw him. Sparrow, who looked even taller on the set than he had at the coffee shop, stood still for a moment, then blew the whistle. At the same time, he raised both arms as a football official would when indicating a touchdown. Then he took a bow.

The audience loved it and continued their wild reception of him. He allowed the show of appreciation to continue for a short time, then blew the whistle again and placed his hands in a "T" formation, as if he were indicating a time out on the football field. The entire audience placed their hands in that same "T" formation, and from there it took the crowd only a few moments to quiet down.

He stepped out of center stage and turned to one side and introduced the two guests.

"While I don't have many rules," he said to Charlee and Throttlebottom, "the few I do have I try to strictly enforce." She tensed again. *Now I have to worry about breaking the rules. Isn't it enough that he actually got me to participate?*

As if Sparrow read her mind, he looked directly at her and winked. "Don't worry," he continued, as part of his spiel, "the rules aren't tough to follow. First, only one person speaks at a time. No one ends up hearing either of you when you both talk over each other. Secondly, it's up to my discretion to call a time out."

At this point he blew the whistle again and placed his hands perpendicular to each other, forming another "T." The audience cheered this antic and mimicked him. Charlee had come to realize this was his signature style. As nervous as she was, she felt a small smile cross her lips as she thought about him being syndicated nationwide and the "T" and touchdown signals becoming part of the national landscape.

"You don't have any real time limit for your answer, but once again, if either of you becomes long winded, you can already imagine what I would do. He once again blew his whistle and as he created the "T." The entire audience imitated him. "You'll get a Sparrow 'tweet.' "

Jared continued without seeming to even take a breath. "In the second half of our hour," he explained, "my assistant, Amy Black, will stroll through the audience with a microphone allowing those who wish to ask questions of both of you."

"Okay, let's get moving then, the clock is ticking." With that, he crossed the stage and hopped on his bar stool. While the stool wasn't that tall, it was just the right height to give an illusion of Sparrow sitting in a nest in a tree, just as the television program's name implied.

"Charlee, since this is your first visit with us," Sparrow said, "I'll direct the first question to you. What made you tackle the fracking industry?"

She laughed. She explained how the anti-fracking group had asked her to run and described her astonishment at the conditions near the fracking sit. "I couldn't sit back and do nothing," she said. "We need a city-wide moratorium."

She wrapped up her remarks to the cheers of the anti-fracking proponents. Sparrow allowed the response to continue for a short time before he blew his whistle and made the "T" formation. Nearly immediately, the cheers and applause slowed and stopped.

The host wasted no time once it was quiet enough to ask Throttlebottom a similar question about his support of hydraulic drilling. His response ignored the potential health hazards and environmental concerns the activity inflicted on the environment.

The councilman emphasized the much-needed revenue the industry brought to the city coffers. "It's been nearly forty years since we've seen economic activity like this in Prague. It's exciting to see our citizens, many of whom who have struggled financially for so long, now have an improved standard of living and a happier life."

Sparrow shot questions at each of them until the first commercial break. While everyone waited for the show to re-start, he jumped off his "perch" and strode over to her.

"You're doing great," he told her. "I told you I don't ask tough questions. I just want to lay out the facts."

Once the director started the countdown to the return to the live broadcast, he jumped back on his barstool.

"One more round of my questions for today's guests, and then we'll give the studio audience a chance to get their own questions answered," he told the audience. She became more at ease and realized that her anticipation of being on the show was far worse than actual participation.

But her mind quickly reprimanded her. *Don't get too comfortable, you still have Whiffler to contend with. What type of questions will he ask?*

Sparrow finished his questions and immediately blew his whistle, and then loudly proclaimed, "Halftime!" The audience roared its approval.

"When we return from commercial break, we'll open the floor and take questions from the studio audience. I'm sure you won't want to miss that," Sparrow said to the viewers at home.

During the commercial break, she felt Whiffler's stare. Soon, she would know what surprise he had saved for her.

"The second half is about to begin," Sparrow said. "Just raise your hand if you'd like to ask a question. My co-host Amy Black will bring a microphone over to you after. We'll get to as many questions as possible."

The process started easy enough. Charlee's friends asked a few questions of Throttlebottom, which he did his best to sidestep.

"A local geology professor from the University of Northern Ohio has enough evidence to link the epidemic of earthquakes directly to the fracking activity. Does that not make you pause about what is happening to the environment?"

"My dear," Throttlebottom began condescendingly, "there is no conclusive proof that the hydraulic fracturing in Prague had one iota of influence over that."

"Then how do you account for the more than a dozen earthquakes we've experienced within a sixteen-month period?"

Throttlebottom flashed a smile and said with a straight face, "Climate change."

The anti-fracking side of the studio audience groaned, while those on the opposite side laughed and applauded.

She fielded a few questions herself and gradually grew at ease as the second half continued and Whiffler made no motion to contribute.

Then it happened.

Whiffler raised his hand, and Amy headed his way; Charlee held her breath and once again wrapped her hands around the arms of the chair. The bile rose in her stomach. Her instinct told to her to run to the closest restroom and throw up. Her brain commanded her to stay.

Remember, Charlee, you're in control. She summoned her strength.

"This question is for Ms. Charlee Lightheart." He enunciated this clearly, as he stared right into her eyes. She returned his glare.

She re-tightened her grip on the arms of the chair to the white-knuckle pose. She felt every muscle in her body tense as she clung to the chair like it was part of a space capsule and she was waiting for lift off. *To boldly go where no woman has gone before.*

Okay. So, I'm not going boldly into this adventure, she thought. *I'm really going into it quite meekly and, in fact, definitely cowardly. But I'm not about to let Whiffler know that.*

She reminded herself that she had decided she would not cower as she wondered about what question he would try to knock her down with. She nodded her recognition of him.

"It's been said that one of the items that make you uncomfortable with the fracking activity is no one seems to be able to discover the parent company of Natural East Energy which is performing the drilling."

"That's right. The corporate representatives we talk to claim the activity is out of their control. When we press to get into contact with their supervisors who make such policy decisions, they claim they don't know. When we tried to find a parent company, all our attorneys found was a shell corporation licensed out of the state of Delaware."

"I think I may be able to help you with that information," he said. His voice held the same monotone that he had when he was at the coffee shop.

Evil.

Demonic even.

He paused for only a minute, before he continued. "With the help of investigative reporter, Gretchen Carlyle, we were able to discover, not only the parent company, but the majority shareholder. And we'd very much like to enlighten you."

Something was wrong, but Charlee couldn't pinpoint what it was. Whiffler's eyes exuded evil. *So, what kind of information did he have?* She sucked in a deep breath and asked, "Who owns the company?"

"Amalgamated American Green," he said slowly. He paused and asked, "And do you have any idea who owns this corporation?" He paused.

He showed a snarky pleasure in keeping Charlee in a tense, uncomfortable state of suspense. The entire audience sat still and waited along with her.

Then he said, gleefully, "I'll let the investigative

reporter who finally broke the story tell you. Gretchen, dear, please inform Ms. Lightheart."

"Thank you, it would be my pleasure," she replied. Whiffler strung this discussion for all as long as he could, and Gretchen appeared to follow suit. "It's a pleasure to see you again, Ms. Lightheart. I'm glad we could clear this issue up for you."

She paused a beat.

"Fifty-one percent of the stock of this corporation is owned by…

Chapter 36

"Brockton Enterprises, specifically Riley Brockton."

Riley jumped from his chair in Quinn's office. "What the..."

"Holy smoke," Quinn said, as he and Riley watched the revelation unfold on television. Riley couldn't attend the broadcast because of a meeting he couldn't rearrange.

Charlee had said she understood and didn't push him to be there, even though he knew she wanted him there. So, he already felt badly about that. He knew he disappointed her.

He took several strides to Quinn's office door, stuck his head out and called to Renee, "The green folder, do you still have it at your desk?"

His voice carried an urgency that was unmistakable. Renee retrieved it from a drawer in record time. "Thank you." He then backed into the office and slammed the door shut.

"I thought something was wrong with this, Quinn, but never in a million years did I think the company was responsible for fracking. Damnit. They stuck it in here with solar and wind energy, all that good stuff." He rifled through the folder and let out a low growl. "What the hell have I done?"

"Riley, I was right there with you. You asked for

my opinion. I said go for it. If you're spreading blame around, I'm just as culpable as you."

"On the plus side, I did buy fifty-one percent of the shares, which gives me the final say." He found the documents he had been looking for and laid them out.

"And I'm exercising my authority now. I have to do something fast on this before that company does any more damage to this town."

Chapter 37

Riley owns the fracking company. Riley owns the fracking company. Riley owns the fracking company.

The accusation echoed through Charlee's mind. Reverberating louder and louder every time the words bounced around in her head. The color drained from her face.

The audience gasped. Even though she was sitting, her legs turned to rubber. She wanted to run into the women's room and vomit as the bile rose up her throat.

It took her a moment to regain a semblance of calm before she looked at Sparrow. He, too, had lost the color in his face and appeared uncomfortable. He would make a miserable poker player.

"Mr. Sparrow," she hoped no detected the quiver in her voice, "may I respond?"

Sparrow nodded, pulled himself together, and said, "Of course, Charlee. Please do."

She forced herself to stand; at first, she was unsure if her putty legs would allow her to walk a bit closer to Whiffler and Carlyle.

She took the first tentative step and found it easier to walk than she originally had thought. Still, she didn't stray far from her chair. Charlee noticed that Throttlebottom had started to get up and was halfway out of his chair. She nodded to him. He sat back down. She grew more stable as she walked.

"The two of you seemed to take great pleasure in telling me all of this." She inched closer to center stage and met their gaze. "I'm indebted to you both for your discovery of that information. I know that the Citizens Against Fracking and their very able attorneys have searched for this. I don't know who or what your sources are, but I'm very pleased to have that final layer of duplicity pulled away."

She knew she was just getting started. She also knew she didn't have a lot of time before Sparrow tweeted that darn whistle, but she wanted to get as much of her information to the public as well. *Two can play this game.*

"This is obviously an attempt to use my relationship with Riley Brockton to discredit not only myself, but Citizens Against Fracking." She paused. While she needed to collect her thoughts, she was well aware of the dramatic effect the momentary silence created.

"Why? Oh wait. Mr. Whiffler, both you and I know why. So, let me tell the studio audience and the viewers at home."

"The other day Mr. Whiffler visited me at my coffee shop."

She knew her voice was growing stronger. As she began to tell her story, she looked around at the studio audience, ignoring Whiffler and Carlyle. "As some of you may remember, I received several threatening calls during my campaign for the council seat."

She had barely revealed that he was behind the threatening calls when he quickly jumped up and nervously said, "I never said that. It's my word against yours."

"No, not really, sir," she said politely, as she whipped her cell phone out of the back pocket of her pants, "I recorded it all on my smart phone."

A low murmur spread throughout the audience. Even Sparrow let out a gasp.

"As interesting as that fact is," she continued, "I can't allow that to detract from the real reason you wanted me to drop out of the race in the first place. The real reason you couldn't lose your seat."

She quickly scanned the audience. Every eye was trained on her, and she swore more than half of them were sitting at the edge of their seats.

"Mr. Whiffler couldn't bear to lose the election because he knew he would lose a nice chunk of his...shall we call it your income, Myron?" For just a half a heartbeat, she hesitated to continue, he looked abjectly defeated. But she quickly got over that.

"Yes, Mr. Whiffler, who tried to make everyone think he sincerely believed in the need for hydraulic drilling, was only concerned with his own personal bottom line."

She took a deep breath. "But wait, there's more beyond that. Oh, Ms. Carlyle, you're not getting away Scott-free. You, too, have ulterior motives for digging up dirt on this company. Or more specifically, the owner of its parent corporation. You appear to have a personal vendetta against the Brockton family.

"You've been harassing both Riley and Quinn Brockton for several years. Not only them, but you've badgered their employees and even members of their family. You're out to prove that the family shape shifts. That they are lion shifters. Does their family lineage matter that much? The family has demonstrated their honesty and integrity, to say nothing of their generosity to the city and its residents."

Her courage grew by leaps and bounds. As she talked her legs grew stronger. She took another step forward and wagged her finger at Whiffler. "I promise you this, I am going to press charges over your threats."

The audience broke out in applause and cheers.

Chapter 38

"What did you have in mind?" Quinn asked.

"Dismantle the entire corporation." Riley shared his initial thoughts.

They sat on the leather couch in the office. "I hate to bring this up at this point, right now," Quinn said, "but you—we—have to figure that there are going to be lawsuits or class action suits at the very least."

He dropped the document on the coffee table in front of the couch. "I stepped right into this one."

"What do you mean?"

"Why else would anybody try to bury a company? We learned this in Day One of business school. Buy the company, you not only buy the assets but the liabilities as well. I can't even begin to wonder what kind of lawsuits are already pending against this company."

Quinn nodded his head in agreement.

Quinn was the first to speak. "But we have a more immediate concern."

Riley already had his cell phone out, poised to start the necessary phone calls to alert his legal department and set up meetings with attorneys in order to discover the best method to divest his firm of Amalgamated American Green.

"What's that?"

"Renee is going to be in here any minute with some reporter on the phone requesting a statement from you. We've got to come up with something."

He let out a low whistle. "You're absolutely right. Come to think of it, I'm surprised she hasn't been in yet."

No sooner had the words left his lips they heard a knock on the door and Renee stuck her head in. "I have a reporter from TV 5 requesting to speak with you, Riley. He wants a comment on your ownership of that fracking company. And..." She hesitated for a moment.

"And..." he repeated, in an attempt to coax it out of her.

"And he wants a statement about how you square that with your relationship with Charlee."

"It's none of his business..." He roared, stood up, and paced. Renee waited at the door.

"Renee," Quinn said while his brother calmed himself down, "both Riley and I are sorry to have to put you through this. I know your job today can't be pleasant."

Then Quinn turned on his lopsided smile. "I do have one consolation in all of this. They're not demanding any statement of me. I'm not sure what I would tell them. Well, let me rephrase that. I do know what I would tell them, and it wouldn't lead to any good publicity, that's for sure." Quinn paused and gave him a brotherly jab.

"You've hit the nail on the head," he said. "Right now, I'd love to give all those...bast...uhm...ladies and gentlemen of the fourth estate an earful. But I have to remind myself they are only doing their job."

"Would you please tell him that at the moment I'm unavailable for comment, but Brockton Enterprises will issue a statement in the foreseeable future?"

"Yes, sir, it will be my pleasure. And I'm to assume when the other media call, I'm to tell them the same thing, until I hear otherwise."

"Precisely. Thank you, Renee."

She backed out with the door nearly closed when he called her back.

"Yes, sir?"

"I love you." He winked at her.

"I know you do," she replied with a tilt of her head.

"Well done, Riley, "Quinn said, "you've handled this like the professional you are. Now, you only have one more task facing you."

"What's that? I think I've kicked the entire process off fairly well."

"Have you even given any thought how you're going to explain this to Charlee? What are you going to tell her? 'By the way, love, want to hear a funny story? I accidently bought a fracking company a couple a days ago. I thought I was buying a green company and got it home and unwrapped it…funny, huh, sweets? And, oh yeah, not just any company, but the one you've been fighting all these months.' "

He laughed. "Actually, she was my first thought. To tell you the truth, she's going to give me an earful when I see her. Oh God, all these plans to divest myself of it mean nothing if I can't think of a gentle way to tell her that those two nutcases are right. I do own the company."

Neither brother talked for a moment. He broke the silence.

"I'm a dead man."

****

"And it's a wrap. Good job, everybody."

212

Charlee slouched in her seat and closed her eyes. *Good job, my eye! I never should have agreed to this.*

She knew it wouldn't be long before she would have to open her eyes again, because she was sure that Karen and her anti-fracking group would descend on her any minute. If she were lucky, she thought, they would club her to death with the signs they held during the show. *Kill me now before anything else happens.*

She formed a smile. *Kill me before I kill Riley would be a more accurate thought.*

She heard a male voice. Not wanting to expend too much energy on anything, she opened one eye to check out who wanted a piece of her now.

Sparrow.

She quickly opened the other eye and sat up.

"I can't apologize enough," he said. "I've never had anything like this happen before."

With his voice nearly an octave higher than normal and his hand trembling, he continued, "I wanted to break for a commercial. But my director wouldn't let me. He said we were gaining ratings by the minute and then when you started in on them, well, the show was a smash hit. Took us to a new level of success."

"I'm glad I could be of service," she said quietly.

"That's not what I meant," he said. "I get solid ratings anyway. I would rather be known for my style and talent, not for hosting people like Whiffler and Carlyle who only want to use my show to bully others and muck them over with accusations."

She could see Karen Manning and her group standing behind Sparrow. All of them held their signs upside down, as if the position represented a distress sign, like when the American flag was hung upside down.

"Besides, I told you nothing like that happened on my show. I feel as if I lied to you. I don't want you to think I manipulated you into appearing. I know you were hesitant from the start."

He apologized again before he walked away.

"Charlee, are you okay?" Karen said. "That was the last thing I expected. How dare they humiliate you like that."

"Don't worry about me, Karen," she said. "I'm just pretty sure the fracking ban isn't going to pass. I had no idea that Brockton Enterprises owned the parent company. I never would have agreed to any of this had I even an inkling that something like that were even possible."

"We know that. I'm sorry you were put in that position."

Charlee stood up. "I've got to get back to the coffee shop," she said. "Why don't you guys come on down. Lunch is on the house. I think we all need to unwind. I probably won't join you, but I'd love to make this fiasco up to you."

As they walked out of the television station as a group, Karen asked, "I know this isn't any of my business, but I'm curious, female to female, how much trouble is Riley in with you right now?"

She laughed. "He's a dead man."

Chapter 39

"You must have called her at least five times, Riley," Quinn said. "I don't think she's ready to talk to you yet. "

Quinn paused a beat and reached for his coffee cup. "Charlee was just slapped in the face. You know how I felt when that Carlyle woman poked around our family business. She's so arrogant that just the sound of her voice is like fingernails screeching down a blackboard. It's only been a few hours since the end of the show. I'm sure she's trying to digest everything."

Riley nodded. Deep down in his heart, he knew his brother was right. But his brother wasn't the person who signed the contract that added Amalgamated American Green to their portfolio. It wasn't his lioness who had locked herself off from all social contact. Well, at least from contact with him. And it certainly wasn't his conscience that felt as guilty as anything.

"I wouldn't blame her if she never wanted to speak to me again," he said, but yet he checked his texts and voice mail compulsively. Every minute that passed without some type of contact from her felt like an hour. His heart ached, and he grew angrier with himself with every fleeting second.

He was the one who decided that folder of green companies represented a socially responsible investment. By the same token, he was the one who had that gut feeling that something didn't feel right about Amalgamated American Green. He should have listened to his gut.

"Should ofs, could ofs, and would ofs." Quinn's voice knocked him out of his thoughts.

"What?" he said.

His brother repeated the phrase. "You remember, that was Dad's favorite phrase when we started to wallow in our mistakes. None of those is going to change what you're facing right now."

"You always had a way reading my mind, bro."

"Just give her a day or so. Then she'll be ready to talk to you—or at least listen to your side of the story. In the meantime, this gives us plenty of time to cripple that company and make sure it never fracks again."

"Us? What do you mean us? This is my debacle. I got myself into it; you're not obligated to get me out of it."

"I know, but we're family. You asked for my opinion, and it was wrong. I'm not going to let you go through this alone." He paused. "Besides, I really want to stick it to that Carlyle woman." He paused a beat. "Oops! Did I say that out loud?"

"Who am I to argue with someone who volunteers to help me? It's time to get busy."

****

It took every ounce of energy she had to swing her lead legs out of bed the following morning. Charlee looked at what she was wearing. The same clothes she wore the day before.

I must have fallen asleep with my clothes on last night. The last thing I remember is sitting in the living room while I watched the local news. It was pretty bad, but it could have been much worse.

Hell, she thought, no, it couldn't have. It was a train wreck. The television station pulled file clips of the anti-fracking meetings Riley had attended and played every one of them—not just once, but over and over again. The reporter drew out the drama as long as he could.

For a nanosecond, she considered not going to work. She thought better of it, though. If she stayed home, she would wallow around in self-pity. At least at the coffee shop she could pour coffee, serve food, and wallow around in self-pity. She was a multitasker to the core.

She walked into the shower. The beads of hot water soothed her aching shoulders. When she turned and faced the shower head, the water pummeled her and refreshed her face. She scrubbed her body thoroughly in an attempt to get the grime of the prior day's events off of it.

She stepped out of the shower, dried herself, and told herself that today would be better. In record time, she was ready to go because she wasn't nearly as fussy about her makeup and what she wore. It took all her strength just to throw on any clothes.

She briefly considered not wearing any makeup. But when she looked in the mirror, she recognized the infamous raccoon eyes, the dark circles she always got when she had been crying or hadn't got enough sleep. Yesterday, she experienced both. A double header. *Lucky me.*

Charlee drove to work on autopilot, her body still numb from the events of the day before. She willed herself not to think about yesterday, but the more she willed herself to push it out of her head, the more her monkey mind chattered endlessly about it.

When she unlocked the back door to the coffee shop, she recognized the distinct signs her baker, Carolyn, was in the house. The smell smacked her senses. Coffee, the singularly satisfying aroma of freshly brewed coffee. Bless her soul, she thought.

The fresh, all-consuming, ambrosial aroma of muffins tickled her nose. But wait... She was sure the unmistakable smell of bacon also floated through the air. *Was Marco here already?*

As if in answer to that question, Carolyn walked out of kitchen, wiping her hands, and approached the counter. "Good morning, Charlee?" The baker raised an eyebrow.

"Good morning, Carolyn. Don't worry, I'm not going to bite your head off. You're not the source of my anger."

Carolyn relaxed.

"Smells like you've out-baked yourself this morning, and that coffee aroma is close to giving me an orgasm. You don't normally make the coffee. Why today? Not that I'm complaining."

"My mother's instincts told me that you probably didn't make any before you left for work."

She nodded. "Bingo."

"Sit down at the counter, and I'll pour you a cup."

"Is Marco here already?"

"No, why?"

"I smell bacon."

"No, I made it for you. I have some eggs already beaten waiting to see if they're going to be turned into an omelet or scrambled eggs. My intuition also told me you probably didn't have any nutrition yesterday except for a handful of grapes."

"Grapes?"

"In the form of wine."

"Absolutely right. Your breakfast offer is awesome. Normally, I would argue, but not today. Bring it on."

Carolyn placed a cup of coffee on the counter.

Charlee shrugged off her coat. "I'll get the papers at the door, and I'll be right back."

She came back shaking her head. She had begun to read even before she sat in front of the coffee and took her first sip. *Boy, I sure wish for the days when I never even looked at the front page.*

In no time at all, the baker had whipped her up an omelet, toasted two slices of bread, and tossed a side of bacon on the plate.

"Here you go; it's probably not as good as Marco's, but you can at least eat without interruption."

She bit into the egg dish. "Delicious—why aren't you a cook, too?" she asked with a wink.

She turned her attention back to the newspaper. The headline read: *Brockton Brothers Behind Drilling.*

The article hit the brothers hard for the ownership of the fracking company and especially their concealment of it. In addition to the front-page article, the paper also wrote an editorial about the lapse in judgment in the normally socially responsible Brockton Enterprises.

Just at that moment, the bell on the door rang, signaling the first customers of the day. Charlee usually had a handful of regulars who came for coffee and muffins on their way to work.

She took another gulp of coffee, wiped her mouth with her napkin. As she stood, she saw it wasn't one of her to-go regulars, but Ed and Fred. "Hey, Charlee girl," Ed said, "I was hoping you'd be at work this morning. This place isn't the same without you."

"Give me just a minute, and I'll get you your coffee."

"You're early," she told them as she poured their coffee. "I must admit, I'm a bit taken aback. You're deviating from your well-worn path of habit."

Both of the men smiled at her sarcastic humor.

"Do you want your customary muffin?"

They both nodded vigorously before they asked if she would sit with them for a while.

"Sure, let me get your muffins, my breakfast, and the newspaper, and I'll be right over."

Carolyn appeared from the kitchen. "I heard the bell. You go and join them, Charlee. I'll bring the muffins." Charlee didn't argue.

She came back with the newspaper under her arm, pressed against her side, her omelet and coffee. The men, who usually beat around the bush, got straight to the point.

"You've seen the article, then," Fred said, pointing to the paper before he took a bite of his muffin.

She nodded. "It's pretty much what I expected."

"Did you happen to get to page three, yet?" Ed asked immediately.

Just then, Carolyn came with the muffins and more coffee, then left.

"What does it say?" Charlee saw the somber looks on the men's faces. "How bad is it?"

"I think only you can decide that," Ed said.

She put her fork down and lifted the first page up slightly to get a peek. Her face turned pale as she hurriedly opened the paper all the way and folded so the entire page three was visible.

The upper half of the page was devoted to a graphic: a triangle that linked her, Riley, and Amalgamated American Green. The headline for the graphic: *Why, Charlee, Why?*

Riley's photo was on the left side of the graphic, and on the right was the logo for the Amalgamated American Green. Her photo was positioned below them both.

The story below detailed Charlee's political trajectory and its effect on the complexion of Prague city council. Then she got to the zinger:

Throughout her campaign, Charlee never mentioned the man she was dating, Riley Brockton, of Brockton Enterprises, owned the fracking company. This revelation came to light during yesterday's live broadcast of the local talk show, "The View from my Perch," with Jared Sparrow.

When questioned at the show, she professed ignorance. "I had no idea he owned the parent company," she replied.

This leaves us—and should leave the rest of the city—asking two crucial questions: What did Charlee know, and when did she know it?

Is impeachment in her future?

But that wasn't the end of the story. The reporter then dug into Riley. The photo which accompanied the article featured Riley as he held Karen's protest sign.

Charlee remembered that moment well. He held it for Karen for less than two minutes; in that short time the photographer snapped it.

How could a man who owned the company that was destroying his neighbors sit there and pretend he opposed the drilling? the caption read.

She let out a big sigh.

"Damn that man," she said. "Why in the world didn't he just come clean and tell me he owned the company? I wouldn't have stuck my neck out like I did."

Ed was the first to speak. "I know this looks bad."

"Bad? It's beyond bad. He not only betrayed me, but he betrayed the entire group and worse yet, he is destroying the neighborhood and literally sucking the health and life out of those families. He is nothing at all like the man I thought I loved." She paused a beat, closed her eyes. She didn't mean any of that to spew out in front of the two men, but emotion overcame her.

"Fred and I came over after we read this. We know you didn't ask for it, but as two old guys who've been through a lot in our years—especially when it comes to matters of the heart—we feel you might be able to benefit from our take on things."

"Did you or your wives ever own a fracking company?" she asked. She smiled as she took her napkin and dabbed her eyes.

"No, but both of us have survived more than one crisis of the heart," Fred jumped in. He apparently knew Ed was having trouble finding the right words. "There are two things working here, much like we experienced in our past. The first is the misunderstanding between you and Riley about the ownership of the company.

"Before you decide he purposely withheld

information from you, listen to his side of the story. He might actually have a reasonable and solid explanation for not telling you. Together, the Brocktons own an awful lot of companies. Buying and selling companies is second nature to them.

"Before you judge him, please hear him out. In the end, you don't have to believe him. But you do owe it to your relationship to at least listen. From what we've seen, it sure does appear like you two have something special."

Ed added a quip of his own. "Yeah, Fred and I are two old geezers. We could even recognize the chemistry you two have when he's in here. That's saying something."

Fred agreed. "And that brings us to another aspect of this. If two people love each other, then it doesn't matter what anyone thinks about you and him. The only two opinions that matter are yours and Riley's."

By the time the men had their say, she felt a bit better. "And you tell me all this from your experience?"

"Yes, we do. We've experienced relationships throughout our lives that we refused to show to others."

"I can't imagine that you guys ever needed to hide anything in your lives," Charlee said.

Ed took another sip of his coffee. "'We did, both of us, and each of us almost hurt the ones we loved most."

Fred added. "Someday we'll tell you our stories. But this isn't the time. Right now, our mission is just to help you get through this."

"Just promise us one thing, Charlee girl," Ed said.

"Depends on what you want me to promise," she said.

"Listen to his side of the story. It might be a bunch

of bull, but then you'll know for sure. And then you can kick him to the curb. But listen. Just listen."

"I'll try." She sighed. "For once, I thought I had found the love of my life."

She couldn't believe she confessed this to two of her customers—the most unlikely two. "To be truthful, I have a hard time imagining my life without him."

The small bell on the door rang. Charlee cringed. Nearly two o'clock. It had been hours since she had talked with Ed and Fred. But the topic still preyed on her mind. So, somehow, she wasn't surprised by his appearance. She knew exactly who had just walked through the door even with her back to it.

Charlee swore she could smell his fragrance the moment the door opened. She chalked her sensitive nose to her lion-shifter ancestry. At this point, Riley was the last person she wanted to talk to, regardless of what Ed and Fred had advised. Maybe in day or two, but not now.

She wanted nothing better than just to blow him off. But then she thought better of it. She looked at the pair who, uncharacteristically, had returned for lunch. She had no idea about their background except they were both widowers. She now began to wonder a bit about it. That kept her, for at least several seconds, from thinking about her future.

Since they seemed to speak from experience of some sort, she decided to give them the benefit of the doubt and trust them on this one. *I won't make any rash decisions until I hear Riley's explanation.*

Chapter 40

"Hi." His voice was low, husky, and probably more seductive than he had intended it to be. Her heart nearly jumped out of her chest. *God, he was a one-in-a-million man.* And up until yesterday, she loved him more than she imagined she could love anyone.

"Hi." She answered back, not knowing what else to say. The snarky side of her wanted to ask, *So, have you opened any other fracking wells to destroy our neighborhood lately?* She bit her tongue to prevent that from coming out of her mouth. And not just in the figurative sense.

Then she immediately regretted the decision and knew why it was just a figure of speech.

"Ouch!" She covered her mouth with her hand and bent over slightly; she didn't expect her tongue to be that sensitive.

"What happened?"

"I bit my tongue," she said as she gave him a slight smile. "Don't even ask why. It was stupid."

"Could we talk?" he asked, again his voice low, his tone repentant.

Her initial reaction was to blow him off. Then she remembered the promise she made. She must have been lost in thought because he asked again, "Could we, please?"

"Yeah, sure," she said, "but let's not talk here. Can

we go someplace where my employees won't be staring at us?"

"Sure, how about something nice and simple like Pat's Pizza. They have that great booth in the one corner that is perfect when you need to hide from the world."

"You read my mind."

"Let me tell Mel I'm leaving. My relief is here, so they'll be fine."

When she returned, she saw Riley still stood in the same spot. He placed his hand under her elbow and led her out the door.

They walked in strained silence. The sounds of the city seemed distant, as if the entire experience were a dream. More like a nightmare.

He broke the silence. "I tried calling you several times yesterday after the television show aired. Did you get my messages?"

"I was in no mood to talk to anyone after that fiasco," she said. "And just because I'm talking with you now, doesn't mean we'll continue to talk in the future." She tried hard to stop the flow of anger out of her mouth.

"Don't think you're special just because I ignored you. I ignored the Bugle, TV5, and even a couple of national media outlets."

Riley chuckled. "At least I'm in good company."

"I'm still in shock," she said, more to herself than to him. "I need time to process what happened yesterday and what it means."

They entered the pizza place and the back booth, secluded from nearly everything, was open. The shop was a landmark in town. A long, narrow stand-alone building along Liberty Street, it had been an integral part of the Prague food scene for nearly sixty years. Charlee was grateful they made it to the back of the room and slid into the booth without anyone taking notice. Except, of course, the server.

The server set the table and placed two menus in front of them. They ordered drinks.

Riley immediately ventured an explanation. "I know what I'm about to say will sound like the adult version of 'the dog ate my homework,' but I swear it's God-honest truth." He raised his right hand.

She involuntarily cocked her head. He was interrupted by the server who delivered their drinks and took their order. When the server left, he continued.

He explained that he didn't even know that he owned the company. "By the time I bought it, you were already a member of council."

"That's even worse," she exploded. She tried to keep her voice down. Anybody who heard her and not know she was furious was clueless.

"So, let me get this straight. You bought it even though you know full well how transparent your life is, not to mention our relationship? What's wrong with this picture?"

He touched her hand that rested near her plate. She pulled it back faster than a flash of lightning. "Please don't touch me," she said.

"I'm sorry, I was…"

"I know what you were doing," she said, "despite everything that has happened, your touch still moves me. I'm beginning to believe our relationship has got to be a thing of the past." She fought back tears as she spoke.

"Please, believe me. I had no clue it was a fracking firm. The language on the documents was vague. My attorney, who's been with our family forever, agreed it was a safe investment. He checked the entire folder out. We all agreed it was an incredible opportunity. A 'green' company that made an incredible profit. I felt good about it. Not only would I make a fistful of money—which is what people expect greedy capitalists like myself to do…"

Riley paused a beat, as if he hoped she would find that humorous. But she didn't. So, he continued. "And I sincerely thought every company in that portfolio contributed to the good of the earth, not to tearing it apart."

She rolled her eyes. "And the road to hell is paved with good intentions."

The pair turned quiet as the server brought their pizza and carefully placed one slice on each of their plates.

"I'm talking with a host of lawyers to discover the quickest way to divest myself of the firm. In fact, it may take a while—"

"Too little, too late. In the meantime, none of that helps Marco, Karen, Jayne, or any of the others."

She took a bite of her pizza and then slapped it down on her plate.

"I've lost my appetite. I think it's best I leave now." She rifled through her purse briefly, pulled out some money, and tossed it on the table. "I'm sure that covers my half of the pizza," she said. "I don't want you to get the idea this was a date."

"At least, let me walk you back to the coffee house," he offered.

"No, I think you've done more than enough already." She kept her eyes down as she exited the booth and took several steps toward the door.

"Charlee, look at me."

She let out a big sigh and looked down at him. *How was she going to live without him*? She knew she couldn't be a part of his life now. She found it difficult to think such an accomplished businessman as Riley would accidentally buy a fracking company.

His actions endangered her friends and threatened the entire fracking movement in Prague and, really, worldwide. The press labeled her as the trailblazer. Yeah, she just went up in flames.

Worse yet, his actions put her at odds with the promise she made to her father. To help others. She felt as if she tarnished his memory.

"What?" She wanted him to speak swiftly. She felt herself melting as she gazed into his large amber eyes. As she drew in the scent she had come to call Riley, she imagined the touch of his curly, tawny hair.

"Is this how you want to end it? Do you really want to end our relationship?"

She knew if she gazed at him much longer she would cave. It was bad enough she soaked in the scent of his cologne throughout their meeting. It only weakened her resolve. *God, if I stand here any longer, I'm going to cry.*

"I don't know. I can't make a decision right now, not the way I'm feeling."

She took in a deep breath, raised her head high, and then walked out of the restaurant.

Chapter 41

Charlee hadn't gone several blocks before the tears streamed down her cheeks. She refused to stop and continued walking even though she struggled to breathe. By the time she got to the coffee shop, she was sobbing so hard, she alarmed Mel.

"What in the world happened?" Mel asked as she ran up to her. "What did that man do to you?"

"Nothing. He did nothing." She reached into the napkin basket on the counter and wiped her cheeks. "At least, nothing more than he already did."

Mel told her to sit at the counter and she'd whip up her favorite latte. "I want to hear what happened."

"That's good, because I really need someone to talk to."

After she recounted her and Riley's conversation, she stopped for a minute to catch her breath.

"It's all my fault," she finally admitted.

"How do you figure that?" Mel asked, as she took Charlee's cup without asking and made another latte.

"I thought he truly loved me. But he's just out for himself. I never should have trusted that billionaire to begin with.

"And because of that, I've failed my constituents, the Citizens Against Fracking, and, well, especially Marco and those other families living in the battle zone."

"Charlee Lightheart, you haven't failed anyone. First, the voting on the ban hasn't even occurred yet. Second, you need to quit thinking you can 'save' everybody."

"I don't think I can—"

"Stop right there. Yes, you do. You blame yourself for your father's death, and you've been using the settlement money to try to save everyone you possibly can. You do a great job, don't get me wrong.

"But you weren't responsible for your father's death. The doctor who prescribed the drugs with those horrible side effects is—and the drug company. You did absolutely everything you could.

"Do you really think your dad blames you for how events turned out?"

Before she had a chance to answer, Mel answered her own question. "Of course not. I'm sure he knows you did everything you could. From what you've told me, you couldn't get a single person to listen to you while your father was alive. And you contacted anyone even remotely connected to your dad's case. That doesn't sound like a woman who should be blaming herself."

Mel held up a finger as a symbol to wait one minute and sidled over to her purse, where she pulled out a book and tossed it in front of her.

"Why does this book smell like...hazelnut coffee?" Charlee asked.

"Because this is the book that you threw into the waste basket on top of the coffee grounds. I saved it from the garbage."

She flipped the book over to see its title. *Something Amazingly Awesome is Going to Happen to You Today.*

"Yeah, it's full of crap. I tossed it in the garbage—where it belongs—when we were arguing."

"And I saved it."

She smiled as she visualized Mel, suspicious as she was about "happy talk," going out of her way to retrieve the book.

"And you actually read it?"

"Not only read it…" Mel said before leaning toward her employer and whispered, "I actually enjoyed it. But please don't tell anyone. I don't want to ruin my reputation."

"Why are you showing me this now? It didn't work for me then. Is it supposed to work for me now?"

"Yes. It has this great exercise that might help relieve you of the guilt you feel. It might take that cross off you: the belief that your penance for past transgressions is to save everyone.

"Admit it, Charlee, you do feel responsible. If you don't want to admit it to me, go home and think about. You always pay for fundraisers. Don't get me wrong. That's generous. I wouldn't want you to stop that. But this anti-fracking crusade, as important as it is, is your attempt to make amends for what happened with your father."

Charlee looked at her latte, the steam rising from the cup. "You might be right, but I can't help it. I made a promise to my dad. If this proposition fails because of my relationship with Riley, I'll feel as if I let my father down."

Mel nodded. "That's where this exercise comes in. You're supposed to write a letter to someone who has passed. Tell them about your life. Ask that person how they think you're doing." She smiled. "It says you'll get an answer."

Charlee laughed. "What? I'm supposed to wait for an email or a text from my father?"

"Not exactly in those forms, but you will get some type of sign—or so the book says. At the very least, you'll relieve yourself of some of your guilt."

"I'll think about it," Charlee said. "But I'm not promising anything. This sounds 'woo-woo.' " She smiled. "Even to me."

"You really have nothing to lose. At the most, it won't work. But, if does and you get a sign, you've lifted some of that weight off your shoulders."

Chapter 42

Charlee sat on the couch that evening, her legs curled underneath her, a glass of wine set on the coffee table next to her. She reached for the television's remote control.

She flipped through all the channels but couldn't find a single show that held her interest. Normally, she would curse the cable company. But tonight, she knew that it was her attention span and her patience that were the problems. Namely, she had neither.

She was still furious with Riley. His actions weren't logical. How could a man she trusted implicitly do that? Clearly her sexual desires, her yearning for a happily-ever-after life, clouded her judgment.

Her love for Riley crashed into her desire to help her neighbors. The result? A major disaster. And a feeling of major failure. She couldn't forgive herself for not living up to her neighbors' expectations. Sure, the vote was still several days off. But too few individuals seemed to take the ban seriously. And fewer yet, she thought, planned to vote for it.

And it's all my fault.

At some point in her desperate attempt to make sense of the situation, she found herself talking to her father, reaching out to his spirit.

Dad, what have I done this time? I tried to help. I saw a wrong, and I tried to make it right. Usually, I'm at least partially successful. But this time everything blew up in my face.

For all of their hard work, my neighbors won't see improvement in their living conditions, their health isn't going to get any better, the houses still rattle and shake from earthquakes causing dangerous living conditions—and the list goes on.

And in the process, I've lost the one person who I thought could possibly be my one true love. But, Dad, you know what makes me feel even worse? It's knowing I let you down. I broke a promise to you. I told you I would never knowingly allow anyone to suffer due to the wrongful actions of a corporation again. I'm sorry I couldn't save you. But I've tried to redeem myself and make you proud of me.

I certainly mucked up this time, Dad. I'm so sorry. Please forgive me.

She felt hot tears pour down her cheeks. As she wiped them with the back of her hand, she rose, then took the last small sip of wine. She changed into pajamas, climbed into bed, and pulled the sheet and comforter over her head. *I just want to hide from the world.*

"Charlee."

Did she hear someone call her name? She opened her eyes. She was in bed. Alone. She checked the time on her cell phone. Three a.m.

Of course, she didn't hear anyone talk to her. She rolled over and closed her eyes again. At least as she slept, the dual fiascos looming in her life felt like a bad dream.

As she drifted back off to sleep, the sound of her name jolted her upright. She couldn't dismiss the fact that someone wanted her attention—urgently.

She looked around the dark bedroom. What the...? Fear gripped every one of her muscles. She saw a figure standing near the bedroom door. She thought, at first, it was Riley.

She squinted, barely able to see the form of a silhouette. The man spoke again.

"Stop punishing yourself, Cupcake," he said.

Cupcake? Only one person had ever called her Cupcake.

"Dad? Dad, is that really you?"

"Of course, it is, Cupcake."

"How? Why?"

"The how I have no idea. You don't get any orientation on the how when you get here. But why? Isn't it obvious? You talked to me this evening."

I'm dreaming. But, if it were a dream, it was one she never wanted to wake from.

"I have so much to tell you, Dad. I really screwed up this time," she said, ready to pour her heart out to him.

"Hang on, there," he said. "You already did tell me quite a bit earlier tonight, remember? It's my turn to talk to you."

She had never seen an apparition before. She hated to call her dad a ghost; he appeared so clearly now that her eyes had fully adjusted to the dark. She crossed her legs.

He strode over to her desk, pulled the chair, and positioned it so he could straddle it. He braced his elbows on its back. *Just like he did when he was alive.*

"You need to know I am proud of you. You give back to the community every chance you get. You unselfishly ran for city council after you learned about the problems of your neighbors and your employee. What's his name, Marco?"

She nodded, and he continued. "Your friend, Mel, is right, Cupcake," he continued. "You can't save everyone. You can't save the world. All you can do is give of yourself. And you give more than anyone I've ever known.

"The anti-fracking proposition hasn't even been voted on yet; you've already blamed yourself for its defeat. If I didn't know better, your words would have convinced me you singlehandedly contributed to its failure.

"Think about it. That isn't even in the realm of possibility. If it does fail, then you know there are any number of reasons for it. The least of which, I would say, is you. In fact, even with what you went through the other day, your efforts and your composure on the television show could be one of the reasons people want to ban it more than ever."

"You saw all that?"

"I'm always with you, Cupcake."

She started to respond, but her father ignored her and continued. "And as for Riley's ownership of the company, perhaps you should believe what he told you earlier today. Wait to see what his next moves are. His future actions are far more important to your relationship than his past mistakes. Don't you think?"

"Dad, I don't think there is a relationship anymore."

"That's a shame, Cupcake, because I like the man. A lot. I think he loves you. And I believe he would do anything to make this fiasco up to you. He wants to make this situation right. And not just for show. I think he believes it's a major step in making amends with you.

"Let me just put it this way, your relationship with Riley has my blessing. And if I were you, I would think long and hard about giving him a second chance.

"Baby, I got to go now. I've used up my time. Think about what I've said."

And with that he slowly faded away. Like a dream.

Chapter 43

It seemed as if Charlee no sooner fell asleep than the alarm rang. She couldn't even pretend to know how long she slept. She lay awake most of the night after what must have been a dream. *It seemed so real, though.*

She pulled herself out of bed, her eyes still only half open, groggy from lack of sleep, and dragged her body into the shower. She wished that all of this crap would just go away. She wanted so much to go back to her life with Riley when they had nothing like a stupid fracking company separating them.

As she stepped out of the shower, she wondered if it wasn't fracking, would it have been another issue that tore them apart? Then she thought about her parents. *How did they stay married for thirty-five years? And the marriage only ended because Mom died.*

"I should have asked Dad about that." Then she smiled. "I'm acting like Dad was really here. I'm sure it was a dream. I needed someone to tell me those things, and I dreamed about Dad."

She walked out of the bathroom into the bedroom and dressed for work. This was one of the few times she dreaded going in. As she turned to leave the room, she noticed the chair in the middle of the floor. "That's where Dad sat in my dream last night," she said out loud. A cold chill ran through her body. She tried to shake it off. She felt an ominous clammy fear overtake her.

Clammy hands. Hard to swallow.

"What the…?" Charlee shook her head vigorously. "No, that's not at all possible. What I experienced last night was a dream. Bottom line."

If that were the case, what is this chair doing here? Once her eyes locked on the chair, she couldn't take them off of it. She backed out of the bedroom deliberately with measured steps.

****

She opened the back door to the coffee shop; the comforting aroma of coffee engulfed her senses. Carolyn. She was the only person to arrive before Charlee.

Charlee stepped over the threshold. "Good morning, Carolyn. Do I smell coffee?"

Carolyn stuck her head out of the kitchen to return the greeting and added, "I knew you had a tough day yesterday. I thought it's those little, thoughtful actions people take that help you feel better, regardless of how small."

"Coffee? Ready to pour? Nice and hot? That's no little thing in my book. You should know that already. Thank you."

She realized that in her fog over her father's "visit" and the chair in the middle of her bedroom, she had left the house without making coffee. She sprinted behind the counter and poured herself a cup. She set it on the counter while she retrieved the house newspapers. On her walk back, she checked out the headlines. The newspapers wouldn't let the issue go—not with the vote for the fracking ban hanging in the balance.

She still had to endure three more weeks of this. The sooner the vote occurred, the sooner she could put this nightmare behind her. *Maybe when it fails, I could resign from the council. I fulfilled my promise to the ladies. And I failed. Surely, they could find someone to fill the spot.*

Then she remembered what her father told her. "You take too much upon yourself. You can't save everybody."

Charlee couldn't wait to talk to Mel, who wasn't scheduled to be in for several hours. She was tempted to call her, but her friend had assumed so many of her duties lately, she thought better of it. Thankfully, the morning flew by. A busier-than-usual breakfast crowd meant she didn't have time to think of fracking or her father.

Charlee got a glimpse of Mel as she entered. Her friend approached her as she was headed to the kitchen to place a lunch order. She greeted her warmly before she said, "There's something I must tell you when this all dies down."

She passed the coffee pot she had in her hand to Mel. "Do you think you can take that four-top that just settled in the corner?"

"Will do." Mel took the pot and gathered the menus and silverware for the group.

They didn't get the time to talk until after the lunch crowd had cleared.

"I hate to admit it," Charlee said, as she poured herself a cup of coffee, "but your advice worked."

"It did? Good." Mel smiled, but quickly knitted her brow. "Wait. What advice?"

"You told me to contact my father."

"Oh, that. And it worked?"

"You seem surprised?"

"I am."

"You were so sure of the advice yesterday," she said. "What happened?"

Mel's cheeks turned red. "I was desperate. My God, I had to think of something to tell you. I'm not even sure that exercise is in that book or if I just made it up."

Charlee glared at her friend.

"What? I was just trying to help." She paused. "So, tell me. What happened."

"You're not going to believe this. Instead of writing a letter to my dad, I talked to him. Told him how I felt." Charlee looked at her friend over her cup as she took a long sip of coffee.

"Annnd? Don't leave me hanging. Tell me what happened."

"I saw him in my dream last night. At least, I thought it was a dream."

She told Mel everything; she tried to leave nothing out. When she got to the part where her dad pulled the chair out, she hesitated. "You're not going to believe this." Mel listened silently. Charlee worried she might laugh.

"When I woke up this morning, it was still where Dad had put it."

Just then the bell on the door signaled a customer. Mel turned to see who it was. "I'll be darned. He's the last person I expected to see here."

Chapter 44

Of course, Charlee's mind shot to Riley; she turned quickly to see for herself. She felt relieved—and yes, a bit disappointed—to discover it wasn't Riley, but Jared Sparrow.

"He has some nerve," Mel said, "to come in here after what happened to you on his show."

"I heard that Mel," he said as he approached.

"I know, I'm one of the last people both of you want to see," he said, "but could I get lunch?"

"Of course, you can, Jared," Charlee said. "Here, sit next to me. My shift is over in a few minutes, and I'm not feeling overly ambitious today."

"Are you sure? I feel I'm responsible for the 'disruption' in your relationship with Riley Brockton. I can't tell you how very sorry you got trapped like that."

"How do you know about Riley and me?" She knitted her brow.

"A journalist doesn't have to divulge his sources." Jared smiled. "But I can't apologize enough. I've never had anything like that happen on my show. I pride myself on having a show that doesn't stoop to headlines like that."

Mel brought coffee and a menu. Jared took a quick glance at it and ordered.

"I know you do," Charlee said.

He sipped his coffee. "That's why I'm livid at what

happened today. I walked out of the meeting." He paused. "I just started walking aimlessly and well, here I am."

Mel served his food. "What happened?"

He took a deep breath. "Gretchen Carlyle now has her own television show."

"What?" Charlee and Mel said at the same time.

"Oh, wait. That's not even the best part. She's taking to the streets live to get the opinion of Prague's average residents on 'the most pressing issues of our day.' " Jared gestured air quotes for the last phrase. Then shrugged.

Charlee shook her head in disbelief. "That woman is ruthless. I don't see how this can be anything but a disaster."

Mel, who had been watching Jared all this time, spoke. "Her idea of news is discovering lion shifters."

"You're not wrong, Mel," Jared said. He nibbled at his grilled cheese sandwich.

"As a broadcaster who tries to be responsible—"

"And you are," Mel said.

He smiled at her and continued. "I'm uncomfortable with the whole situation. And what's even worse, I'm her lead-in show. I sure hope people don't get the idea I endorse her."

"That could be a good thing," Mel said.

"How?" Jared took his eyes off his sandwich and looked at her.

"You don't attract the type of audience that goes in for tabloid news. Let's face it, that's all Gretchen is about. Maybe they won't stay tuned for her."

Jared nodded. "That is a possibility, I guess. Yeah, thanks Mel, that gives me some hope."

Charlee marveled at the seemingly immediate connection that two of them had created over a grilled cheese sandwich. She checked Jared's left hand. No ring. Mel didn't have a boyfriend, and her last relationship ended disastrously. Something good just may come out of Gretchen Carlyle's show after all.

****

The following week Channel 5 barraged the air with commercials for Gretchen's new show. Promoted as "the program for how we view news today," the tag line, Charlee thought, was all Carlyle: Unfiltered. Unfettered. Unflagging.

Goosebumps surged through Charlee each time she watched them. She empathized with those unsuspecting residents who would be, well, accosted. She wouldn't wish that on anyone.

She also noticed Mel's reaction to the promotional spots. It was subtle, to be sure. Nothing more than a raised eyebrow or a roll of the eyes. On rare occasions, Mel winced. Charlee wondered how Mel felt about Jared. And how Jared felt about Mel. He often ate lunch at the coffee shop and always made time to chat with Mel. Charlee kept her fingers crossed.

Chapter 45

When nagging thoughts wouldn't allow Riley to sleep, he rose in the middle of the night and headed for the office—specifically his brother's office. He reviewed all of his options in dealing with the fracking company. When he finally glanced at his watch, he discovered it was already 7 a.m. Quinn would be in soon.

Yet he was no closer to feeling good about any of his decisions. He knew he needed to dismantle the company. But, in doing so, he would throw hundreds of innocent people out of work. But that wasn't the only worry weighing on his mind.

"Knock! Knock!" He heard his brother's voice.

Riley stopped pacing and greeted him. Quinn settled in behind his desk, and Riley sat opposite him in a receiving chair.

"What brings you into the office so early?" his brother asked.

"I have an appointment with our lawyers at two," he answered absentmindedly.

He laughed. "Okay, that's more than six hours away. Now tell me the real reason you're here." Riley didn't answer. Instead, he stared off into space.

Thud.

The noise jolted him. He saw that Quinn had dropped a heavy book on his desk.

"What?"

"Earth to Riley. I know you've got a lot on your mind. But talk to me, bro. You don't have to go through it alone. I'm here."

"I've lost her." His voice, far from being sad, contained an edge of anger, even rage.

"She's my lioness. I know that. Not only did I lose her, but I royally screwed up her life. She gave everything she had helping those affected by the fracking." He paused a moment and whispered, "My fracking."

He closed his eyes for a minute. "I know I can divest my interests in the corporation. But I can't divest my love for Charlee."

When Quinn didn't say anything, Riley rose. And paced. "I'm open to any suggestions, bro." He turned on a heel and gave his brother a hard look before he continued. "I don't see any way I can resolve this that satisfies the fracking predicament and restores my relationship with Charlee."

"Sit back down for a moment," Quinn said. "Let's analyze this one aspect at a time." Riley grudgingly complied.

"First, have you had any coffee this morning?"

Riley smiled. "You do have your priorities right. No, not yet."

His brother picked up the phone. "Renee, I apologize for asking you this. I know it's not your job; could we please have two large coffees?"

Quinn turned his attention back to the situation. "What do you have planned with the lawyer today?"

Riley told him he wanted to get rid of the entire portfolio. He knew the other companies in the group he bought were good; he just wanted to rid himself of any memory of it.

Shortly after Riley started laying out his plans, Renee knocked at the door, walked in with the coffee and several donuts and muffins. "Thought you guys might appreciate a little bit of food, as well."

Then she left as quietly as she arrived.

"You said you have fifty-one percent of the firm, right?" he asked.

Riley nodded as he took a bite of donut and sipped his coffee. "This coffee still sucks."

"That gives you the right to do whatever you want with the company, including shutting it down for good."

"That's exactly what I intend to do. But I also have to help those employees losing their jobs.

"And I keep second-guessing myself. With each move I consider, I wonder what Charlee would think of it. I feel as if I'm playing a game of chess. I dissolve the company and I'm off the hook for owning a fracking company, but…"

Riley left the rest of the sentence unspoken.

"But you still haven't won Charlee back because she'll be teed off you knocked so many people out of work."

"Yeah. I'm still the average cold-hearted venture capitalist in her eyes. I'm damned if I do and damned if I don't."

"Do you have any other options?"

"There are no other options. I have to do this. I just have to admit, I've probably lost Charlee for good."

"Could I ask you a question?"

Riley nodded.

"Don't you ever use your own office?"

He gagged on his donut. He picked up his coffee and tried to wash the food down. "I thought you were going to ask me a serious question."

"That was a serious question. I know you have an office. I've seen your name on it, and I've even been in it once or twice. Is it haunted or something that you're never in it?"

Riley took several moments to recover. "If you must know, I feel removed from 'where the action is.' I get lonely. That's a long hallway you have to go down to get to my office."

Quinn rolled his eyes. "You sound like a four-year-old boy."

****

Riley closed the conference room door after he and Attorney Michael C. Morris, entered. He deliberately pushed the folder toward him. "I outlined the problem to you on the phone, Mike," he said.

Riley and Quinn had used Mike as their attorney since Day One. Mike was the son of Allen Morris, who had been their dad's lawyer. The relationship was more than professional. The Brocktons often hosted the Morris family at their parents' summer home in Rehoboth Beach, Delaware.

But the brothers didn't use them solely because of the close family and professional history. Riley knew Mike was a damned good lawyer. If anyone could get him out of this mess, it would be him.

He smiled. "Does your expertise as a lawyer extend to giving sound advice on women."

The response was immediate and loud. "Hell, no! I haven't a clue when it comes to the opposite sex. If you knew how many times my wife has gotten mad at me and I have no idea why, you wouldn't be asking me."

"I tried."

Mike nodded thoughtfully as he scrutinized the contents of the folder. "I remember your concern when you closed the deal. I'm sorry I didn't listen to your intuition."

"I own enough of the firm to shut it down completely, right? Not just the Natural East Energy Group that's doing the fracking, but the entire Amalgamated Corp. The problem is, it will put so many people out of work."

The attorney looked over his reading glasses at Riley. "A venture capitalist with a heart."

"You sound like my brother now."

"You own more than half of the shares. You can do whatever you want. But you need to know it's going to cost you. And I'm not even talking about my fee. You're opening yourself up to a myriad of lawsuits. From those who may have been injured from the fracking and those who are about to lose their jobs."

"I know. I can't get out of this without lawsuits, but would it be possible to find these displaced workers jobs within Brockton Enterprises?"

The attorney thought long and hard. "Off hand, I don't know. I have no idea where these people live. I'm sure you want an answer as soon as possible."

He laughed. "Of course. Yesterday, if possible."

"Let me get our attorneys and paralegals on this. We'll tear this corporation apart on paper to discover who's affected, what their occupations are, and where they live. Once we know their demographics, then we'll have a better idea of what exactly we can do."

"That's all I can ask for. Thank you."

"No, problem. I'm just going back to the office and issue a code red. You have my promise everyone at the firm will drop everything they possibly can and start working on this."

"I'm going to owe you big time, aren't I?"

"Don't you always?"

Chapter 46

Charlee poured herself a glass of wine and prepared a small plate of cheese and crackers. No, she didn't expect company—certainly not Riley. She prepared herself to watch the coverage of the fracking proposition. Alone.

Why am I putting myself through this flagellant self-pity? She set the cheese plate on the coffee table. *What are the chances of the proposition passing?* Then she recalled the words of her father. She always did try to save the world. There were battles you just can't win regardless of how hard or long you fight. This may be one of them.

She replayed those words over and over in her mind as she listened to the votes slowly trickle in. She had done her best and now the rest was out of her control.

Even the Citizens Against Fracking wasn't gathering tonight, she thought. The group initially was optimistic about the election, based on several polls. Of course, they were all taken prior to her appearance on *The View from my Perch*. After that fiasco, the numbers dropped precipitously.

Initial election reports gave the moratorium an edge. Charlee allowed herself a moment of hopefulness. She knew she was grasping at straws; the night was young.

She sipped some wine, stood up, and walked around as the television anchor droned on about the other issues on the ballot, including a school tax. That issue, even at this early point, seemed as if it would pass easily.

The school tax reminded her of the flaming well perilously close to the elementary school. As she continued to wander about the house, she wondered how parents could even think of voting for fracking if they had kids in school.

Her movement didn't calm her, as she had hoped. Instead, she grew more agitated. She sighed as she sat down and waited for the remainder of the results.

By the end of the night, she witnessed the inevitable. The fracking moratorium failed. But it did so by a surprisingly small margin. It fell short, nonetheless. Fifty-two to forty-eight percent.

Some people understood the harm the industry did to the environment, and to their neighbors, she thought. But she was also aware others voted with their wallets. The economy was the best the area had experienced in nearly thirty years. And she got it. If you benefited from the fracking it would almost be stupid to vote against it. Almost.

Shortly after the final votes were announced, her cell phone rang. She checked the caller identification before answering it. If it were Riley, she didn't want to talk to him. Not yet, at least, she didn't want to hear his insincere apologies.

She wondered if she could ever forgive him.

The number that popped up was Mel's. She smiled as she swiped her screen. *She's probably checking on me to make sure I'm okay.*

"Hi, Mel," she said, as she tried to sound cheerful.

"Cut the crap," her friend snapped back.

"What? We haven't even started talking yet."

"I can already tell from those two words that you're trying too hard to be happy."

She laughed weakly. "You do know me."

"I just called to say I'm sorry about the proposition and remind you not to take it personally."

"Thanks. But I've got to take the blame for some of it. My relationship to the owner of the company certainly didn't help the cause."

"Charlee, there are any number of reasons why it failed. And did you ever think it may have had nothing to do with you?"

"Now, that you mention it…" She paused a beat. "No, I never once thought that."

"Just remember that dream or vision or whatever you had the other night. It really doesn't matter if it were just a dream. Even a dream version of your father gave you excellent advice."

Leave it to Mel to check on me, she thought after she disconnected the call. She hated to think that the fight was over. Sure, they could put the proposition up again for a vote and, in the meantime, they could continue to hold educational meetings, put out press releases, and hold protests at the site. Well, as close as they could get to the drilling site. The company forbid anyone on their property even though the entry gate was a good distance from the drilling.

She had just finished her glass of wine when her phone rang again. She presumed it was Mel. *She probably forgot to tell me something.* The caller ID surprised her. It was Karen. Her curiosity beat out her trepidation.

"Charlee, did you see those results?" From Karen's tone, you would have thought the issue passed.

"I'm sorry, Karen," Charlee said, "but on the bright side, if there is a bright side, the vote was closer than I would have imagined it to be."

"Yeah, that's the best part," the head of the anti-fracking group said.

" 'Best part?' There's something good in all of this?"

"There sure is."

"Karen, I've had a glass of wine tonight. Okay? Maybe two. So, pardon me if I don't have a clue as to what you're talking about. Please explain it—slowly."

She heard some noise in the background. "It sounds like you have people over," she said.

"I called some of the group over to hold a quick strategy session to plan the soonest we can get the moratorium back on the ballot. If we could get this many votes with so many other events clouding the issue, I'm sure if we're given another chance, the ban can pass. No question about it." Karen paused a beat as the background noise became louder. *Was that Marco she heard in the background?*

Then, she heard him yell over everyone else. "We couldn't have come this far without out you, Charlee. I think what we accomplished tonight was close to a miracle."

"That pretty much sums up what I wanted to tell you, too. We'll be in tomorrow sometime to talk to you about our next steps."

Next steps.

Charlee was at a loss for words. "Don't worry,"

Karen assured her. "If you can't help, I understand. We just want you to know we've gotten this far because of you. If you weren't on the council backing us, there wouldn't have even been a vote."

That was the last thing she expected—the group excited about the loss. If ever there were a positive thinker, it was Karen. *I bet she could find a good reason why she was in the middle of a tornado.*

She padded around the house until nearly one in the morning, as she reviewed her conversation with Karen. She was torn. She couldn't see how she would be an asset to the group. Yet they still wanted her help. Charlee's brain told her to play ostrich—stick her head in the sand. But her heart told her not to give up.

Somewhere during her wandering throughout the house, she had entered her bedroom. She had finally exhausted herself out. She climbed into bed and closed her eyes.

****

The following morning, Charlee walked through her morning coffee shop duties and took care of customers like a robot. While she was polite and friendly, her mind was clearly on the failure of the fracking proposition.

True to her word, Karen, and several others from the Citizens Against Fracking appeared after the lunch crowd rush cleared out. "Got time to sit with us?" Karen asked, in a voice that showed no animosity for the hideous events of the last several days.

Mel assured her she'd get the coffee and their orders. "Charlee, after we talked to you last night, we got so excited. We lost by such a narrow margin—even after Sparrow's disastrous show. We think we struck a nerve."

"What nerve was that?"

"Even as much as everyone prays NIMBY, the well and the horrendous conditions are just a bit too close to their back yard. And they believe they need to do something before they find the same thing in their back yard."

Jayne added, "And while the turnout was great, it seemed like those who voted were more concerned with the economic impact than the environmental impact. At least, that's what the *Bugle* said this morning."

"We're too close to quit now. We need to continue to educate the public and put the issue on the ballot again."

She couldn't believe what she heard. "I was ready to resign my position on the council, if you guys thought it would help. And I know the fact that Riley owns the company did nothing to further the cause."

Karen laughed. "I'm sure it didn't further Riley's cause, either. I can only imagine how angry you are with him right now." She paused a beat and took a sip of coffee. "But in the long run, it seems your connection with him didn't sway the vote one way or the other."

Karen paused, drank the last of her coffee, and asked, "I know this really isn't any of my business, but have you had the chance to talk with him since the show aired? Have you asked him why he would put you through all of this?

"You know, this really does seem out of character for the Riley I know—or thought I knew. We all have our reasons for doing things. I hate to think that he's that good of an actor...or that two-faced that he could fool the lot of us."

She shook her head. "Once. He tried to explain his actions. But it sounded like an excuse. Totally unbelievable."

She cleared the table after the women left. She couldn't believe what she had heard. They had told her over the phone the night before they were excited by how narrow a vote they lost. She had assumed they would wake up this morning and come to their senses. Mel strode over with a bus tub ostensibly to help her, but it was apparent her ulterior motive was to learn the thoughts of the group.

"Well?" Mel asked. "Come on, tell me what they said. I know you were worried about them holding you responsible for the results, but from the little I heard, they sounded happy."

"They were extremely gracious." She recapped the conversation.

"I'm glad they feel that way, but I can't help but think you're ready to just walk away from the entire issue."

"Trust me, part of me would love to resign." As she placed a few more cups in the tub, she slid into the chair she had been kneeling on. She sat there, rested her hand on her chin, and stared into space. Her eyes widened, and a smile crept over her face.

"Oh, no, Charlee," Mel said. "That's your classic I-have-a-plan look. And as I recall, that can only mean trouble. What are you thinking?"

"Just a vague idea. It's something that's sure to get the attention of the entire community. It could be called a bit far out. You may even want to call it radical. I need a little time to mull it over." Charlee flashed her friend a smile. "In fact, if I do this, I'll probably need your help."

Mel moaned. "No, not again. I remember the last scheme of yours you dragged me into."

"This one will be more fun. Besides, it's for a good cause."

Chapter 47

Riley and the company's attorney met again in the soundproof conference room.

"I have bad news," the attorney said. "You only own fifty-one percent of the company."

"Yeah, a bit more than half. I did that—"

The attorney broke in. Riley was taken aback at how quickly he got cut off.

"You don't own enough to shut the company down."

"I own more than half of the shares of the stock. It's right there in black and white." He pounded his fist on the table. He closed his eyes and then apologized.

"What do I need to do in order to shut Amalgamated down?" He felt emotionally and physically drained but was determined to stop the fracking. He was ready to call checkmate on this absurd game of chess.

"The by-laws of the Amalgamated American Green state—not so clearly by the way—that in some cases, an act that deliberately and substantially alters the structure of the company requires a vote of sixty percent of the shares of the stock."

He opened his mouth to speak, but Mike instantly shut him down. "Don't even go there," the attorney said playfully. "My staff is already finding you more shares to bring you to sixty percent." He looked directly into

Riley's eyes. "Is that what you were going to instruct me to do?"

Riley leaned back in his chair and tilted it on its two back legs. "Precisely." He thought for a moment, then asked, "How long do you think this will take? And do you think we have any potential sellers?"

"I'm sure we can find at least the minimum for you. With your permission I would love to try to find you even more, if you were so interested."

"I do love the way you think. Yes, please buy up as much stock as you can. The more I have above sixty percent, the more leverage it will give me." He paused a beat and gazed into space.

"That sounds perfect."

The attorney left, and Riley headed straight for his brother's office. He walked in after a quick and unanswered rap at the door. Quinn was transfixed by the television show, *The View from My Perch*.

"Listen to this," Quinn said without looking up to verify who had walked in.

He padded over to a receiving chair in front of the desk. Jared Sparrow was interviewing Karen Manning, chairperson of the Citizens Against Fracking. "Of course, we'd encourage everyone who cares about the environment and our town to join us next week."

"You do know, Karen, that the fracking company guards its lands as if they were gold. In the past all the protests were held across the road from the drilling area. Are you willing to stand that far away from the land?"

"Jared, normally we would respect that restriction, and I encourage those private citizens who support us to do exactly that. In that way, they are in no danger of violating any of the fracking company's regulations. But the members of CAF are not going to settle for that kind of protest. It was only a few weeks ago on your show that they used veiled threats against one of our most loyal allies.

"We aren't about to accept that. The company threw the gauntlet down; we're about to respond. We will be on their land, directly in front of the gate."

"For those of you just tuning in, this is a special edition of *The View from My Perch.* I'm deviating from the standard debate style that is customary for the show," Sparrow said. "Our only guest today is Karen Manning, chairperson of the local and may I add quite vocal—" Sparrow waited a moment for the studio audience's laughter to fade. "—Citizens Against Fracking.

"It's my way of apologizing for the unfortunate turn of events the anti-fracking spokesperson we had on last week experienced. Being gracious enough to appear, she was treated unfairly by certain members of our studio audience."

Riley listened closely. "What day, Quinn, did they say the anti-fracking group was protesting?" Quinn told him. "Clear your calendar for that day," Riley said, "you're going to be with me."

Chapter 48

Charlee, never one to pay much attention to the television at work, made the exception for this episode. She watched Karen handle herself with grace and dignity. The group had asked her to accompany them and be part of the audience, but she declined. How could she?

She felt like one gigantic and glaring hypocrite. She had spewed the anti-fracking message to whomever would listen. All the while she slept with the man who owned the company responsible for the life-threatening damage.

But she knew she had to be there with them when they protested at the site. That's when her mood brightened a bit. "Of course," she said out loud. "That's it. It's perfect timing."

"Ohhh, Mel," she sang as her assistant backed into the kitchen door, her arms filled with dishes and glasses cleared from the tables. She was ready to disappear to the other side. "When you get a moment, we need to talk." Again, her voice took a melodic tone.

Mel groaned as she pushed the door with her backside and nodded. She couldn't help but comment on Charlee's countenance. "You have that sparkle in your eye. I'm in big trouble now."

"You look worried. Don't be so paranoid." Charlee flashed a smile at her and told her friend, "Just because you're paranoid doesn't mean I'm not out to get you."

"Let me tie up a few loose ends in the kitchen. I'll be right back." Mel sighed. In a few moments she was back in the front of the coffee shop and leaned against the counter.

"Okay, give it to me straight," she said, "I have a feeling this is going to be…let's just say interesting. Why do I think you've finally nailed down the details of that plan?"

"Because I have. And it's a stroke of genius, if I do say so myself." Then she outlined it for her friend. It was so simple, it didn't take much time.

"No, you can't do that. That seems like an unnecessary risk," Mel said in a panicked voice.

"It just might take an extreme action like that to get people to realize the severity of the issue."

Chapter 49

"So, Charlee girl," Ed said, the following morning. "I see where your boyfriend has called a press conference for next week." Charlee poured him and Fred their coffee. The pair frustrated and irritated her at times. Their interest in her personal life grew with each visit. But…there was something irresistible about these two.

"He is not my boyfriend any longer. And you know that."

"No, what I do know, though, is that we old curmudgeons still like to see a 'happily-ever-after' ending. We'd like nothing better than for you to have one—with that Brockton boy."

"Happily-ever-after between the two of us is completely out of the question now."

Fred laughed. "When in the world did you get to be so cynical? It seems like just the other day you were Ms. Optimist."

"You know when it happened, Fred. And just so you know, sarcasm doesn't become you."

Ed had the newspaper in front of him. "I read he's holding the press conference during the protest at the drilling site. He must have some important announcement to make."

"So I've heard," she said. "But even before you ask, I have no idea what it is. And quite frankly I could care less." She hadn't anticipated Riley's presence at the protest, but she wanted him to see what she had planned.

****

Charlee threw her shift stick in park, wrapped both hands around the steering wheel, and took a deep breath. Mel sat in the passenger seat. They were the first to arrive; Charlee parked across the road from the fracking site. "Well, I either do what we've planned—"

"No. What you've planned." Mel took the cue from her friend and made no move to exit the car. "I'm not convinced this is one of your better ideas."

"Trust me. The only factor I hadn't figured into the equation was Riley. But I'm never going to get a more fitting opportunity."

They got out of the car and approached the drilling site. "Tell me again why you're doing this?"

"A couple of reasons, really," Charlee said. "First, there's no better way to keep the public's attention on the problem. And I believe it's an extreme enough action that even Riley will understand how horrific the effects of fracking are."

Mel tilted her head at Charlee and offered, "This doesn't have a thing to do with your feeling personally responsible for the failure of the vote?"

She remained silent for a moment, so Mel filled that silence. "You can tell me. This is your form of penance you and you alone think you need to perform. Didn't that vision you have of your dad have any effect on you?"

"Yes, as a matter of fact, it did. But I've come to terms with Riley's presence here today. That gives me a new level of motivation. It's about me wanting to punch him in the balls for what he did to me. When he sees me on his land in defiance of his company's order, he'll have to contend with the idea of having me arrested."

"Okay. I'm finally satisfied," Mel said between her belly laughs. "I can totally support you on this now. Give me that extra key. I'm ready to be your accomplice in this insane plan."

"I'll do it when the group arrives," Charlee said. "I really don't relish being in that position any longer than I need to."

The pair arrived at the fence. Since there were only the two of them, Charlee used the opportunity to enjoy the crisp, cold air of the early December morning.

The sun shone on the wooded area where she had parked her car. She loved the morning light. The soft radiance of the few hours after sunrise promised a day of infinite possibilities. A fresh start.

She shivered, despite the fact she had several layers of clothing on, topped off with a jacket. She thought her winter coat would be too bulky for her purpose. She contrasted the day's frosty morning to the hot, humid day the group of women asked her to run for office. Weeks turned into months too fast.

As she waited for the group, she and Mel made small talk, mostly about Ed and Fred. While she spoke, she paced and kicked the dirt in front of the fence up like a bored little kid. Even though it was December, there had been little snow. At this rate, she thought, in a deliberate attempt to take her mind off what she was about to do, there wouldn't even be snow for Christmas.

The sound of familiar voices brought her back to the present. She knew their voices anywhere. Ed and

Fred. She waved to them as they ambled toward her.

They were clad in their "uniform," the same style they wore to the coffee shop every day. Plaid.

"Well, when you guys mentioned you might stop by," she said, "I thought you were only being polite. Standing at the fence of a fracking well, watching a group of protesters usually doesn't rate high on Friday morning events."

The pair agreed. "But then, Charlee girl," Ed said, in his slow, easy tone, "it's not every day you're one of the protesters."

"Did you come out to laugh at me and enjoy a good show?" she asked them. "Or are you just tired of getting all of your news about me 'from the street'?"

"You know us better than that," Fred said, as he flashed a smile. "We're here to support you. We're behind you a hundred percent."

The longer she knew Ed and Fred the more she liked them. When they first started asking about her personal life, it irritated her. She thought they were a couple of lonely old buttinskies, as her mother used to say. But these two men seemed to genuinely care for her. They reminded of her father more every day.

"I do appreciate your concern as well as all our open and honest discussions about—"

At that moment, Charlee heard a vehicle's door slam. She turned to see Karen had parked her van behind her car. It looked as if the entire anti-fracking group was piling out. Once they all had exited, they unpacked eight or nine protest signs. She laughed; it reminded her of a tiny clown car that miraculously held an unimaginable number of clowns.

"I'm so glad you're here," Karen said. "This

protest wouldn't be complete without you and Mel."

"Don't say that until you see what I have planned. You may think I'm a screwball. But I'm willing to take my chances."

"I'm ready, Mel," she said. "Let's get this done."

Charlee and Mel marched to the fence. Charlee took a pair of handcuffs from her back jeans' pocket. She clicked one cuff through the gate. Mel helped her click the other end to her wrist.

With her free hand, she plopped the key into the front pocket of her jeans. Mel, in turn, took her key to the cuffs out of her pocket, showed Charlee she had it, and pushed it back into her jeans' pocket. It had the flair worthy of a Houdini escape trick. The protesters' eyes were riveted to her actions.

"Anytime you need me to unlock you if you can't do it fast enough for whatever reason," Mel said, her eyes piercing. "All you need to do is call me."

It took several seconds before Karen fully grasped the situation. Their eyes locked, and she could tell that Karen panicked. The head of the anti-fracking group ran up to her and just shook her head.

She flashed a big grin as she tried to find a comfortable position. "Those trucks won't get past me. They're not dumping any waste in our water supply today."

"Who do you think you are?" Karen asked her. "What you're doing is so radical I wouldn't even consider it."

A car pulled up the gravel driveway of the well, interrupting their conversation. Two men got out of the car nearly simultaneously. Riley and Quinn. Their movements were so synchronized she thought they could have shared one mind. That and the similarity in their looks struck her again. She thought they could pass as twins.

Definitely the family resemblance was there. *It's amazing the strange thoughts that run through your mind when you're handcuffed to a fence waiting to come face-to-grill with an eighteen-wheeler tank truck.*

"Hell, no! We won't go!" Jayne began the chant.

Immediately, the others joined in. "Hell, no! We won't go!"

The chant referenced the fracking company's no-trespassing rule.

"What does he think he's doing here?" Karen said. "I resent his presence, but I'm not sure why. It's either because he owns this company and has taken us for fools, or it's because of all the humiliation he's caused you." She paused. "Or both."

Nearly instantly, the members of the group formed a protective circle around her. The action reinforced their respect and support for her. While she was grateful, she wondered if she deserved either.

Silently, she cursed herself. She cursed where her thoughts—even in the middle of all of this—sent her. She tried not looking at him, but it didn't help.

She sensed his presence. Surprisingly, she could even distinguish his distinct fragrance despite the fact they were separated by some ten to fifteen yards among people who had their own scents.

It seemed as if she had a keener sense of smell recently. She recalled the day Riley walked into the café to explain himself. She recognized his scent the moment he opened the door. She pushed this out of her mind as she concentrated on the conversations around her.

Riley worked his way through the protesters to get to Charlee. He scrutinized her hand cuffed to the fence and tilted his head. He raised it slightly as he looked it over. The touch melted her heart. A tsunami of desire rushed through her body. His touch was as gentle as she remembered it. She whimpered softly.

"Did you say something?" He flashed his lopsided smile. For a moment he held her hand perfectly still. If it hadn't been attached to the fence, she would have pulled it away. *Who am I kidding? If I wasn't cuffed, it would take all my strength not to wrap my arms around him and feel his body against mine.*

She shook her head. She tried to speak but couldn't.

"That's funny," he said, "because I thought I detected a small moan." He winked at her. He still had hold of her hand. "Many a woman has had to handcuff herself to something to keep from wrapping her arms around me. I can't tell you how many times a week that happens."

When that didn't get a laugh out of her, he then went for truthful and serious.

"I've missed you, Charlee. Terribly so."

"I miss you too, Riley. If you only knew how much."

She felt as if someone had ripped her heart out and dangled it in front of her. How she wished they were a couple again. She didn't feel whole without him by her side at night, without him listening to the mundane details of her day.

This raced through her mind as the protesters continued their chant despite the fact neither Brockton made an effort to disperse them.

Chapter 50

"Do you always spend your early mornings handcuffed to a random gate, waiting for a ride from a tractor trailer?" In the next breath, without allowing her to answer, Riley continued, "Charlee, what in the world are you doing?"

"Making a statement."

He shook his head and laughed. "You do know that most women make statements by buying shoes, not acting like a one-woman radical environmental organization."

A short silence fell between them. Finally, he said, "I, for one, am glad you did this, at least for the moment."

She could tell by the glint in his amber eye that he was about to say something even more unexpected.

"It's the only way I can get you to stay in one place long enough lately to talk to you."

"Darn, I knew there was a downside to this plan."

"I know you don't believe me, and you may never come to believe me. But everything I told you at Pat's was true. I had no idea what Amalgamated American Green did—until I heard it on the Bird Man's show."

She squinched her face in disbelief. "Please, don't lie to me. At least respect me enough to tell me the truth. I know you're far too good a businessman to buy a company blind."

"Basically, I screwed up," he confessed.

His back to the protesters, he all but pleaded with her. He didn't see the media arrive. Charlee watched as they walked up to Quinn, who pointed toward Charlee and Riley. "Incoming at one o'clock," Charlee said. "The media are arriving at record speed, it would seem."

"Riley Brockton?" one of them asked as he hustled up to the billionaire and identified himself as David Chinwag of the Zen, Ohio *Daily Meditation*. Zen was located about 5 miles north of Prague.

Fresh faced and enthusiastic, he looked as if he just "got released" from journalism school and saw every event as a chance to change the world. Riley smiled despite the circumstances, because the cub reporter acted as if he had just landed the best assignment ever. And who knows? Maybe he did.

"What is the purpose of your presence here today? Are we to assume you have some statement to make since you alerted the media of your actions? Can you give me a heads up on what you plan to say?"

He shot the questions at him so quickly, Riley wouldn't have had a chance to answer, even if he wanted to. When it sounded as if the reporter had run out of steam, Riley politely declined to comment.

"You'll have to wait with everyone else," he said. "But good try. I admire your assertiveness."

That's when the reporter noticed Charlee. "Excuse me, Ms. Lightheart, but I can't help but notice that you're...uhm, handcuffed to the gate?"

Riley was off the hook. He no longer felt obliged to the reporter, who found someone who might make an even better headline.

As Chinwag began to interview her, Riley winked at her and backed away. He didn't want to abandon her, but it looked as if Quinn was drowning in a sea of reporters. He knew his brother had volunteered to accompany him. It wouldn't be fair to allow him to face the media alone before the actual start of the press conference.

As he hurriedly walked toward his brother, he couldn't help but notice that the crowd was growing by leaps and bounds, which explained the crescendo of the chorus of "Hell, no! We won't go!"

Not only was the anti-fracking group present, but a large crowd of spectators had formed across the street. Apparently, they weren't willing to trespass on the company's property.

While Riley anticipated heavy local media coverage, he was initially surprised by the national and international media present. Then he reminded himself of the attention Charlee's race had received.

"Gentlemen, ladies," he said loudly, as he walked up to his brother, slapped him on his shoulder, and whispered a thank you in his ear. "You're all wondering why I called you here today." He stopped, grinned from ear to ear, and chuckled.

"Sorry. I've always wanted to say that," Riley said through his laughter. His momentary silliness caused Quinn to laugh as well. It seemed to have lightened the mood, as some of the media joined in.

****

Then Charlee's moment of decision arrived. The tanker truck rolled up. This would be the first of several trips that carried wastewater from the site. The waste supposedly was headed for a self-contained well to avoid polluting Prague's drinking supply. More often than not, the drivers were ordered to take the wastewater to the nearest water source.

There was no turning back. Charlee was about to find herself face-to-grill with the tractor trailer. Okay, so that was a bit melodramatic. After all, she had more than a dozen people—no it looked like two dozen people now—separating her and the truck. She was hardly in any danger of getting run over.

She was more likely to get thrown in jail for a night. While she knew that wasn't a desirable outcome, she thought it might wake Prague voters to the horrid conditions of her constituents.

She took several deep breaths. The group, just by presence on the company's land, no, she corrected herself, Riley's land, broke one of his sacred commandments, "Thou shall not stand on the property of the hydraulic drilling company for any reason at all."

No, that wasn't really how the warning read, but certainly that's how she translated it in her mind. She also half expected to see some outrageous penalty to go with that. Perhaps she'd discover the consequences of breaking the rule today.

She noticed the truck arrived with a police escort. That signaled the company...no, Riley...had little patience with the protesters. Perhaps that's why he hadn't chased them off yet. He waited for the police to do it. Charlee just hoped she didn't get arrested before she heard Riley speak.

Every time she thought "company" she replaced it with Riley. He was the owner. But she couldn't reconcile those actions and commands against the man she knew and...damn it...still loved.

Another vehicle followed the police onto the property. A black SUV. Three individuals exited, stood next to it, and glowered at Riley.

They were not in a good mood.

Though Riley wasn't standing near Charlee, she could hear what he was saying.

The police approached the Brockton brothers. "I'm sorry to tell you this, Mr. Brockton," Police Chief Harlan Davis said. "But the officials of the company would like you leave the premises. They said you are more than welcome to speak to the media across the street."

Chapter 51

Riley and Quinn both laughed in his face. "Sir, I have every right to be on this land."

The chief stammered for a minute before he came up with a cogent reply. "The CEO of the company said you and your brother are interrupting the workflow."

"I hope you understand," he said with a smile, "it's not my intent to undermine your authority. I'm merely here to establish control over property that is rightfully mine. If I choose to interrupt the workflow of my company, I have every right to do."

The police chief didn't—couldn't—say another word. Riley filled the awkward silence. "Would you do me a favor and inform me which of those gentlemen in dark suits and sunglasses next to the SUV is my CEO."

"Certainly Mr. Brockton," the chief said, sounding relieved. "Only in this city would the owner of the company want me to point his CEO out to him."

He agreed. "I can't even tell you how embarrassed I am that I even have to ask you."

"He's the man in black in the middle."

"Thank you."

He took several steps toward the gentlemen but had second thoughts. "Mr. Oswald, would you and whoever you have with you please step over here. I don't think any of the media will bite you. But I would like to talk to you."

Riley and Quinn exchanged glances. He had been in enough negotiations and discussions to know that he had just gained the upper hand.

"Good job, Riley," Quinn told him. "They thought they were going to dismiss and blow you off, just like they do with everyone else."

The trio hesitated momentarily, but then approached, slowly and deliberately, as if they were large cats stalking their prey. Their body language screamed arrogance, Riley thought. As they approached, his anger rose. *If they only knew what was about to hit them.*

He was sure they didn't know the trick he had up his sleeve. While his attorney and his staff had purchased all the available stock, they also discovered loopholes in the company's by-laws so the transactions would not have to be reported to the CEO immediately.

He had no idea how Mike pulled it off, and frankly he didn't care. He was about to knock them down a peg or two.

The men, still in a near-perfect line, stood in front of the Brockton brothers, their back to the press.

He addressed the media first. "You're about to discover why I called you all here today." He felt his anger dissipating some, but enough of an edge was left to enjoy the upcoming discussion.

"First, I would like to offer my apologies to Citizens Against Fracking." He paused a beat and waved an arm behind him where they were gathered.

"I've stepped on their toes this morning and took the spotlight off their protest. My purpose here is make sure they'll never need to stage a protest again."

While the protesters fell silent, the media buzzed

with excitement. Before he could continue his presentation, reporters hurled questions at him. "Mr. Brockton, what do you have planned?" "What are you thinking?"

"This man," Oswald said, "doesn't own enough of this corporation to do much of anything. You may be a stockholder, but—"

The media didn't let Oswald continue. It sounded as if every reporter shouted questions at the same time. None was intelligible, but they did throw Oswald and his men off balance momentarily. Not to mention that these men—and not him—were now the center of attention.

After several minutes, Riley restored order. He explained he was unaware of the true nature of the company when he purchased it. "Because I failed to research this firm thoroughly, I've hurt many people and embarrassed a great many more."

He turned around and looked for Charlee. Despite the people and protest signs that separated them, he was able to get her attention. He knew she would never love him again, but he had to let her know he understood the pain he had caused her.

He brought his attention back to the media. "It was an irresponsible move. I should never have relied on the word of others, regardless of their intentions. We judged the firm by its name and the other companies in the same portfolio.

"But with this short announcement, we can finally begin to dismantle Amalgamated American Green and compensate my neighbors who have been injured by its deceitfulness. I know my actions in the latter portion of the process will be meager compared to everything this company has done to you. But I will do everything within my control to compensate you."

He took a deep breath to ensure his composure. Silence blanketed the gathering.

Chapter 52

The silence didn't last long. A voice from the back of the crowd shouted, "Mr. Brockton, you need to stop now before you make a bigger fool of yourself."

Riley tilted his head as the man worked his way through the members of the media. When he passed Oswald, he nodded. Riley thought it looked as if it pained the gentleman to wear an expensive suit in such a dusty location.

"I'm Attorney Robert Skinner, head counsel for Amalgamated." He extended his hand. Skinner looked around before he asked, "Where is your attorney?"

Riley shrugged. "Don't know. Didn't invite him. Why would I need him?"

"I'll cut to the chase, Mr. Brockton," he said, using a tone as if Riley didn't have a clue as to what was about to happen.

"Oh, you're going to cut to the chase? How kind of you."

"Rumor has it that you came today because you're under the delusion that you can shut down this company. And while I appreciate the fact that you do own fifty-one percent of the stock—"

"That's not enough to shut the company down. Is that's what you want to tell me?"

"Then you already know that you have power within this corporation, but not nearly the amount you need to kick us to the curb."

"Oh, I wouldn't be so sure about that. I'm only kicking a few people to the curb."

"I don't understand."

Quinn who had stood by his brother silently for this whole time, chuckled. "Of course, he doesn't understand."

"But he will soon." Riley couldn't help himself as he allowed a smile to cross his face. A low buzz swept through the protesters, who up until this point had been rapt in silence.

"I do understand the situation, Attorney Skinner," he said, pulling his stature to his full height. "And that's why within the last couple of days, I advised my attorney to act as my proxy and purchase another twenty-five percent of the shares of Amalgamated."

"You only needed—" The attorney began to stutter.

"I know." He cut him off. "I only legally needed sixty percent of the stock to do what I please with the company." He paused because he could feel his anger growing toward this groveling sycophant.

The attorney took several steps back, as if it finally hit him that he no longer held all the cards.

"Are you quite done with your empty threats?" Riley asked. "Because if you would just allow me to say what I came here to announce without your meaningless interruptions, we can get over this pretty much painlessly. Well, at least on my part. It might be a bit more painful for you."

The CEO of the corporation whispered something to his attorney at his side before he stepped up to the Brockton brothers. "We have yet to be informed of this change of ownership. I personally think you're bluffing. I can't believe all of this could happen without my knowledge."

Riley growled at Oswald. "It could occur the same way this corporation found its way into a portfolio that had nothing but 'green' companies in it. Now, how could that possibly happen? Perhaps someone—and I'm not naming names—would purposely do this in order to cover the real nature of the firm."

The CEO turned pale. Right there, Riley knew he struck a nerve. He had wondered whether the inclusion of the company in the portfolio was merely an administrative error or a sincere intent to deceive. And he contemplated it all the more once his attorney told him the number of celebrities who owned shares. Once these Hollywood "green" advocates discovered the true nature of the firm and Riley's reason for the purchase, Morris said, they were more than happy to sell.

"If you're not willing to move, Mr. Oswald, I can have the police over there move you."

Oswald whispered something to Skinner. They were stalling. *After all, I've done it plenty of times in negotiations.* He read the man's body language and would have laid a tidy sum of money on the fact he was searching for something that could give him the upper hand, if only for a moment, while he came up with a game plan.

Oswald and his team stammered for what seemed to be a long moment. Finally, Skinner blurted out, "Who's the freak handcuffed to the gate? I'll run her over in a heartbeat to get this workday started. The company loses money every minute we stand here arguing, every minute we're denied legal entry onto our property."

Riley's eyes blazed with anger, and he leaped over to the man, grabbed a hold of his starchy collar and his tie with his left hand, and balled his right hand into a fist.

"You're going to be sorry you said that." He drew his arm nearly all the way behind him and propelled it to the side of Skinner's face. The punch knocked the man down. "Sorry about getting your suit scuffed up," he said. He paused a beat and then by way of an explanation, shouted at him, "She's the love of my life, you no-good low-down coward—"

He could have gone on and would have if Quinn and the police hadn't rushed over to pull him off of the man.

Riley lowered his voice to a whisper. "That woman is no freak. She's my soulmate. How surprising it is that I don't take kindly to you calling her that." He wriggled out of the hold the police had him in and sprinted to the other side of the tanker truck. The truck, its engine still idling, served as the perfect cover for Riley as he growled like an animal.

His actions drew the attention of the driver and his partner in the truck, who looked out the driver's side window. The pair screamed, loud enough that everyone could hear even though the windows were only open less than an inch.

The growl, loud and low, subsided, and Riley returned to the other side. He knew exactly what he had done. He hadn't planned this transformation and he knew it would cause untold complications, but he also knew his brother had his back.

Riley appeared before the group again, this time as

a lion, singing a low, constant growl while his eyes appeared fixed on the quartet of men from Amalgamated.

In his newly transformed lion body, he padded over to the attorney who was just getting up with the help of the others from the corporation. Riley nudged the man's butt with his muzzle, causing him to stumble and fall again. He lay prone for a second, then he rolled over on his back and tried to get to his feet. He couldn't. Riley had placed his paw on the man's leg.

Chapter 53

"Mel! Help me!"

Charlee's cry ripped through the air almost immediately after Riley's growl. The protesters swung around toward the city councilwoman just in time to see Mel bound toward her.

She couldn't remember when her body turned on her. Was it when she heard Riley referred to her as "the love of my life"?

Or when she heard the agonized growl of what sounded like a wounded animal? All she knew for sure that a growing unrest, a dizziness, and sweaty palms and brow overwhelmed her. Up until that moment she thought she was feeling good.

She knew instantly the large African cat was Riley. The moment she saw him chills shot down her spine, her fingers and toes tingled, and the hairs on the back of her neck stood up. She could barely stay in her own skin.

As she struggled with her emotional and physical reactions, she could clearly hear the bewildered voices around Riley.

"Brockton," the attorney called to Quinn, "call him off."

"Who? The lion here?" he asked, appearing to fully enjoy the transformation of the man from cocky SOB to groveling, quaking sycophant.

And yet during all of this, her thoughts still lasered in on her relationship with Riley. At the very least, it made the physical uncertainty of the moment a bit more endurable.

She hadn't seen him since...wow, it seemed like forever before they talked briefly this morning. As much as she had tried to push him out of her mind—every single day—she now understood why it was so difficult for her to get past him. She still loved him. Darn that man.

Sweat trickled down her forehead as another tidal wave of physical distress washed over her. Shortness of breath. She tried repeatedly to take a long, deep breath, but her body refused to cooperate. The more she tried and couldn't, the more the panic shot through her. *Surely this reaction is more than just my sorrow and pain over a love lost.* What was going on?

After several excruciating moments, a thought struck her. *Could it really be?*

She had heard enough of her family's descriptions of these events. She had been told women sometimes had their first shift when their adrenaline level was extremely high.

No, it couldn't be.

Charlee fumbled for the key. She knew she had stuffed it in her pocket. She specifically remembered it was in her right jeans pocket. But in her heightened state, she couldn't feel it. The last thing she needed was to shape shift in front of all these people—if that's what was really happening. And if it was, she wasn't sure what would happen if she shifted still handcuffed to the gate.

A tidal wave of impatience, frustration, and sweat

overrode her senses. "Get me out of these as quickly as possible," she said, once Mel got to her side. Her body shook violently as her friend unlocked the cuffs.

She allowed Mel to take her to one side of the tanker truck, then she chased her away. "I know," Charlee said breathlessly, "it's against your better judgment, but please, just do it. I need to be alone." *I feel like a clump of cow dung.*

As the sweat evaporated in the cold of the morning and the tide of frustration diminished, she slowly gained control over her body. She tried to stand up. She couldn't. Not all the way, at least. Her hands refused to push her into an upright position. *Am I paralyzed?* Something about her body felt fundamentally different.

She looked down at her hands, uhm...her paws. Her yellowish-brown, furry paws. Then, she looked around. She didn't know what happened to her clothes. They just seemed to have magically disappeared.

She stood up and involuntarily stretched. She laughed at herself as she felt her lion's body move. And after what she had endured in that short period of time, the stretching was a welcome action.

She really had shifted. She stood for the first time as a lion, on all "fours." Just the idea of it overwhelmed her. She never allowed herself to think that she would ever experience the transformation. What an incredibly alive and freeing feeling.

She walked to the other side of the truck and took a quick, cursory look around. She saw him just as he saw her. She wasn't sure how she appeared to others, but in her lion state, she felt a sense of confidence she seldom felt as a human.

She walked toward Riley, whose large paw still

made sure the man on the ground wasn't moving. That's when she heard it...no, that wasn't possible. How could she have heard Riley's voice?

There, she heard it again. Distinctly. *Telepathic, telekinetic communication?* She thought a moment. Of course, her parents said they could do this when they both shifted. She had forgotten about it. And it was wild to actually experience it. She knew it would take a bit to get used to it.

"Think of it as you and me slinging pizzas at each other," Riley said, gently. "You need no words; you just need to think of what you want to tell me. Toss the pizza, in this case a thought, my way, and you can be sure I'll get the pizza."

"That's just like you," she told him. "Always finding food analogies."

Some of the media and the protestors noticed her— at least had the courage to admit it. "Oh my God, there's two lions now." She heard the speculation of where the second lion came from. She felt the panic of not only a few of the protestors, but some members of the media.

There, that voice, she thought. She couldn't have mistaken it for anybody else but Gretchen Carlyle. She looked up, and Gretchen bounded toward her, pushing all the other media people out of her way. Her videographer tried to keep up with her, but it was nearly impossible. This evidently was the moment she had been waiting for.

Not only could she now confirm that Riley was a lion shifter, but it would also only be a matter of time before she learned who the second lion was.

Charlee felt a twinge of happiness for her.

Gretchen had been chasing down the Brockton family for years, on the outside chance that someone, somewhere would reveal the news.

Gretchen walked up to her. She wasn't sure what she should do. "Don't panic," Riley said, "Just let her approach you. People can read fear a mile away." Charlee laughed—at least she tried to laugh on the inside.

Gretchen walked around Charlee. "Go ahead, it's okay," Riley said, "I know exactly what you're thinking. That should give her something to think about."

When the rogue reporter began to encircle her again, Charlee mimicked the motion. The two of them took deliberate steps around each other. "Looks like that lion wants to eat that reporter for lunch," Charlee heard someone in the crowd say.

No one present could take their eyes off the scene. They acted as if they were hypnotized. Parents picked up their toddlers so they could watch the action without struggling to peek through the legs of adults. "They must have spent hours rehearsing this," someone said.

"Well, they did a darn good job, because this is so entertaining."

Throughout this exhibition, Quinn urged Gretchen to stop. "You never know how a wild animal will react. I wouldn't get too close to her if I were you." Her camera person, though, didn't need to be told twice. He hung back. Finally, the journalist looked back at him and screamed at him, "For cryin' out loud, Mark," she said, "get up here and get a close up." She paused a beat and then laughed. "Maybe you can finally get the Emmy you've been whining about."

At that moment Riley took his paw off of the attorney and allowed him to stand. The unexpected motion startled Gretchen, and she jumped back several feet.

When Gretchen rocked back, she knocked her videographer on his butt. He had been right behind her, using her as a shield.

The crowd laughed even louder; they still thought it was part of a comic routine prepared for the day.

With her pride wounded, Gretchen couldn't stay in the forefront. She retreated and directed the camera man scan the protesters. "That's Charlee Lightheart," she cried out. Charlee thought Gretchen was a little slow. She could tell by their reactions that most of the Citizens Against Fracking had already figured it out.

"Close-up on the gate," she snapped at the camera man. When he questioned her judgment, she practically screamed at him, "Because that witch, Lightheart, isn't cuffed to it anymore, there's no one there." She pushed him into the crowd.

He looked back at her and said, "I don't get it." Clearly, he didn't see any news value to a gate. He already had a quite a few with Charlee cuffed to it.

"The lion is Lightheart!" He did as he was told and got it over with as quickly as possible.

Chapter 54

"Charlee, I'm going to shift quickly back to human form, to lay down the groundwork for the fate of the company. Can you hold down the fort for me in lion's form?"

"What do I do?"

"You're doing it. You just standing there makes them nervous. If you want to circle them and give them a look in the eye every now and again that would be fine. If any of them begins to complain or interrupt me, simply place one of those paws—which are quite sexy, you wear them well—on his foot. That'll keep him quiet for a while."

"I can do that," she replied.

He walked around the back of the tanker truck and disappeared, only to return on two legs, looking his usual fresh and handsome self. He threw her a lopsided grin, then got down to business.

He approached Gretchen and stood behind her. "I'm about to tell these fine gentlemen the consequences of their extended stay on my land." The unexpected voice startled the woman, who was clearly already unnerved, and she jumped. "I do believe it's something you should be aware of, too."

Riley took a deep breath and explained to the crowd that he did own a large enough percentage of the company to shut it down.

"That's exactly what I intend to do. With regards to personnel and salaries, though, I can't go into the full details here."

Oswald tried to interrupt several times, but when Charlee's paw landed on his foot, the executive obviously thought better and stopped in midsentence.

The truck driver and his partner had rolled their windows at the start of the confrontation. They were visibly shaken by the announcement.

"What's going to happen to me?" one of them asked. "Are you saying you're throwing me out on the street? I have a family to feed."

"We're developing a process to match you up with other businesses of Brockton Enterprises closest to your homes. While we're hammering out the details, you'll receive your regular paycheck right on time. Until we find you a job that pays what you're making now—or something better—you'll get your base salary. If you want to go to school to learn a new skill, I'll pay for a hundred percent of the tuition and the books. But we'll discuss that in a private meeting with all employees in a couple of days. I don't have it all laid out today. Some of this takes time to ensure everything falls into place correctly."

He strode quickly to the truck and pulled a couple of business cards out of the back pocket of his jeans. "Here is my office number as well as my personal cell phone number. If at any time you need anything, call me. Even if you find yourself running out of food," he said a bit more quietly. "I will personally make sure you're never lacking for anything."

The crowd reacted with applause and a few cheers. Riley pivoted on a heel and waited for the response to subside. "I'm sorry to have to put you through all of this. Brockton Enterprises is in the initial stages of finding a way to compensate you. I know it's small solace considering what you've been through, but I'll do the best I can."

Skinner spoke out. "I appreciate your passing out condolences and empty promises, but I have to inform you that I am not prepared to walk away from this situation just because you claim to have seventy-five percent of the stock."

What happened next was a one-in-a-million chance. Riley thought the odds were better that he would be struck by lightning. A red SUV pulled up next to the tanker truck. All eyes were on the man who stepped out.

"Mike!" Riley and Quinn exclaimed together. Their attorney, Morris, walked up to them shook their hands.

"I've got it all confirmed on paper. I knew you said I didn't need to be here, but I had a hunch they wouldn't believe you." He handed the folder to Riley.

"Would you mind telling everyone what this contains?" He waved the folder.

"You want Oswald and company to hear it from your attorney? Sure." He nodded and cleared his throat.

"It's with great pleasure that I announce Riley Brockton now owns seventy-five percent of Amalgamated American Green." He looked at Oswald and his small contingent. "Mr. Brockton has the legal right to make structural changes within the corporation." The representatives grumbled among themselves.

Attorney Skinner took several steps forward. "I

wish to see the documents."

"Certainly." Morris handed the folder to Skinner. It was as if everyone held their breath as Skinner reviewed them. Reluctantly, he handed them back.

He turned and told Oswald, "The documents are authentic. He has a legal basis for his actions." He paused a beat. Sighed. "Even a right to dismantle it."

The crowd cheered. "Riley! Riley! Riley!"

Riley asked the crowd to calm down. "This is the moment I've been waiting for." He looked directly at the anti-fracking group. "Beginning immediately, drilling will cease. There will be no more hydraulic fracturing by Amalgamated American Green doing business as Natural East Energy ."

Cheers rang from not only the protesters but the members of the media as well—with the exception of Gretchen Carlyle. She looked as if she had been kicked in the face.

"Well, I never heard of anything so stupid in my whole life. Riley Brockton, you are nothing but low-level pond scum. You have not heard the last of me. You can't be as squeaky clean as you try to make out."

Chapter 55

Charlee eased her sore and tired body into the bathtub already filled with water and a splendidly refreshing bath bomb. Eucalyptus and spearmint. Her favorite combination of fragrances. Both healing and relaxing. That's what she needed at the moment.

The only light in the room was from several candles.

A glass of wine sat on the edge of the tub with the bottle on the floor just within reach. She sank as low as she possibly could, the bubbles covering much of her body and the warm bath soothing, not only every muscle, but her mind as well. She reviewed the day.

It was unlike any other she had ever had. Well, of course, silly, she thought. She had never fastened herself to a gate before waiting for a truck to run her over.

But then to have shifted for the first time. She wasn't sure when her body would recover, but she had a wild guess it wasn't anytime soon.

She took a second sip of wine and sighed. While she appreciated the celebratory lunch that extended out to dinner, she wished she would have heard from Riley. He had indicated before they parted ways that morning he would call her. It was nearly 11 p.m., and she still hadn't heard from him.

She knew he was deluged with the attorneys and

details of the divestiture of the businesses. She could only imagine what a nightmare that was.

The moment she morphed into a lion, she knew the depth of her love for him. She had told herself repeatedly when it looked as if their relationship were over, that other men would walk into her life. Men she would love with the same fervor. She recalled that she chastised herself for giving her heart away so easily. She now understood everything clearly.

As she poured herself, yes, another glass of wine, she felt a wet, salty liquid run down both cheeks. God bless this, she thought. *Earlier today I was in tears because I thought our relationship was over. Now, I'm crying because of how much I love that man, regardless of his actions.*

She sighed contently as she realized the full embodiment of the words, lioness and lion. It was a deep metaphysical, mystical bond that was instantaneous. She now appreciated what her presence in Riley's life meant to him all along. She no longer feared heartbreak, no longer feared his abandonment. He was her lion. Who knew the confidence she felt when she shifted would remain with her even now?

And her lion faced a mound of work following the press conference to ensure the well was shut down. He hadn't made it clear what his former company would do to help with the bills and health care of the affected families. But he did promise he would execute a plan. He begged everyone to be patient while he spent several weeks finalizing it.

And then she wondered how many other families Amalgamated American Green had ruined in how many other cities across the country. Her ringtone snapped her back to here and now. She recognized the voice and tried hard to remain calm, but her heart was racing like a Porsche engine. It went from near zero to sixty at the blink of an eye. "Oh, Riley," she said.

Silence.

"Riley, are you still there?"

He stammered and then said, "The thing is, uhm Charlee that…well, I'm still here. Yeah. I'm sorry I didn't call you sooner. I didn't want you to think that after you shifted and helped me this morning that I wasn't grateful." Silence for a moment. "I'd still love to see you tonight, even though it is rather late."

"Of course," she said. "Could you give me about ten minutes? I'm in the tub. I need to dry off and throw a robe over me."

"Oh. Well…I'm not so much there as I'm here. And I bet I can help you with that bathtub visit." He sounded less nervous and more spirited.

"What? What do you mean 'here'?"

"Right outside your door. I've been in meetings and arguments with people telling me what I can't do all day. I didn't have a moment to call you. But you were on my mind today and that sexy lioness body of yours."

Though he couldn't see it, she cracked a smile.

"And well, I'm loaded down with…things."

"What kind of things?"

"If you let me in, you'll find out."

"To paraphrase one the classics," she said, "Riley, you've had the power within you to enter the house all along." She paused a beat. "It's the key on your key chain." She barely finished her sentence when she heard the key in the door turning.

"I take it you still do have the key," she said through the cell phone even as she heard a thud on the kitchen table.

"Whatever you do," Riley said, "don't get up. I'd hate for you to interrupt your relaxing moment for me."

"Okay," she said, "just make sure to bring an empty glass for the wine I have in here."

"You've got it. It sounds like an ideal way to end an unbelievably long and stressful day."

She heard his phone click off and, by the time she clicked hers and placed it on the floor, he stood in the doorway. He held a glass in one hand and a bouquet of Star Gazer lilies in the other. And, yes, he was utterly and completely naked. He looked like a Renaissance sculpture.

Chapter 56

"May I?"

He held the wine glass up. She nodded her assent, then held her glass up as well. Riley's lopsided smile seemed more out of kilter than usual.

"I have so much to tell you." She needed to tell him her shifting was more than a physical process; it also touched her soul.

"Shh." He put a finger to her lips. "Not tonight. At least not right now. Let's get back to the important stuff. We have a lot of time to make up for, and I don't want anything to get in the way. We'll talk later tonight or in the morning over breakfast. I brought breakfast supplies. Is there any way Mel can work for you?

"I know I'm assuming a lot waltzing back into your life, like I never left. But I hope you realize I did tell you the truth—as incredulous as it sounded. And perhaps you can see your way to forgive me." He paused. "And if you can't, well, at least I'll have this last evening we spent together."

She immediately called Mel, despite the late hour. She gave her friend as few details as possible.

"Is he there now, are you getting back together?" Mel whispered. "Take the entire weekend if you must. Of course, I've got you covered. I'm rooting for the two of you."

"Thank you, Mel."

"I can do breakfast and talk almost all morning, but I have one meeting I can't rearrange, even though tomorrow is Saturday. This meeting is to discover how best to handle the payments I need—and don't get me wrong—want to make for the families affected.

"But we'll talk about that later. Right now..." his voice trailed off, he placed his wine glass on the tub and took the bath scrub out of her hands.

Then he dipped it in the tub to make sure the water was as warm as possible and caressed her back. He used slow, sensual strokes, and her body responded enthusiastically.

As he leaned in closer, she recognized his familiar cologne, the one that had made her putty in his hands on their first encounter. She inhaled slightly, and it brought back memories about everything good she loved about him. And there was so much, from his silly lopsided smile to his genuine concern for her and his interest and concern for others.

He stroked the rest of her without saying a word. He circled her breasts, placing a bit more pressure on them until she let out a soft, low growl. He seamlessly worked his way toward her pelvic area until she involuntarily lifted her hips. All this time, Riley was silent, a small smile wrapped around his face; his eyes never strayed from her for a moment. He even made sure the scrubby found its way to her feet, the sensation to her a blend of pure relaxation and sexual expectation of what was to follow.

He offered his hand as she got up out of the tub. He lightly dried her off and picked her up as if she weighed less than a feather and carried her into the bedroom.

Chapter 57

He knelt above her and said, "I know we still need to talk, but I want you. Right here. Right now."

His eyes locked with hers, and she thought for a moment he was about to hypnotize her. No, that had already happened—the first time they met. His eyes pierced her soul, and her heart melted like a stick of butter on a hot summer sidewalk.

He caressed her breast and lightly continued downward to the inside of her thighs. With a slight lift of his body, he rubbed against her with an erection so hard it shocked her. She reached for him and asked if he were ready, knowing full well what the answer would be.

They exploded together, their bodies finely tuned. He collapsed on top of her, and she felt every beat of his heart. The more she listened, the closer her heart beat in rhythm with his. She closed her eyes. *This is the closest any two people could come to feeling like one.*

He rolled over on his back and pulled her close to him. She placed her head in the crook of his shoulder and wrapped a leg over his waist. They embraced; Charlee had no words to express the serenity that enveloped her.

Chapter 58

"A foundation?"

Charlee poured the coffee Riley made before she woke up Saturday morning. "That's brilliant."

"I'm not too sure about it being brilliant, it was my idea." He sat at the dining room table as he ate his breakfast. "But I sure had no idea it would be this complicated to put together."

She gagged on the coffee she had sipped and quickly passed his cup on to him.

"Charlee, are you all right?"

She nodded and took a long sip of orange juice.

"Complicated?" she asked between gasps. He patted her on the back.

"Riley, how long have you been working on this idea?"

"Actually, I thought of it all along as part of my divestiture program, but just mentioned it to the lawyer yesterday and asked him to implement it. He seemed to have the same reaction when I suggested we get it up and running within the next couple of days."

"I don't really know much about these things, but doesn't it take a bit longer than a day or two to pull one together?"

"That's exactly what the lawyer said, down to the gagging on his coffee," Riley said flatly, "and he specializes in foundation launches."

There's that little boy look that I love so well.

"But there are some snags in the plan in addition to my timing," he said. "The biggest of which is that I'm offering everyone who works for these fracking companies their regular paycheck, re-education programs, and moving costs depending on what jobs they accept."

"But you've got billions, don't you? Can't you pull some change out of the couch in your office? I bet between you and Quinn you two have more lost change in the couches in your offices than most people have in their checking account."

"I wouldn't be surprised. But the lawyer expects a boatload of claims, at least at the beginning. He has warned us not to pull money from other resources to cover the claims. That starts the foundation off without a strong base. And without those resources, we run the danger of running out of money."

"What about donations?" She took a bite of her toast.

"That looks like what we're going to have to do," he said. "But let's face it. There are few corporations that can afford to donate as quickly as I would like to get this thing going."

He paused as he took a forkful of hash browns. "I know we'll eventually get the foundation started, but I feel as though I owe it to everyone affected to do it as soon as possible."

He took a sip of his coffee. "But my attorney reminded me that we haven't discovered all the other cities the company has been destroying. I need to be able to take care of them as well. My intentions, I've been told, keep my attorneys and accountants up nights."

"Just out of curiosity," she asked casually, "if I could ask without getting too personal, what's the minimum you need to get these claims started?"

"No question you ask me, babe, is too personal." He rattled off a number, and she blinked incredulously as she heard the sum.

"I told you it was a lot. Not many companies have that kind of money—lying around at least, not tied up in stocks, invested in other programs—just ready to hand over to me."

Without saying a word, she picked up her cell phone and scrolled through her contacts. "There," she said, "I knew he was in there somewhere."

"Hey, Don," she said lightly as someone answered the other end. She didn't have to identify herself, he called her by name immediately.

"What can I do for you?"

She heard loud strange noises in the background. She was unable to identify them at first. Then she remembered.

"I did it again, didn't I?" she asked. "I called you during your bowling league. Don, you're the only accountant who is worth millions himself, runs in all the right social circles, and then bowls in a league as well. Isn't it a bit out of character for a man of your means?"

"Aren't you the sports snob these days," he said. "Give the young lady a little bit of money, and she'll never go on a bowling date with you. As much as I love you, I know you didn't call just to distract me from getting a strike on my next turn up." Before she could answer, he added, "Or, on second thought, maybe you did."

She told him what she wanted to do. "It's about time you found some real investment for your funds," he chided her. "I've been telling you to do this for years."

She squinched up her face and then told him the minimum she wanted to invest.

"Does this have anything to do with this fracking business you've been fighting lately?"

"Everything. It has everything to do with it."

He assured her that she not only could afford it, but it would be a very healthy financial move for her in the long run. "Great. And just offhand, what would be the upper limit of what I could donate, invest, whatever you call it?"

The financial planner gave her the amount.

"Really, wow. Who would ever think I could do that?"

"I'll let you know my plans in a couple of days. How long would it take to get the money to the foundation?"

"Thanks, I appreciate it."

She disconnected the call and turned to Riley.

"Could I donate to the foundation?" she asked. "I can donate at least the amount you need to get you started, but I'm thinking I should probably give the maximum of what my accountant suggests."

His eyes opened wide. "H-how much is that?" he stammered.

When she told him, he got up and paced.

"Is something wrong?" she asked. "Did I violate a protocol by not reporting my net value when I first met you? I told you I won that settlement."

He stopped and laughed. "No, nothing's wrong. I just never…"

"Thought of me of having that much money available to me, living in a house like this and running a coffee shop in a town like Prague, Ohio?"

She paused and, when he didn't continue, said, "You still love me, don't you?" She said it in a teasing manner, but suddenly felt it was a problem.

"Of course, I do. I'm just a bit stunned."

"You're incredible, you know that? My financial adviser has hounded me to do something with the money. It was important to me that whatever I chose made a difference in people's lives. I just didn't want to donate to a nonprofit that would spend more money on lining their pockets than helping people. I thought I would eventually find the right organization. And I certainly have. That is, if you're willing to accept my offer. I would love to see Karen, Jayne, and the others get the money they deserve, the health care they so need. And the sooner that could be done the better."

"I couldn't agree with you more, babe. Of course, I accept your offer." It only took several steps to get to her. He knelt beside her and kissed her. "I have more than enough time before my meeting. Let's continue talking business in your bedroom."

Chapter 59

Charlee decided to go to the coffee shop after Riley left for his meeting that morning. Now that the initial exhilaration of shifting was over, her mind turned to the inevitable fallout—the reaction of her friends and her employees. Her mind raced as she tried to figure out how Mel and the other employees would treat her, not to mention Karen and the Citizens Against Fracking. And then, there were Ed and Fred.

"Hell," she said on the drive to the shop, "I might as well just wonder what the entire town thinks." She stopped the car for a traffic light. "Because I'm sure the media had a grand time covering it."

As the light changed, she laughed. "I know one person who is very happy today: Gretchen Carlyle."

She held her breath as she opened the door to the café and braced herself to expect the worst. Instead, her entrance prompted applause and cheers. Mel sprinted over to her and hugged her. "You were friggin' awesome yesterday." Her friend released her and held her at arm's length. "I didn't know you shifted."

Charlee had no time to comment because Karen and several others gathered around her. "You were great," Karen said. "I loved Carlyle's face when she realized the second lion was you."

Jayne agreed. "I pulled out my camera and recorded it. Do you want to see it from our point of view?"

Charlee held up her hands. "Stop. Just everyone, stop for a minute." They laughed but refrained from saying anything more.

"I'm overwhelmed," she said. "I didn't know what to expect. Let's sit down. I've got a lot to tell all of you." She eyed Mel. "I could start with a cup of coffee."

"Coming right up." She turned on a heel, then looked back. "But don't you start explaining a thing until I get there."

"So that was really the first time you shifted?" Mel asked after Charlee told her story.

Charlee nodded. She didn't know how to express her relief and gratitude for her friends' acceptance of who she was.

"Thank you," she said, as she felt tears well up. "I wasn't—"

"Charlee Lightheart," Karen said, "you're our friend. We accept you as you are." There was a short silence. Then Jayne added, "It's really cool to know not one, but two shifters."

"I'm not sure the *Prague Bugle* feels the same way," Charlee said.

Karen quickly pulled a copy out of her purse. "No, they were quite pleased." She handed her the newspaper.

"Wow, they were gracious." Mel's cell phone chirped, and the conversation distracted Charlee.

"Yeah, Jared, she's here with us now. We'll definitely watch. Thanks for the heads up."

Mel disconnected the call. She didn't look happy.

"What?" everyone asked nearly at the same time.

"That was Jared," she explained, "he just found out that the television station is broadcasting a special *Gretchen Carlyle Live Saturday* edition."

Charlee groaned. "Let me guess. She wants to see what people think about Riley and me being lion shifters."

Karen looked more upset than Charlee. "How dare she."

"I have to admit," Charlee said, "it is news."

"Aren't you worried about what the residents think?" Jayne asked.

"I hope they're accepting, but if they aren't, I have all the acceptance I need right here."

Mel stood up. "If you want to watch it, I'll flip it to Channel 5. It's on in ten minutes."

Charlee chuckled. "Of course, I want to watch it. Don't you guys?" They all agreed. "Well, bring it on."

Mel retrieved the remote control. Once she had the proper station, she hurriedly refilled everyone's coffee. Then the moment came.

"I'm Gretchen Carlyle with a special edition of *Gretchen Carlyle Live*." She reported on events at the protest site. While she mentioned the halt of the fracking operation, she focused on Riley and Charlee's shape shifting.

"To think the two major players in this months-long drama were shifters. I'm here on the street to discover what the average Prague resident thinks about this deceitful behavior."

The journalist attempted to stop several people before she found two who were willing to talk to her.

"What the hell?" Mel said. "Do you see who that is?"

"Ed and Fred. And it looks like they're going to talk." Charlee felt nervous. "I wonder what they'll say?"

Mel shot her a look. "Those two old guys—"

"Shh!" Karen shushed them.

"So, you want to know what we think?" Fred said. "I'll tell you what we think. We think it's none of our business whether Charlee girl or that Brockton boy are lion shifters. The bottom line is they are good people. They aren't hurting a soul by being shifters."

Ed added. "From our perspective, it appears they're helping a hell of a lot of people. That's what we need more of—people with hearts, regardless of their lineage."

Karen, Jayne, and Mel cheered. Charlee felt tears well up.

"Wait," Mel said, "she's cornered another person."

They focused on the program. "Ma'am," Carlyle said, "I see you're a mom to a lovely little girl."

"I'm not little," the child corrected her. "I'm eight. And I'm smart for my age. That's what my teacher told me."

The mom nodded while Gretchen attempted to ignore the child. "Tell me, what do you think about yesterday's revelation that Charlee Lightheart and Riley Brockton are shifters."

The woman spoke immediately. "I think it's great."

"Excuse me?" Apparently, Carlyle couldn't believe that another person wasn't as upset as she wanted them to be. "What kind of example does this set for your daughter?'

"A wonderful example," the mom said, "it shows her that the most important thing in this life is to care for others. Charlee fought hard for her neighbors—and by the way got a lot of flak for it." The woman paused and glared at the journalist. "Shifters are no different from any other residents of Prague. I welcome the diversity they bring to the city. And I would love it if my daughter grew up to be as compassionate and caring as Charlee and Mr. Brockton."

"I want to be just like Charlee when I grow up," the girl said. "She's like a superhero. She changes into a lion and saves the day."

Chapter 60

"I'd like to start now." Riley spoke loudly. Quinn stood by his side at a far corner of *That Coffee Shop*, just as he had at the fracking site.

The chatter of the media, Citizens Against Fracking, and others slowly quieted. Riley realized he was uncharacteristically nervous. *It's not like I'm a rookie. I've done hundreds of these, easily.*

This press conference, though, was different. A minimum of three months in the making and, in his opinion, long overdue. In addition to the weeks he and his attorneys fervently worked on the foundation's launch, there were several weeks of inaction, which he felt were merely thrown in to appease some bureaucratic whim.

He looked to see what forms of media had shown up. Of course, the local newspaper appeared as well as Chanel 5 TV. The Prague news station, in fact, had all its bases covered. In addition to a beat reporter, he recognized Sparrow.

There was at least one reporter from every news organization within 150 miles, he swore. *Must be a slow news day.*

That's not even counting Citizens Against Fracking. He looked at the group, as they sat together three rows back. They had waited expectantly for the help he had promised. *They had been divinely patient during this time. They could have been much more demanding in me fulfilling my promises. It was almost as if they trusted me to do what was right.*

To his surprise, the group hadn't disbanded with the announcement of the halt of the drilling. Instead, it expanded its focus nationwide to help others who faced the same issue. "It would be negligent not to," Karen had said on Jared's show after the protest. "We know the dangers of life near a fracking well. We're here to help get this hideous activity stopped regardless of where it occurs."

The coffee shop's regular customers were in attendance as well. They had pulled chairs to the area where the event would be held. He thought the rest of those present had just walked in off the street out of curiosity.

He grimaced when he saw Carlyle enter. She positioned herself in the front row and opened a notebook. Since the announcement at the site, she had approached him frequently concerning the "alleged plans" for the foundation. She accused him of dragging his feet and said he reneged on his promise.

He took a deep breath as he realized the chatter had died down. "It's my pleasure to announce The Brockton Enterprises Foundation is now ready to accept applications. We are eager to start the reimbursement process for those adversely affected by the fracking activity."

The anti-fracking group and others cheered. He flashed his signature smile at the group.

"I apologize for the time lag. My lawyers were the hold up." The group laughed. "But we finally overcame all the bureaucratic obstacles. We're ready to get to work. To this point, we've hired a temporary director. Her job is to ensure the seamless flow of applications and answer the flood of questions I'm sure you have." He paused and smiled. "You already know her. Melanie Milan. Come on up here, Mel."

"You hired a barista to fill such a vital position?" Carlyle screeched, sending shivers down his spine.

He stared at Gretchen and, as calmly as he could, said, "Mel has an MBA from Ohio State and has worked extensively for various non-profit organizations in Columbus."

Thankfully, that shut Gretchen down, and Mel stood up to talk. She started off a bit shaky at first—and who wouldn't after that woman's remarks—but quickly found her stride and voice.

More than satisfied that Mel could handle the crowd and the questions, Riley went in search of Charlee.

He kissed her on the cheek and, with a heavy whisper, said, "There's more where that came from after we both finish our days."

She nodded. "I'll be waiting with bells on."

"Please, don't overdress on my account." He took her by the hand and guided her closer to the press conference. It appeared to be wrapping up. Mel was passing out applications when they approached.

"I think we've covered the preliminaries," Mel said. "Please don't hesitate to call me. Now, I'd like nothing more than to have Riley finish up here. I was told there is one more item on the agenda."

He was only a few steps away when Mel had finished her talk; he could tell she was relieved her portion of the meeting was done. She sat with the anti-fracking group.

He stepped squarely in front of the crowd. Somewhere along the way he had let go of Charlee's hand.

****

She leaned against a wall as she admired his body, his demeanor. And did she say his body? The thought that someone, Riley in particular, could love her unconditionally made her heart swell.

"Charlee? Did you hear me? Come over here for a minute." The crowd applauded. She had no idea what he had told them, she was so absorbed in her thoughts.

She hesitantly approached him. She felt naked. This wasn't how she usually saw her customers, all in one area, every eye upon her.

"Charlee Lightheart." She looked over at him at the sound of his voice. Riley took her hand and quickly got down on one knee. She gasped, but before she had a chance to protest, he whipped out a blue velvet ring box, opened it, and said, "I love you. And I want nothing more than for you to marry me. I've made some really dumb mistakes in the past, and I can't guarantee I won't make more really dumb mistakes in the future."

He paused. The crowd remained amazingly quiet.

"No, that's one thing you can take to the bank, I'll probably make more really dumb mistakes in the future. The only thing I can clearly say I've done in my life that was not a mistake at all is to love you, Charlee Lightheart, with all my heart. If you think you could stand me and if you would have me, I would love for you to marry me."

Every media outlet had its microphones as close to

the couple as they could get and withheld comment.

She shook her head side from side slowly, producing a collective whispered gasp from the group.

She answered through sobs. "Of course, I will. Of course."

He placed the ring on her finger and gave her a kiss that she knew she would never forget.

After everyone had left, the post-press conference lunches that had been ordered eaten, and the tables bused, Charlee sat with Riley at the counter, a cup of herbal tea in front of her. Something caught her eye.

"Mel, the picture next to the cash register is gone. What's up with that?"

"Oh, that," Mel said. "I thought we needed to hang something else there."

"And what might that be?"

Mel ducked under the counter. When she popped up, she had a new wall hanging in her hands and hung it where the old one had been. It was a gorgeous photograph of a sunrise with the saying:

Have an amazingly awesome day.

Through tears of joy, Charlee explained to Riley that was her mantra the first day he walked into the coffee shop and they felt that electric surge.

She gazed in his eyes, still stunned every time by the clear, crisp amber, and whispered in his ear, "Little did I know, how amazingly awesome it could be."

A word about the author...

Terry Newman always loved words. As the editor-in-chief of a national natural health publishing company, she ghostwrote books on a variety of topics as well as direct mail advertising. She's also been a reporter, a communications specialist, and a freelance writer. She's had clients worldwide and has researched and composed hundreds of eBooks and print books as well as ghostwrote novellas and short stories for others. Terry has taught workshops on writing and character development locally.

She has one daughter and a grandpuppy, and lives in North Lima, Ohio.

http://terrynewmanauthor.com